THE OBLIVION TAPES

One, the infection is not contagious. By this, I mean that it is not transmitted by human beings. Like the common cold, for instance.

Two, we believe that the infection is transmitted through the air and not through water supplies or contaminated foods.

Three, as it is transmitted through the air, the infection attacks the body through the respiratory system. In our many autopsies we have discovered clotting in the lungs. There are also indications that paralysis has occurred in various parts of the body. We are not as yet sure what exactly happened in the body once the air entered the lungs.

Four, we are following the line that the infection was a mutant strain of virus. We have as yet been unable to isolate the virus. Until we can, and until we identify it, it will be impossible to invent an antidote. Thank you.

Timeri Murari

The Oblivion Tapes

MAGNUM BOOKS
Methuen Paperbacks Ltd

A Magnum Book

THE OBLIVION TAPES
ISBN 0 417 03850 X

First published Berkley Publishing Corp, New York
Magnum edition published 1979

Copyright © 1978 by Timeri Murari Ltd

Magnum Books are published
by Methuen Paperbacks Ltd
11, New Fetter Lane, London EC4P 4EE

Set, printed and bound in Great Britain
by Cox & Wyman Ltd, Reading

To my sisters, Nalini and Padmini, with love.

There is reason to believe that population growth increases the probability of a lethal world wide plague and of a thermo-nuclear war. Either could provide an undesirable 'death rate solution' to the population problem; each is potentially capable of destroying civilization and even of driving 'homo sapiens to extinction.

– Paul Ehrlich
and Anne Ehrlich,
in
Population
Resources
Environment
(W. H. Freeman & Co,
San Francisco)

1

The soldier with binoculars, a stocky young man of nineteen from the northern provinces, stood on the narrow catwalk of the control tower three hundred feet above the ground and watched the Pan Am 747 from New York descend to the tarmac. The roar deafened him and he pressed his palms against his ears. It was the fifteenth he'd watched that day and he was bored and hot. For the last two days he'd watched nothing but aircraft land and take off. He wiped the sweat off his face with a damp handkerchief; there was little he could do about the dark patches under his arms and around the belly of his uniform. He glanced back. He would have liked to stand inside the air-conditioned control room, but the busy, technical men barely tolerated his presence. They'd made him feel gauche and unwanted, so he suffered in the heat.

The stairs were being wheeled to the the open doors of the aircraft, and the soldier pulled a postcard-size photograph from his back pocket. There was a deep crease down the center of the face he stared at, and the edges of the photograph curled. He glanced at the photograph to refresh his memory and then squinted through the binoculars at the disembarking passengers. The man he was looking for was in his mid-fifties, clean-shaven, and had receding hair. His face wasn't memorable. It had a straight nose, high cheekbones, and shy eyes that had avoided the camera.

The soldier swung the binoculars from door to door, trying to find the man. He didn't know why he was looking for this man. He had been given an order and he just carried it out. He shut his eyes for a moment; the glare made them ache. He straightened hopefully and glanced at the photograph. He sharpened the focus on a man descending the stairs and then lost interest. He cursed softly to himself and wished he were back in the cool mountains. The passengers were down to a trickle now but he kept the binoculars to his eyes. The last man to come out held a briefcase in his right hand.

The stewardess held his case while he took off his light summer jacket and slipped on a pair of sunglasses. The soldier watched him smile his thanks at the stewardess, take the case, and slowly descend the stairs. As he crossed to the terminal building the soldier noticed that the man made no effort to hurry and in fact deliberately trailed as far behind the other passengers as possible. The soldier reached back to the wall and picked up the walkie-talkie. His eyes never left the man as he switched on and said: 'He's just coming in.'

The soldier waited until the man entered the terminal building and then happily took off the binoculars, scooped up his machine-gun and headed for the elevator. In an hour he would be back in his barracks, standing under a cold shower and drinking a cold beer.

The interior of the terminal building was cool and gloomy and smelled of fresh paint and varnish. The whole building was brand new and some sections of it were as yet unfinished. It wasn't built to look like an air terminal but rather like a spacious, fountained *hacienda*. No expense had been spared to make it the best-looking airport in the world. There were doubts by those who passed through it whether it was the most efficient.

Some of the passengers who had just disembarked were moving through to the transit lounge to wait for their connections to Rio and Lima and other cities on the continent. The majority, however, tiredly queued up at the three immigration desks. It looked as if it were going to be a long wait, as the officers were taking great care in passport inspection.

The man the soldier had been watching sat down by one of the windows and lit a cigarette. He ignored his reflection and halfheartedly tried to flatten the stray hairs on his head. He slumped back. The long flight from New York had exhausted him, and though he needed to be alert for the authorities he felt he just couldn't summon the energy. Through the window he saw the aircraft he'd come in being unloaded. He bit his lip briefly in worry at the thought of his suitcase being opened by customs. There was nothing to do but hope for the best.

It took forty-five minutes for the queues to dwindle, and the man chose his officer carefully. It was going to be the one on the left. The immigration officer looked impatient and in a hurry to finish his work. The man crossed to him and dropped his passport on the desk.

'Mr . . .' The officer thumbed through the slim, green US passport. '. . . Whitlam. How long will you be staying in the country?'

'Four . . . five days. Then I return to New York.'

'Business?' He flicked through and stopped at the entry visa. An eyebrow rose. It wasn't an ordinary embassy one. This visa had been issued by the foreign office. Gratefully, the officer stamped it, and returned the passport to Whitlam. Important visas meant less work and that meant he could be off five minutes earlier.

Whitlam nodded his thanks and passed through to luggage collection. His battered blue case was forlornly circling around the conveyor all by itself. He grabbed it and carefully studied the line of customs inspectors. It was impossible to pick the right one, as they all looked busy and thorough. He joined the shortest queue and as he shuffled nearer, he realized he'd made a mistake. The inspector he was about to meet was trying to be extra efficient, and it was too late to change queues. He found himself standing between a pretty woman whom he'd admired on the plane and her mother, a bulky, floral-patterned duenna. Whitlam stared straight ahead and gripped his suitcase tightly. He looked through the man and woman standing a few feet behind the zealous customs inspector.

The man was around the same age as Whitlam but physically different. His black hair was touched with gray and his face was proud and handsome. He looked fit, and he was impeccably dressed in a light fawn suit. The woman beside him should have looked beautiful. Unfortunately her near-perfect-oval, sensual face was marred by a sullen pout.

If Whitlam had known the identity of the man who was

the cause of all the extra activity of the customs inspectors, he would have turned around and reboarded his flight.

Fortunately for him, Colonel Carlos Lopez had his own problems. He should have been a very happy man, for he was about to take his first vacation in three years, and every detail had been meticulously planned. In an hour and a half, he would be by the jetty in Fortaleza, and five minutes after that on the chairman's luxury cruiser. It would be stocked with cold beer, enough good food to last a week, and a very attentive crew to look after his needs. For seven glorious days he planned to just laze in the sun, fish, and drink the cold beer.

One flaw was Inez. He glanced at her. She looked even more sullen, and he was sure by the time they reached the coast, she would have thrown half a dozen tantrums. Lopez was a widower, and Inez was his mistress of a year. She knew her time to leave was coming, and she intended to make as much fuss as possible. She was a city girl who hated the idea of a week away from her friends, the shops, the clubs, and the cafés.

'Look,' Lopez whispered fiercely. 'You really will have a good time. All that sea . . .'

'I get seasick in my bathtub,' Inez snapped, and Lopez gave up. The holiday was also intended as her final treat.

He would have left her behind but a man needed company apart from the fish.

'Your flight will be announced in two minutes, sir,' a young, uniformed man said and saluted. He withdrew to a respectful distance and waited to escort Lopez to the air-craft.

Lopez nodded and then ignored him. He was aware of the man's deference, and the effect his presence made on all the people around him. He was a dangerous man, he knew, and most men and women became nervous when he approached. As chief of the Special Organization for the Maintenance of Internal Security (SOMIS) they had good reason to worry about Lopez.

Lopez moved restlessly. There was something else bothering him but he couldn't put his finger on it. It was a feeling more than a thought or a worry. For the last ten days there'd been a stillness in his underworld of conspiracies, plotters, and surveillance. It was as if everyone who was working against his chairman had stopped to wait for something to happen. But what? Colonel Lopez had checked and re-checked the grapevine. None of his agents had anything to report, and there was no trouble anywhere in the country. The generals were up north on maneuvers; Chairman Bolivar was going to make a secret visit to the eastern provinces, where he had his strongest supporters in the copper mines, and Lopez was positive there'd be no trouble; the students were quiet and satisfied on the campuses; and those that remained to cause trouble were all in jail.

The unease remained, and Lopez, lost in thought, took a step forward. This made the customs inspector even more zealous. He threw open Whitlam's case and roughly went through the contents. There were the usual things – summer clothes, shoes, toiletries which included two large cans of deodorant. The inspector pushed these aside. Neither he nor Lopez noticed the tic of worry in Whitlam's eyes as the cans were touched. It passed the moment the inspector shut the case and scrawled his chalk mark.

Whitlam locked the case and started to move away quickly. 'Mr . . .' The inspector glanced at the passport. '. . . Whitlam, your passport.'

It took a second or two for Whitlam to realize he was being called, and he returned flustered. As he took his passport he met Lopez's eye by accident. For a moment, Lopez thought, the man hadn't known his name. He shrugged – it was noisy in the hall – and forgot him. The next time they came face to face, one of them would be dead.

'Your flight is ready, sir,' the young man whispered, and Lopez nodded. He was determined to enjoy his vacation, and he thrust the unease he'd felt to the back of his mind. He moved away and didn't bother to check if Inez was following him.

The man, Whitlam, cursed himself silently for forgetting his passport. Still, no one had noticed. He paused for a moment, before the exit doors, took a breath of cold air, and then walked out into the heat. It felt like being punched in the gut, and he gasped. He called a taxi and climbed in.

'The Carlton,' he said, and sat back. As the taxi pulled away, he glanced out of the window. A soldier was staring straight at him. Whitlam was startled. For a moment, he felt, the man seemed to know him.

It was a six-mile drive into the capital of Menaguay, Sao Amerigo, and Whitlam peered eagerly out of the window. It had been seven years since he'd visited the country, and so much had changed. The airport was new, and there were buildings along the roadside. Mile after mile; there wasn't a vacant site to be seen. Two miles outside the city, the landscape abruptly changed. It became ugly and squalid with *barrios*. They'd sprung up like obscene weeds in what had been a beautiful garden. The sight made Whitlam sick and angry. The poor always looked the same: scrawny and dirty and numerous. They lived in the same tin shacks; clustered around the same dirty pumps; and the children played in the same muddy, garbage-strewn lanes. Whitlam felt sad when he saw them. Half of them would die before adulthood from some awful disease or just starvation; the other half would eke out their miserable lives in grinding poverty. He felt, briefly, happy. He was going to change their future; the children would be given a chance.

The taxi entered the suburbs of Sao Amerigo and was soon enmeshed in the noonday traffic jam. It has changed, Whitlam thought. It's become richer and busier and looks like any American city. There were skyscrapers and tunnels and flyovers and all the unpleasantness of urban living. But the city also had managed to retain its old beauty. There were parks and quiet plazas, and in the poorer parts, the old, Portuguese-style houses were still to be seen. Midtown, however, was glass and concrete and expensive stores, and, it seemed to Whitlam, nearly the whole city's population of six million.

The taxi turned down Avenida Peron, and Whitlam shut his eyes and sat back. He hated Sao Amerigo. It had been a quiet, sleepy town seven years ago. Why did man always want to grow and change and destroy his world in the

14

process? Coming in on the plane, he'd seen the jungle receding farther and farther back, like his own hairline. He knew there were men down there cutting down the trees, destroying the land, killing the animals, wiping out the primitive tribes so that they could become rich.

It had, he supposed, been happening gradually for many years, but the pace had been accelerated by the new ruler of the country, Simon Juan Bolivar. Whitlam thought of him in dismay. Bolivar was a barrel-shaped man with the instincts of a street fighter and the mind of a Napoleon. Facts about him were few and far between; only stories and myths abounded. He had no father, and it was said his mother was a *puta*. He was an aggressive, ambitious man who had climbed out a *barrio* and gone to work in one of the great copper mines. There he'd fought and schemed his way to the top of the Unión de los Trabajadores, and the next natural step for him had been politics. He was a fanatical socialist, bordering on communist, and he'd won the last election by the skin of his teeth. That had been two years ago, and the world had not been the same since.

The taxi stopped with a jerk, and Whitlam saw they were outside the Carlton. It was a small, neat-looking hotel three blocks south of Avenida Bolivar, the center of the city. He could have stayed in a Hilton or a Sheraton, but this quiet, back-street hotel suited his purposes. As long as it had a shower and a comfortable bed. The Carlton looked as if it had both. He followed the bellboy to the reception desk.

'I think you have a room for me, Charles Whitlam.'

The girl behind the counter flicked through a list and then silently slid a card across to him. As he filled in his passport details, he felt her studying him. He glanced up quickly and caught her eye. There was a nervous, almost frightened curiosity in her face, which immediately went blank. He signed the card with a flourish, and she held out her hand for his passport.

'When can I collect it?' Whitlam asked.

'In the morning.' She handed a key to the bellboy.

Whitlam followed him to the elevator and stepped in. He

15

turned. The girl was still watching him, and with the same curiosity, as the doors closed.

As the elevator rose, she picked up the card Whitlam had just filled in, tore it into pieces, and dropped the shreds into the wastebasket. She slipped the passport, without even looking at it, into an envelope, sealed it, and handed it to another bellboy. He took it without a question and hurried to the manager's office.

The room was all Whitlam needed. The bed felt comfortable, and there was a shower in the bathroom. He tipped the bellboy and immediately began undressing for a shower and, what he needed most, a long sleep.

When he awoke, it was dark outside. As he drew the curtains he saw that the streetlights were on and the pavements crowded with strollers. He dressed quickly and went down to dinner. He had a steak and baked potato, and when he finished the simple meal he thought of joining the strollers. He decided against it. He had a very early start in the morning, and he still had a few things to get done before he went to bed.

From his room, he ordered a self-drive car. He made sure they were going to give him the latest model with a full tank before he asked reception for an early call and room service for breakfast at six. He unpacked his suitcase and carefully hung up his suits and put away his shirts and underwear into drawers. His actions were all economical and neat. When the case had been emptied of clothes, all that remained were the two large cans of deodorant. He snapped open the briefcase and emptied the contents onto the desk. There were a couple of books, a magazine, and note paper. He frowned. In between the loose paper were two neatly typed pages covered with graphs. He picked them up in irritation. They belonged to a file which should never have left his office. He studied them. Unless one understood the whole report, these pages were incomprehensible. He balled them up and looked around for a wastebasket. It was near the bed. He pitched the ball, missed, and watched it roll under the bed.

He took the cans out of the case. They looked exactly like a popular brand, except, as he hefted them, they felt marginally heavier. If the customs inspector hadn't been so flurried, he would have noticed the difference. Whitlam placed the cans carefully in the briefcase and locked it.

By seven the next morning he was ready to leave his room. He stubbed out the cigarette, drained the coffeecup, and picked up the briefcase. He made sure that he had everything he needed for the long journey. It was going to be a tiring day, and he didn't want a false start. He picked up the road map with the two tiny crosses he'd marked on it and let himself out.

As he waited for the elevator, the floor waiter, a short, sleepy man in an untidy white jacket, came down the corridor.

'May I have the key to clean your room, señor?' he asked.

Whitlam tossed it to him and got into the elevator. The waiter didn't move but watched the indicator. Ground floor. He yawned and leaned against the wall and waited.

Whitlam crossed the foyer to the reception desk. A young man was on duty.

'My name's Whitlam. May I have my passport?'

'We haven't as yet completed the formalities.' The man shrugged and smiled apologetically. 'Maybe by this evening . . .'

'I'll pick it up tomorrow.' Whitlam was irritated. He would have liked it for the journey, just in case he had to stay somewhere overnight. 'Where do I pick up my car?'

The man pointed. 'Down the corridor, sir.'

The man, an assistant manager, waited until Whitlam turned the corner, and then strolled to the top of the corridor. He just caught a sight of Whitlam entering the rental office. He sat down and waited.

Whitlam quickly filled in the form and signed his name with an extra flourish. He was feeling buoyant as, finally, he was starting out on the journey. The girl took his charge card, ran it through the machine, and handed him the car keys.

'The car is just outside.' The girl smiled. 'Have a good trip, Mr Whitlam.' She turned away.

'Can I have a copy of the form?'

'It isn't necessary, Mr Whitlam.'

'Oh, yes, it is. When I return the car, you'll slap on extra mileage, and I'll have no proof. Give.'

The girl suddenly became unsure, and it puzzled him. He rented cars often, and he'd always been given a carbon of the agreement. He snapped his fingers impatiently. The girl looked around. She was alone. She shrugged and gave him the carbon, which he tucked triumphantly into his pocket. In Sao Amerigo you really had to be sharp.

The car was a locally made two-year-old Chevy. From the outside at least it looked in good condition. He put the brief-case in the trunk and climbed in behind the wheel. The car started immediately, and he cautiously moved down the driveway.

The girl saw him turn out and immediately tore up her copy of the agreement.

'You followed your instructions?' the assistant manager asked as soon as he entered the office.

'Yes, sir,' the girl said quickly. 'The license plates were changed, and the car cannot be traced here. But . . .'

'What?' the manager snapped.

'He insisted on a copy. I couldn't prevent him from—'

'You fool!' The manager didn't seem so much angry as frightened for himself. 'It can't be helped now.'

He hurried to the elevator and got off on the seventh floor. The room waiter seemed asleep, and the assistant manager snapped his fingers and hurried to Whitlam's room. The waiter hurried ahead and opened the door.

'Everything.' The order was snapped out.

The waiter quickly opened Whitlam's case and piled the suits and neatly ironed shirts and toilet articles in. The assistant manager followed him around making sure everything was cleaned out, including the books and magazines. The waiter forced the case closed, and the manager picked it up and staggered to the elevator. He took it down to the basement and opened the furnace door. Piecemeal he fed everything from the case into the fire. Within a minute he was pouring with sweat, and he wished he could have delegated this menial job to someone else, but he'd been ordered to do it personally. When he finished, there was little he could do with the empty suitcase except throw it in the garbage bin. When he finished, he wiped his face and went to the phone. He called the manager at his home.

'We have done as you ordered, sir, except that stupid girl in the car rental allowed him to take a carbon of the agreement.' He listened patiently as the manager swore at him, and then put down the phone. As he washed his face in the bathroom and cooled off, he wondered to whom the manager would be reporting.

Whitlam reached the southern outskirts of Sao Amerigo in half an hour. It had been an easy journey. From the hotel, he'd turned into the axis of the city and joined the major eight-lane highway. As it was early, the traffic was still light. Once he cleared the city he settled back for the long drive. He had nearly three hundred and fifty miles to cover by two in the afternoon. He didn't expect the journey to be difficult. The roads were wide and excellent. One of the boons of Bolivar's civilization of the jungle was the network of highways and roads.

Whitlam's route followed one of the tributaries of the river which ran south into the Serra dos Paroces. He knew it wouldn't be a monotonous drive; there was too much to see since he'd last visited this part of the country. He shook his head in sadness. It had all changed, and in his opinion for the worse. It was all so ugly and crowded. Nothing ever remained the same. A trading post had become a village, and a village a town. The jungle had had no chance against such greed for space and food.

And everywhere there were people. They were on cycles, in buses, on horseback, walking or just squatting by the roadside. In seven years, he knew the population had doubled, and it shook him to discover how visible the people were. Where were they all going? What were they going to do with their lives?

Admittedly, Menaguay was a rich country. There was oil to the northwest, and the rich copper mines to the east, and, a year back, a rich seam of molybdenum had been struck

19

150 miles north of the copper mines in the foothills of the Andes. It had all the minerals and energy that the western industrial nations desperately needed, but the soil wasn't as generous as the earth deep underneath. There was only a 200-mile-wide belt of land to the south where the soil was fertile enough and there was adequate water to grow wheat. It wasn't enough to feed all the people.

Bolivar, on his election, had promised a miracle for his people, and to deliver it he was on the verge of destroying the industrial world.

By 11.30 Whitlam had reached Manicore. It was a small, busy town situated by a small lake. He decided to take a break and pulled up by the water and bought a bottled cold drink. As he sipped it, he watched the urchin fishermen languidly trying their luck. He wanted to touch them because they looked so vulnerable and innocent; they didn't know that for many years they would be the last children. He turned away quickly and climbed back into the car. Soon, he knew, he would be driving through a blazing, semi-deserted landscape. The sky and land would be almost white with the heat of the sun, and the road a shimmering mirage in front of him.

He stayed on the main highway for another half-hour until he reached Porto Beilha, and then swung west. The scenery didn't change much, and he lounged back and tried to make himself as comfortable as possible.

He sighed quite suddenly. It was a sad, nostalgic sound, as if an old, almost forgotten memory had passed through his mind and he wished he could relive it again. He shook his head. He was getting old, and the world was changing too fast for him. The world had been a simpler place when he'd been born in 1931, it had had an innocence, like those children he'd seen.

Since then, everything had seemed to go wrong; and in the last five years it looked as if the whole ordered structure was disintegrating. He wasn't sure who was to blame. All of us, I suppose, he thought. The earthly paradise we'd dreamed of in the western countries has turned to ashes. The problem, Whitlam thought, was really quite simple. The rich wanted to remain rich, and the poor didn't want to remain poor. The first danger signal was the OPEC embargo and price hike in 1972. Once the crisis passed, the people in the industrialized nations forgot the problem. But it had opened a Pandora's box. The Third World suddenly realized that they did have power to force concessions and over the last five years had begun to use it brutally. In 1975, the two world blocs had tried to have a dialogue in Paris – the industrial world of the United States and Europe and Japan faced the Third World nations of India, the OPEC countries, and a few others. The discussions hadn't succeeded because neither would compromise.

In 1977, with the signing of détente, the USSR had joined the industrial nations in the meetings (it was also because the Third World nations no longer had any faith in the Soviets), and nearly all the remaining Third World countries had joined the others. In 1979, the industrial nations lost a valuable, though embarrassing ally – South Africa. In a bloody revolt that had shocked the world, the white government of South Africa had been overthrown by the black nationalist, Odu, and he'd immediately aligned himself and the chaotic economic resources of his country with the Third World. In the same year, Bolivar had moved suddenly. He had nationalized the oil wells and the copper mines and thrown all the US companies out of his country without a cent in compensation. The more right-wing members of the US Senate and the army threatened invasion, but to date nothing had happened.

But Bolivar hadn't left well enough alone. He had cut the flow of oil and copper and molybdenum to the United States, and all economic hell had broken loose. His reasons were valid in a nationalistic way – they had more need of their precious natural resources in order to develop industrially.

The crisis he'd triggered had brought the world economy to a halt. Bolivar was now trying, with Odu, the oil sheiks, Mrs Gandhi, and Liu of China to widen the embargo. Checkmate was to take place between the Third World and the industrialized nations any day now. And then what?

Whitlam thought sadly. We've run out of ideas of how to live with each other.

Whitlam felt drained; the driving and harsh glare were exhausting. He straightened. It would be over by tomorrow, and he'd be back in his home with his wife in West Caldwell in two days. Porto Velho was reached by one-thirty. It was a large town, and rather than drive through it, Whitlam swung west. He stopped at a small café to stretch his legs, refuel the car, and eat lunch. He ate a few bananas and drank a cold Coke.

He now kept heading west. The land seemed deserted at this time of the day, but he knew there were people everywhere. They had built the towns and roads and factories that he saw around Porto Velho. Countless people, millions. The world just couldn't support them all, he knew only too well. Another five years was the most the earth could take, and he knew that after that it would be just too late.

Another hour and he'd reach his first destination. He passed through Rio Zinho and stopped twenty miles north of Rio Branco. Rio Branco was on the edge of the plain. From there the land rose slowly into gentle hills and gradually became the towering Andes. He hesitated. The main road was too open. He swung the car onto a narrow road, the sign pointed to Cochos, and drove for a mile. He stopped and got out and shielded his eyes. Cochos was beyond the next bend. Looking north, the land was flat for miles. The first of the small hills began half a mile to the southwest. In the distance, he could see a group of peasants coming toward him, but there was no one else around as far as he could see.

Because he and his horse were standing so still under the shade of the tree on the slope southwest of Whitlam, Xinhama wasn't noticed. He watched Whitlam with an expressionless face, which was flat and wrinkled and sunburned. He was an old man who had been born north of the great river. Sometimes, at a time like this for instance, he would try to remember his people. They had been a small tribe, not more than fifty, who had lived deep in the forests. When he was eight or ten or twelve – he had no idea how old he was – the hunters had come and killed all the adults. He'd been transported down the great river and sold to the rancher for whom he now worked. One day had flowed into the next, and now he was old. He thought of those killings and believed that one day the people who had destroyed his people for their land would in turn meet their own destruction. It was the way of the gods.

He watched without curiosity as the man below him took a case from the back of his car.

Whitlam opened the case and hesitated and then in an act of defiance which only he understood, he took out only one of the cans. To hell with instructions, he thought. I still believe that my plan of two locations is better than one. It means another hour of driving, but I'm going to prove I'm right.

He flicked off the white plastic cap and wrenched at the spray section of the can. It came off easily. He carefully slid out the metal flask and threw away the hollow can. The flask was made of smooth, almost silky metal and was the color of dull silver. Its cap fitted flush with the main body and was locked in by two parallel rings which were held by a linch pin. He spent five minutes working the pin loose; it appeared to have jammed, and by the time he succeeded he was pouring with sweat. The pin popped out and the rings now unscrewed in opposite directions. Once he had them off, all he had to do was shake off the cap.

He closed the briefcase and locked it in the trunk. The peasants were closer, and he decided to drive a little way back to the main road so that he wouldn't be seen. He lifted his head. There wasn't a drop of breeze, and he hoped it would start soon.

He started the car, and holding the flask carefully, drove up the road. On the slope looking down on the car, Xinhama felt the faint breeze touch his cheek. It was hot but welcome, and the horse stirred under him.

Whitlam was nervous and awkwardly lit a cigarette. He was a hundred yards from the main road now. He couldn't wait longer. He held the flask out of the window and tossed it into a ditch. He saw the cap spin off as a puff of breeze blew the cigarette smoke out of the window . . .

2

Piers Shatner peered through the viewer of his Sony 655 video camera. The butt of the machine rested comfortably against his shoulder as he pressed the rewind button. The Sony was his favorite. It was slightly larger than a 16-mm film camera. He had been using it for the last three years, and though there were newer and better machines on the market, he clung stubbornly to the 655. It was as much a part of him as his hands and eyes. He watched the images skittering backward and stopped them occasionally. He had taped the news before catching the Pan Am flight to Sao Amerigo, and this was his first chance at viewing the recordings. There were messages from President Carter, Giscard d'Estaing, Mrs Thatcher, Mrs Gandhi, Trudeau. He skipped through them quickly as they all sounded the same. He stopped when John Darrigan, the US secretary of state, appeared on the screen.

Darrigan was obviously speaking from Geneva, where he was attending a meeting of the Council for the Economic Stabilization of Industrialized Nations. He was flanked by the other two members, Andrei Solotov of the USSR and Claude Mercer of the European Community. Piers didn't particularly like Darrigan. They'd clashed a year back when he'd been making a documentary on the Council. Darrigan, like his predecessor, Henry Kissinger, was an austere, clever man; academically brilliant, intellectually arrogant, and too confident with the power he wielded through his position of secretary of state, chairman of NSA and half a dozen other security agencies, and permanent representative to his brainchild, the Council.

The Council had been formed three years ago, a year after the breakdown of the Paris talks, as the single negotiator with the Third Nations. Canada and Britain and a few other countries had also wanted to be members of the board, but they'd been gently dissuaded, as it would become too unwieldy. In its three years the Council's power had increased in leaps and bounds as the industrialized world realized it had to present a united front against the increasing hostility of the Third World's demands. It had reached the position now that the Council virtually, though not entirely, dictated the growth and the prices of energy and raw materials in the western countries. Recently, its power had begun to worry the editorial writers on the *New York Times*, the *Washington Post*, the *Manchester Guardian*, *Le Figaro*, and a few other well-informed publications. They all felt, looking into their crystal balls, that the Council would one day totally control the economic lives of the countries it represented.

Piers pressed play, and Darrigan and the other two with him magically came to life. Darrigan was reading a prepared statement.

Television Broadcast Replay: It is with enormous sadness and horror that we have learned of the terrible tragedy that has struck the nation of Menaguay. We, on the Council, send our deepest condolences to all the people who have suffered. More practically, we also send our assistance. The Industrial Nations has reacted instantly to the tragedy and the Council has personally supervised the dispatch of aid and personnel. Over one hundred aircraft from the United States, Canada, Britain, France, Germany, and the other western countries have begun a shuttle service to Menaguay. Over two hundred and fifteen ships, with supplies and food, are now on their way. I can assure all the nations of the Third World that the Industrial Nations will never ever shirk its responsibility to all peoples of the world. Of late there have been many efforts by certain people to undermine the cordiality between the Third Nations and the Industrial Nations. As tragic as are these present circumstances, we are determined to prove that we are deeply affected by the catastrophe. We have airlifted, round the clock, supplies and personnel, and not only medical teams but also technicians who will help Menaguay to recover. The Council has also allocated a one-billion-dollar aid program to help Menaguay to reestablish itself among the nations of the world. I, personally, have had assurances from General Peres that his appointment as chairman is strictly temporary. Once normality has returned to the nation, he will step down in favor of Señor Bolivar.

Piers stopped the tape and rewound it back to start. He ran it over again. It didn't need much intelligence to realize that Darrigan was not addressing the survivors of Menaguay nor the people of the Industrial Nations. His speech was directed at Odu and Liu and Mrs Gandhi and Sadat, and if he really was alive, Bolivar. Piers vaguely wondered why.

Piers was a stocky man in his mid-forties. He looked older, for his face was worn and the creases around his slate-gray eyes, which looked overused, were deep and long. His nose had a bend in the middle, and his hair was cut close to his skull, so that it was hard to tell the color. It looked blond at times, at others brown. His left ear was crumpled, and he had a habit of pulling at the lobe. His actions were efficient, like a man used to conserving time and working well under enormous pressure.

Piers ran the tape forward a foot, and stopped it. The last seconds of a 'conserve food' commercial slid by and the tape stopped on Odu. Even shrunk to three inches, he looked a big man. His face was broad, fleshy, and strong, his gray hair looked white, and the glare of bad lighting hid his eyes. He was speaking from his Cape Town office with the right and assurance of a man who had won a long and bitter battle.

Television Broadcast Replay: I cannot tell you all how happy I am that my friend Bolivar has survived the terrible plague that has struck his country. I send him my deepest condolences, not only for the millions of his people but also for the personal loss of his wife. I am deeply impressed that the Industrial Nations have . . . uh . . . moved so very fast to come to the aid of one of the Third Nations. To be frank, I had not expected this. I am happy to admit it is my fault. I can assure the Council that by their quick reaction, they have won our admiration and friendship. I also sincerely hope that the Council will use its good offices to protect the life of Señor Bolivar and ensure that once the emergency is over, he will be allowed to return to his natural place as chairman.

Piers reran the short tape and pressed the plug more firmly into his ear. The sound was bad, but he thought he detected an edge in Odu's voice. Why hadn't he expected the Industrial Nations to help? Piers brooded about this briefly and then decided that his imagination had run away with itself.

He switched off the machine and slid it under his seat. He settled back to try to sleep. He wasn't looking forward to Sao Amerigo and the countless dead. He had seen too many of them over the last twenty-five years, and he was very tired. It wasn't so much a physical exhaustion; it was much deeper, for it touched his soul. At the beginning, there had been the excitement of witnessing wars, disasters, and the inevitable sight of dying men; in the middle there had been a dull acceptance of his role as voyeur; he was now at the end. It was, he promised himself, going to be the last assignment.

Marion Hyslop watched Piers settle back to sleep. She was in the seat next to him, and she felt wide-awake.

'Comfortable?' she whispered. Piers nodded and settled deeper into the seat. Marion smiled at him, and felt slightly envious. Piers could fall asleep in an instant, even when on a story. She always felt nervous and excited. He had tried to teach her the knack of sleeping, but she couldn't master it. They'd been working together for three years as a news documentary team for Channel 14, New York, and this was their eighth international story. In many ways, Marion thought, the stories are all same: wars, famines, and now a plague.

However, she never got tired of covering another tragedy. She was ten years younger than Piers, and when they'd first teamed up she'd been in awe of him. He was Piers Shatner, war correspondent, and she was a nothing. It hadn't been easy in the beginning. Piers was a man with a lot of machismo, and apart from patronizing her, he also seemed to resent her. He had asked the head of the studio to give him a guy as a second video cameraman, but Marion had screamed 'civil rights', and the studio head had backed down. She worked twice as hard after that to prove herself to Piers, but to her puzzlement, his resentment only increased. It was when they were covering the civil war in Ireland, and she was wounded, that she found out why. She threatened his masculinity by competing with him. Marion was a wise woman. She knew that all he wanted was to feel protective toward her and prove his own strength, so she'd allowed him to nurse her, tenderly, in the hospital. They became part-time lovers after that, and a good documentary team. Piers was a damned good reporter and never ever let a story go; she gave the story they covered a more practical, human touch.

Marion looked around the aircraft, and nodded to many of the familiar faces. There was Lewis Simon of the *Washington Post*, Don McCullum of the *Sunday Times* of London, and with him the ever-elegant Bryan Wharton, Richard Blume of the *New York Times*, Jack Newman of CBS. She knew nearly all of them. They were an exclusive club which met each time disaster struck. She'd even slept with two of them. Under pressure, she'd discovered, one of the releases open to both men and women was violent lovemaking.

Marion pushed her hair off her forehead. She knew she wasn't a beautiful woman; she was an attractive one. She was thirty, quite tall, with good breasts and ash-blond hair which fell to her shoulders. Her hazel eyes were watchful and intelligent, and when she laughed they crinkled tightly at the corners. Since learning her lesson from Piers, she knew most men enjoyed her company, and that gave her an enormous advantage over other women.

She lit a small, thin cigar and leaned back in her seat. She glanced at Piers; he was fast asleep, with his mouth half-open. In half an hour they'd be in Sao Amerigo, and she knew he wouldn't stop running until their story was over.

She'd never been to the country before, but Piers had. He'd made a documentary by himself on Bolivar, and she'd thought it very good, except it had been a bit too sympathetic. If she'd been with him at the time, she was sure she would have been able to balance it, as she wasn't as idealistic as Piers. Bolivar was ... well, not as romantic a figure as Piers made him out to be. He'd won an election democratically, but since then he'd caused nothing but problems.

The engine notes of the plane changed, and Piers immediately came awake and looked around. He raised an eyebrow in her direction.

'Another twenty minutes,' she told him, and he reached under his seat for his video camera. 'Do you want me to shoot as well?'

'No. There's only one angle we can get from this height.'

She touched his hand. 'To be honest, I'm not looking forward to going down. It sounds ... awful.'

'I know.'

The pilot announced they were approaching Sao Amerigo airport, and Piers shifted around in his seat and pointed the camera at the window and down. He spoke softly into the inset microphone.

Video Report: It's a few minutes before dawn and we're at one thousand feet. In fifteen minutes we'll be landing. What you see down below – bright jewels scattered across a velvet cloth – are not campfires. They are the funeral pyres for the countless dead. And countless is the right word. How many have died in the plague that has swept this country is anybody's guess. Estimates put the dead at fifteen million. And as suddenly as it started, the plague has ended. But not quite. A few more thousand will die from the more familiar diseases like cholera and dysentery. So far the medical world has no idea what the nature of this plague is. It has, until now, been confined to the South American continent. But scientists are racing against time to discover its origins and then invent the vaccine – for plagues, as man well knows, are no respecter of frontiers. There have been many over the centuries. The most famous, or should I say infamous, was the bubonic plague which devastated Europe in the mid-fourteenth century. Others, of different nature, have occurred in India, in Africa, in China. The last plague to sweep the world was in 1921. This was an influenza plague whose death toll reached twenty-one million. Plagues are too quick, and they leave too many dead. There is no time for burials, for fear of the other diseases breaking out. So the army has built giant fires and dug lime trenches to consume the victims of this new and terrible disease. This is Piers Shatner, Channel 14, New York, approaching Sao Amerigo.

Piers released the button and sat back. He shook his head to clear the dazed feeling. Fifteen million. The words had spilled out so easily. He punched rewind angrily and fitted in his ear plug. He checked the footage; the picture was fuzzy but adequate. He handed the video to Marion, and she nodded approval.

They both sensed someone hovering over them and looked up. Marion busied herself with the camera to avoid attention. It was Richard Harris of ITN, London. Harris was a red, round man. He had a round, bald head and a round, soft body. He looked as if he would puncture if a finger was poked into him. He and Piers had known each other for many years, having covered the same stories in the Middle East, Africa, Asia, wherever there was trouble, but neither could truthfully say he liked the other man. Harris liked the easy life, and to him an assignment was an excuse to run up expenses and do as little work as possible. He disliked Piers because Piers always rocked the boat – it was his favorite phrase – and would never share any of the hard news he'd found for himself. At the moment, Harris looked far from happy.

'I didn't want this damned assignment.' Piers could smell the whiskey on his breath as Harris leaned across him and peered at the ground. 'It'll just be my luck to catch every disease that's going down there.'

'They wouldn't dare touch you,' Piers said. 'Anyway, it's supposed to be safe now.'

'There's no such thing as safe in these countries,' Harris said, and looked mournful. 'I intend to get the hell out as fast as I can. A few hundred feet of video tape, and that's it, so for God's sake don't you start rocking the boat. Even you won't find a story apart from the plague.'

'You never know.' Piers smiled. 'Maybe one on you eating a poisoned plant.'

'I'm not going to eat or drink down there. And if I were you, I wouldn't either.'

His round face became even more unhappy, and for a moment Piers thought he was about to cry. But it was only the preparation for a belch. Marion stuck her tongue out at him as he left.

The pilot announced he was about to land, and Piers looked out of the window. In the gray dawn, Sao Amerigo looked black from the fires in the city. The smoke rose a few hundred feet and drifted reluctantly and lazily south. There seemed to be little breeze, and Piers expected that the city would be stifling.

It was still cool when they disembarked, and the air smelled clean and heady. But as they made their way to the terminal, a slight breeze brought in the smell of the city — smoke and stench. They all gagged and held handkerchiefs to their noses as they ran to the shelter of the building.

Lieutenant Henriquo Geddes watched them running across the tarmac and smiled. There was no humor in the expression, for once his mouth had twitched, it returned to a thin, flat line. Geddes was a young man in his early twenties and a career officer who wasn't happy with his present job. He looked every inch a toy soldier. His uniform was too immaculate and his face a bit too handsome. He had joined the army because his uncle was General Orantes and his father, retired General Velaz. He himself couldn't think of anything else to do, and the army, even under Bolivar, was a respectable profession. Geddes would have preferred, at the moment, to be attached either to his uncle or else given a command in one of the cities. Instead he was expected to play nursemaid to dozens of reporters from the world over. His orders had been simple: watch them carefully and don't let them stray too far. It was, his uncle assured him, for their own safety. Geddes could console himself that the job would last only a few days.

He waited until they'd gathered together and then stepped forward. He studied each face carefully, and mentally matched them with the files he had in his office. He didn't expect too many problems, as there was nothing secret about the disaster that had struck his country. The only good that had come out of the terrible evil was that Bolivar had been removed from power, and the army was back in its rightful place.

'My name,' he announced, 'is Lieutenant Geddes. I am here to ensure that you are given every facility to report this terrible tragedy to the people of the world. The city of Sao Amerigo and the country are at the moment under curfew: dusk to dawn. This is to prevent looting and unsociable elements taking control of an unstable situation. For your own safety, it is advisable that you do not go out by yourself.'

Piers had heard that phrase often before and had never obeyed it. It was always used for the convenience of the authorities.

'What,' Piers came to the point quickly, 'has happened to Chairman Bolivar?'

Geddes stared into the lens of the video. 'Because of the emergency,' he recited, 'General Peres is now chairman. Only the army, with the help of the Industrial Nations of course, could mount the massive rescue operation. Once the crisis is over, General Peres will step down.'

Neither Geddes nor Piers believed this. Nor did Schmidt of Radio Hamburg.

'When can we meet ex-Chairman Bolivar?' he asked.

'Soon. He is in mourning, for, as you know, his wife was one of those who died in the plague.'

Piers lowered his head briefly. He had spent a lot of time with Madame Bolivar when he was making his documentary on her husband, and he'd liked her immensely.

A few more questions were asked about the situation, and

32

then Geddes led them to a row of telephones. Piers picked up the nearest and raised a questioning eyebrow at Geddes. 'There is no censorship,' Geddes said. 'This is not a war or a coup.'

Piers dialed New York. 'Shatner,' he said when he was connected to recording. He uncapped the mouthpiece and attached the transmit cable from the video and pressed the button. The video was capable of transmitting on its own power pack over a distance of ten miles. Beyond that range the signal needed to be boosted. Piers disconnected when the footage had been transmitted.

'Okay?' he asked New York.

'Some blur, but otherwise okay.'

Piers waited a moment and looked around. The others were still sending. He redialed and connected the cable once again. He transmitted the same pictures, but this time it was sent to his own recording machine in his studio. Experience had taught him to always have a copy, as Channel 14 would, when it thought it best, conveniently lose his tapes. When he finished sending, he, like the others, pressed the erase button.

Geddes made sure they were all ready and then led them out to an army truck. A soldier stood by the tailgate with an armful of gas masks; another stood behind him with a machine-gun in his arms. As they climbed in, each reporter was given a mask.

'We're not going to catch anything, are we?' Harris' worried voice rose an octave as he took his mask.

'It's for the smoke and the smell,' Geddes said abruptly. He didn't like men to show they were afraid, especially as the women had not shown any fear.

For the first couple of miles into the city, the air remained cool and pleasant. The road itself, however, was empty, and the only vehicles they passed were other army trucks. The sun had started to climb, and Piers could feel the first heat of the day on his back. He shifted under the covers. He knew that soon the heat would be unbearable. It became unbearable much sooner. The wind shifted and he felt as if he'd been hit in the face with the heat and smell of smoke. The sickly odor of burning flesh made him gag; it was as if someone was forcing thick, greasy tendrils down his throat. He choked and tried to suck in air and only swallowed more smoke and smell. He could see, through the blur of tears, the others also doubled up and gasping. He slipped the mask on and steadied his breath. The air smelled somewhat clean but dusty. The others were doing the same. He caught a glimpse of Geddes and the two soldiers. It looked as if they were grinning behind their masks.

The truck took a curve, and Piers saw the first of the massive fires. It was raging in the *barrio*, and the noise was awesome. The flames crackled and boomed and the tin of the shanty town bent and buckled, making noises, as they fell against each other, like human screams. At times, because of the heat, the fire didn't seem to exist. It would merge in with the sky and the bright sun, and all one could see was the shimmering waves of heat. The whole scene looked like a medieval painting of hell, for standing around the fire were soldiers dressed in asbestos suits and holding bazookas. Backing toward the edges of the *barrio* were dump trucks piled high with the victims of the plague, rich and poor, man and animal. They were dumped into the fires and the soldiers would fire their bazookas at the fresh pile.

Piers jumped off the truck and got as near as possible to the flames. He shot fifty feet of tape. He would have taken more, but the heat was burning his skin, and he backed hurriedly to the truck. The other reporters remained where they were, shooting their pictures through zoom lenses.

For a moment Piers watched the soldiers at work. The heat still seared his forehead and bare arms. His eyes, however, remained blank and just curious. It seemed as if nothing he was seeing could ever touch his heart. He turned, and Geddes helped him back into the truck.

'Next time tell me you are going to jump,' Geddes said shortly. 'I am responsible for your safety.'

'Okay, okay,' Piers said. 'I'm sorry.' He moved to the back of the truck and joined Marion. She was looking very pale.

The reporters were all silent and one of the women, the Russian, looked as if she were about to cry. Piers touched Marion. She looked specially vulnerable as she tried to compose herself.

'You all right?' he asked.

She nodded. Piers had long since trained himself to remain totally detached from all the tragedy he saw. It seemed as if there was a built-in coldness in him.

'It's terrible,' Marion said, and repeated herself once more. 'I thought I'd be able to take it, but . . .' She shook her head hopelessly.

'You're lucky to feel something.'

'Yes.' She nodded to his video. 'New York won't broadcast those close-ups you took. Viewers don't like to see those sights.'

'If I can, they can. I'm not shooting commercials for them over here.' He stopped angrily and nodded. 'I know they'll never be shown, but I do the job I'm sent out to do, and I don't know how to pull my punches.'

This inability, he knew, was a dangerous habit and had already gotten him into endless trouble with authority. But he was a man who couldn't change for the sake of authority.

The truck started off and passed through the park. It took the final curve and entered Sao Amerigo. The city appeared empty and disquietingly silent. The avenues and plazas and gardens and sidewalks were deserted. Here and there, as he peered through the video, Piers saw movement. But it was too quick and too brief. They passed parked jeeps and trucks filled with soldiers who watched them suspiciously. Yet the city retained its beauty. No doubt it was a desolate beauty, drained of all its life force.

Piers wondered whether Bolivar was really alive, for this city was Bolivar's monument. He had dreamed grandeur for it and for his people. They'd believed totally in him and his vision of the future. It had all come to this mean and unforeseen end.

He caught a sudden movement out of the corner of his eye and reflexively had the video lined up on target. A young

35

man, who didn't look older than twenty, smashed a shop window and grabbed what he could. He turned and sprinted with his armful of tinned foods. He didn't get far. A jeep patrol took the corner, and one of the soldiers fired a short burst at the running boy. The boy seemed to trip and fall, his pathetic haul scattering across the road. He never would get up again.

The truck passed the body, and they all looked down. The blood was slowly spreading into a widening pool. The boy's face wasn't visible to them, but his death touched them more, for his was comprehensible. The others they'd seen piled on the flames were just numbers.

'As I warned you earlier,' Geddes said with satisfaction in his voice. 'The soldiers shoot first and ask questions later. You all must either remain in the hotel or else be accompanied by me or a soldier. Now' – he looked at his watch as they neared the hotel – 'General Peres is giving a press conference at noon. After the conference there will be a tour of the hospitals and the emergency stations. You will be able to see for yourself how the army, with the help of Industrial Nations personnel, is coping with the disaster.'

'I see the army everywhere,' Piers said quietly. 'Weren't they affected by the plague?'

'We are human too,' Geddes said. 'We were lucky, as we lost only a third of our men. Ex-Chairman Bolivar had us scattered all over the country.' He smiled at the irony of Bolivar's strategy.

The rest of the journey was spent in silence. They passed other fires, and they all looked the same as the very first. The smell, the heat, the soldiers, the bodies, the dump trucks; everything was the same. There was also a bit more sign of civilian life in the center of the city. Outside a food shop a small line of people waited for it to open. Their faces looked stunned and withdrawn.

The truck turned up a drive, and Piers glanced out. They were to be billeted in the very best hotel, the Amerigo. It was a graceful, brightly white, circular building. Piers remembered it as the center of high-society living, constantly filled with beautiful men and women. All that remained now were memories. The foyer was gloomy and empty and silent; the swimming pool was filled with dead leaves; and the bars were empty. The reporters whispered as they moved through the foyer as if they didn't want to disturb the spirits of the people who'd once enjoyed life so much. Piers remembered a girl he'd met here, Cecilia. He still had her number and decided to ring her once he'd checked in.

They were given rooms on the fourth floor, and as there was no staff, they carried their own bags. Though there was electricity, the elevators weren't working. Marion joined Piers on the stairs. They always had separate rooms. She still looked shaken, and Piers felt sympathy for her.

'I've got some brandy in my case,' he said. 'When you've unpacked, come up and have some. It'll steady you.'

She managed a nod, and he showed her his key. There were signs of neglect in his room. The bed was rumpled, the dust was thick on the furniture, and the air smelled stale. Piers tried the air-conditioner; it worked. He unpacked what little he'd brought and checked the tape he'd shot coming in from the airport. The pictures were too clear and showed all the horror in detail. He knew there'd be trouble as he dialed New York and plugged in the machine. He lay on the bed while the tape was being transmitted.

He wondered about what he'd seen. He felt some envy for Marion. She'd felt pain and horror; he had felt nothing. It was as if he was moving in a dream and nothing that he'd seen over the years – death and pain and suffering – really existed. He seemed at times on a different plane and too far away for things to affect him. He had been too long on the job, and a kind of death had struck him. This was going to be his last assignment.

He thought about Marion and felt himself smiling. He loved her; at times the love was for a friend, at others it was for a lover. They'd been together a lot, and he trusted her. They were a good team. She was getting to be as good as he was. Yet, finally, she'd never ever match him. She lacked his need for the truth; to find it, and to know it. Nor did she have his curiosity. To her a story was a job, to be done well, and it ended there. When he quit, she would take over. Or maybe, he paused, she'd quit with him. They could do other things.

The buzz from the transmitter interrupted his thoughts. New York was wanting to talk to him, and he disconnected the machine and picked up the phone.

'What the hell are you playing at, Piers?' Frank Kolok, his editor, screamed down the line. 'You know damned well I can't broadcast pictures of burning kids and dogs. It's too emotive. Fifteen years you've been working for me, and you still manage to get up my nose. Keep it to long shots. Now I have to use the Chicago or London pictures. They're more discreet.'

'What do they show? Alice in Wonderland?'

'Long shots,' Kolok shouted. The phone abruptly went dead.

Piers shrugged and dialed his own studio, rewound, and transmitted the tape once more.

He didn't let Kolok worry about him. They spent more time bickering than a married couple, and Piers knew it wasn't Kolok's fault. Television audiences didn't like too much reality on their screens. If the pictures turned their stomachs, they switched channels.

The transmit finished, and Piers erased the tape and rewound. He decided to try Cecilia while he waited for Marion, and thumbed through his phone book. He dialed her number and waited. He counted fifteen rings and then gently replaced the phone. The echoes gave him the answer. He tried to remember what she looked like. She had been beautiful, but the most he could recall was the way she'd laughed, and strangely, the vague odor of her body after lovemaking.

Marion carefully washed her face. The moment she'd entered her room she'd had to dash to the toilet and puke up her breakfast. This story, she thought as she looked at her wan face in the mirror, was different – it was awful. She'd seen men and women die violently in the 1978 Arab-Israeli war, and in the South African massacres, but never in such vast numbers. She wiped her face and spent some time making herself up. It helped to steady her nerves, and gave her stomach time to settle. In a few minutes, she'd have to go out on the street again and see and smell those countless dead. Maybe a shot of brandy would help. She unpacked quickly, scooped up her video camera, checked that it was working, and left the room.

She knocked on Piers' door and heard him get off the bed. She was glad she was with him; she couldn't have done this story alone. There were times, and they were becoming increasingly frequent, that she sensed Piers was wanting to quit. The signs to recognize were an edgy irritableness, but she expected they would pass. Every reporter she knew dreamed of quitting, going away to write a book, make a film, lie in the grass, whatever. They never did. She'd known Piers long enough to feel that his irritability would pass; it would happen once they began to put together the story. She hoped there wasn't going to be much, as her stomach wouldn't last.

Piers handed her the brandy as soon as she entered. She sipped it, gagged a bit, but held it down. It warmed her belly.

'Okay?' Marion nodded. 'We better get going, then.'

They went down to the lobby, and Geddes was waiting for them. He counted heads and found one missing. They all waited a further five minutes for Harris to join them.

'New York's not too happy with you,' Harris said with a smirk as he fell in beside Piers. 'I keep telling you, Shatner; don't make them unhappy. Transmit only what they want. It just makes life easier for you.'

'If I wanted the easy life, I'd stay in New York.'

It was a five-minute ride to the Great Assembly Hall, and they could have just as easily walked the distance. The Plaza Bolivar, outside the hall, was almost deserted of civilians but heavily populated with soldiers. Piers never considered them as people, for they belonged to the same battle-dress-green machine he'd seen in a hundred countries across the world.

They removed their masks once they entered the hall. It was empty, and their footsteps echoed. The tiers of vacant seats looked down on the dais, and their emptiness made the hall look only bigger and somewhat sadder. It was designed to reflect the grandeur of the country and the people. The decor, Piers thought, was too flamboyant for his tastes. An eight-foot-high, gold-and-blue-and-red seal dominated the hall from behind the dais; the seats were made of black leather, and the walls, covered with the flags of the various provinces, were red. The reporters took the front row and waited five minutes before the eight generals and one colonel, the ruling junta, filed out from the wings looking like a chorus of marionettes.

Video Report: When the catastrophe struck this country seven days ago, the civilian adminstration of Chairman Bolivar was incapable of handling the situation. Such a massive relief and rescue operation could be organized only by the army. Due to the emergency situation, General Emilo Peres, the army chief of staff, became temporary chairman of the country and declared martial law. General Peres, a career man with a particularly undistinguished military record, stands in the center. He is the one wearing dark glasses, and the uniform he is wearing looks weighed down with just that much extra gold braid and medals. On either side of him are the other members of his temporary government.

He is first to read a short statement before answering our questions.

Gentlemen. I am a man burdened by a terrible sadness. I mourn the deaths of countless of my people from this cursed plague. The army is working day and night to ensure the country doesn't collapse completely. I would like to take this opportunity to thank the leaders and the people of the Industrial Nations for their messages of condolence and also for the medicine, food, and doctors they have rushed to this country. I would also like to thank the leaders of the Third Nations who have sent as much aid and supplies as they have thought possible. I would like to assure the world that when the normal situation has been restored, I promise to step down from this office and allow Señor Bolivar to continue to rule this country. Thank you.

Harris, ITN, London: Chairman General, do you think

your country could have survived without the help of the Industrial Nations?

No. The help your countries have given is incalculable. Industrial Nations personnel have staffed our hospitals, distributed food and blankets, and restored power supplies. Once we have recovered, we shall take over these duties.

Hyslop, Channel 14, New York: Chairman General, have the doctors as yet found the cause of the plague?

No. It would be best to ask them about their progress when you meet them later today.

Shatner, New York: What has happened to Chairman Bolivar?

Señor Bolivar is safe and well. This is not a coup. The army was the only organization capable of handling the emergency.

May we meet him?

It will not be possible at the present moment. As you know, his wife was taken by the plague, and he has been shaken by the tragedy to her and his people. I repeat, this is not a political matter. Once normality has returned, I promise I shall vacate. Thank you.

The generals file out behind the chairman. The question on Bolivar still remains unanswered. Is he alive? If he is, why can't we meet him? Or maybe he died in the plague. This is Marion Hyslop, Channel 14, New York, in the Assembly Hall of Sao Amerigo.

The conference was over, and Geddes was quick to move them on. It was, Piers realized as they climbed back into the truck, going to be a very long day. Geddes had set up a grueling program. They were shown the army in action – distributing food, manning information centers, tending the sick, burning the bodies. The sun by this time was high in the sky, and the open truck offered them no shelter. They wilted and slowly began to lose interest in the tour. Even Piers found it difficult to lift the video to record the horrors of the plague. By the time they reached the Sao Amerigo

General, they had just enough energy to drag themselves into the auditorium.

Piers removed his mask and wiped his face. The cool air managed to revive him, but Marion looked as if she was going to faint. He helped her to a chair and collapsed next to her. The hospital and research laboratories were part of Sao Amerigo University and were in the education sector of the city. Within this area, which was really one huge campus, were all the institutions from primary schools to the university. There were some ideas of Bolivar's that Piers didn't like, and one was the grouping of all education into one sector. It was like being filed away in a pigeonhole, and this one would hold a child for twenty years.

Three men mounted the steps to the stage. One looked American, the other two South American. Though the American was the youngest, his companions obviously accepted him as their spokesman. At least, he was the only one with notes. He was a young man. Piers guessed him to be in his early thirties, with a smooth, impatient face and a top lip that quivered with superior intelligence. He rustled his papers impatiently to hurry the reporters to set up their equipment.

Video Report: *My name is Dr Kevin O'Brien. These are my colleagues Drs Seguira and Dr Henriques. I would first like to read my statement. I hope it will answer all your questions and we won't be delayed. My work is very urgent, as you can understand.*

My colleagues and I have little to report at the moment. We have been working enormously hard to discover the cause of the plague which has devastated this country. From the extensive tests we have made, however, we have reached a few conclusions.

One, the infection is not contagious. By this I mean that it is not transmitted by human beings. Like a common cold, for instance.

Two, we believe that the infection is transmitted through the air and not through water supplies or con-taminated foods.

Three, as it is transmitted through the air, the infection attacks the body through the respiratory system. In our many autopsies we have discovered clotting in the lungs. There are also indications that paralysis has occurred in various parts of the body. We are not as yet sure what exactly happened in the body once the air entered the lungs.

Four, we are following the line that the infection was a mutant strain of virus. We have as yet been unable to isolate the virus. Until we can, and until we identify it, it will be impossible to invent an antidote. Thank you.

Bruyere, ILTV, Paris: How long will it take to isolate this virus and run tests on it?

It's impossible to say.

What will happen if you cannot invent this antidote?

I am sure we will be able to, given enough time.

Hyslop, Channel 14, New York: In that case, if the plague should recur either in this country or elsewhere, the people will be without protection?

That is assuming the plague does recur. I, personally, don't believe it will. The virus appears to die within its victim.

Shatner, New York: What exactly do you mean by paralysis?

Muscle constriction in the area of the arms, legs, abdomen, and heart.

What exactly happens to the person who is infected? I mean physically.

According to eyewitnesses, the victim of the virus becomes paralyzed.

How long would it take for the person to die?

A minute or two at the most. It will vary from person to person.

Schmidt, Radio Hamburg: Are the facilities here adequate to carry out these tests?

They are excellent. And the Sao Amerigo scientists and doctors have been of enormous help. A few facilities are lacking, but it doesn't affect my work. I'm afraid that is all

I have time for. We have to return to our work. Thank you.

Alexeyev, Tass, Moscow: Just one last question, Dr O'Brien.

Can you make it brief, please?

Of course. In your opinion, would you consider that this ... virus ... may have extraterrestrial origins?

I have not ruled out that possibility in my investigations.

So it is very probable.

I said possible. Please don't put words in my mouth. I'd like to add that to date there have been no reports of meteorites or any unidentified objects falling in this part of the hemisphere. I must end this conference now. Thank you.

Shatner, New York: Would it be possible to question your colleagues? Dr Seguira, could you tell me ...?

I'm afraid we just don't have any more time, thank you.

Though Dr O'Brien, acting as spokesman for his colleagues, who never once volunteered to answer questions, has narrowed down the causes of the plague, he has not as yet discovered the exact nature of the virus that has killed so many millions of people. To isolate the virus is going to take days, weeks, even months. And once he has done this, he will then have to invent the antidote, which in turn may take weeks or months. In spite of his reassurances that the plague will not return, there is no guarantee. It can return here or break out in another country. Plagues are no respecter of national boundaries. Until Dr O'Brien and his colleagues can crack both parts of the problem, we can only hope and pray that no new outbreak occurs. This is Piers Shatner and Marion Hyslop, Channel 14, New York, in Sao Amerigo.

Piers lowered his video and wished that O'Brien's colleagues had also answered questions. It looked at times as if they did understand English, but their eyes, Piers had noticed, had constantly shifted to follow what looked like warnings coming from the left side of the room. He'd glanced once in that direction; they'd been watching Geddes. In spite of his stillness, he had looked menacing and seemed ready to intervene if the questions did become too awkward. Piers tugged his ear lobe and wondered why Geddes hadn't wanted the local scientists to answer questions.

O'Brien also wondered why he'd had to do all the talking. He hated the press conference and was relieved it was over. He was a scientist, not a bloody politician who had to be grilled by reporter idiots. But he was also relieved the conference was over in another way: he wasn't sure whether he'd spoken the truth. He'd been ordered to Sao Amerigo by WHO and told to urgently discover the cause of the plague, and invent an antidote. Nothing more and nothing less. When he'd first been given the order, he thought they meant take his whole lab team and equipment down to Sao Amerigo. No, he was told, by yourself; you'll be assisted by the local scientists. They were asking for a bloody miracle, sending him by himself, or ... He hesitated. Maybe they were not wanting the miracle.

O'Brien removed his glasses and wiped his face. He was a tall, thin man, and as Piers had guessed, in his early thirties. He was a brilliant man in his field, but outside of his subject, he was like a child. At the moment, however, he felt a vague unease. He wasn't sure what it was. Doubts, like wisps of cloud in a clear summer sky, were drifting through the outer reaches of his mind. There was something about the symptoms of the plague he didn't like. It had come and gone too suddenly, and its method of attacking the human were vaguely familiar. If only he was back in his own lab in Boston ...

3

Piers found himself with the others in the Sao Amerigo hospital itself. It was one of two thousand-bed hospitals in the city, which, at one time, were thought adequate. But a crisis like this was unforeseen, and the victims of the plague were lying in whatever space could be found for them. Most, Piers saw, were only partially affected by the plague; they were either semiparalyzed or else in a state of shock. New patients being admitted were suffering more from other diseases that had broken out due to the breakdown in water, food and sanitation. The doctors and nurses looked as if they hadn't slept for weeks, and moved around like zombies. Piers casually detached himself from the group, and lifting his video, approached a middle-aged man lying in a bed.

Video Report: Excuse me, sir, do you speak English?
   A little.
   Can you remember exactly what happened to you?
   It is difficult to speak. My throat . . .
   Take your time.
   I remember little. I am a bus driver. I am going down Calle Allende and suddenly I take a breath and it feels as if my throat has caught fire. It burns.
   And then?
   It turns . . . how you say . . . numb. Like a cold stone. I cannot breathe anymore and I feel as if my chest is being crushed. I can see in the street the other people falling down, and I cannot control the bus. That's all. When I wake, I have crashed into a shop . . . a lot of people are dead in my bus. Not from my driving, you understand.
   Why do you think you lived?
   Ask God.

How have you been affected by the plague?

I cannot move my right leg and right arm. The doctors do not know if I will ever recover.

Can you tell me what time this happened to you?

Eight-thirty-five in the morning. I remember it because I am running behind time and I have to hurry.

Can you describe—?

Mr Shatner, you are disturbing a very sick man with your questions.

Lieutenant Geddes, he doesn't seem very disturbed to me.

You are not a doctor. Will you join the others, please. We must move on.

The authorities have informed me I may no longer question this man. This is Piers Shatner, Channel 14, New York, at a bedside in Sao Amerigo General Hospital.

Piers angrily jabbed the video's off button. The gesture left Geddes unmoved.

'Did you have to include that last remark?' Geddes said. 'I was only trying to save that man discomfort.'

'He seemed to be okay to me,' Piers said. 'Besides, the remark was the truth. You stopped me.'

Geddes shrugged and politely waved Piers on to join the others. Piers moved unhurriedly to join the group. When he reached them he looked back. Geddes was talking to the bus driver. Piers wished he had a directional mike to find out what was being said.

'I wish you wouldn't cause so much trouble,' Harris said petulantly. 'They'll cancel our visas and shove us out if you keep pushing them. Then we won't have a story.'

'What story?' Piers asked. 'All I've got is propaganda on the brave army and the brave Industrial Nations doctors.'

'That's the only story I can see,' Harris said. 'You don't have to push your video into a dying man's face to invent something different.'

'He wasn't dying.'

'So you're a doctor now.'

'And you're a horse's arse.'

For a moment the two men glared at each other. Then Harris wheeled and rolled off in the direction of Geddes.

'He's a creep,' Marion shuddered beside Piers.

Piers shrugged. 'We just don't like each other very much.'

'Did you find out anything from that man?'

'Not much. Only that he caught the plague at eight-thirty-five.' Piers tugged his ear. 'I wonder what time it hit the other parts of the country?'

'Why?'

'Curiosity. It couldn't have happened everywhere at the same time.'

Geddes returned to them and shepherded them down the corridors. He allowed them to film a few more wards and interview doctors and nurses from Paris, London and Moscow. Piers remained at the rear of the crowd. He didn't bother to ask any questions. The answers would always be the same. Every now and then, Geddes would glance around hurriedly, spot him, and relax. Piers grimaced when it happened the third time. He'd made himself too conspicuous, but it couldn't be helped.

It was on the way out that he had a break. Geddes was called to a phone, and for a few minutes they were left in charge of a private soldier, cradling an old machine-gun. Obviously he had not been given any orders apart from being told to watch them.

Piers looked around. Dr Seguira, one of O'Brien's colleagues, was slowly walking toward them. He should have been a portly man, but in the last few days he must have visibly shrunk. The skin around his neck was loose, and his clothes looked baggy.

Video Report: Excuse me, Dr Seguira, would you mind if I asked you a few questions?

I'm sorry. I will have to get Lieutenant Geddes' permission.

He said I could just before he left, doctor. Are you from Sao Amerigo?

No. I come from a small town about four hundred miles north of here. Are you sure that Lieutenant Geddes said I could give an interview?

Positive. What is the situation like there? By being here, are you neglecting the people in your city?

The people there don't need me.

They're all dead?

No. All alive. We have not been affected by the disease which is why I was brought to Sao Amerigo to assist your Dr O'Brien. He's a very clever man, and—

Yes ... yes. You are sure about your city?

Positive. It's only the central area that has been struck by the plague. I would calculate that taking Sao Amerigo as the center, the affected area forms a circle of around three to four hundred miles. Outside this circle, life is normal.

Why do you think this is? Some parts outside this circle you describe must have had a few casualties.

None, from what I can gather. My guess is that the center, being so highly populated, was the hardest hit. As we move farther away from Sao Amerigo, the population thins out.

Do you believe there is a point of origin for this plague?

There must be, but it would be very hard to find. One man catches the disease, and it spreads like wildfire. Only God would know who this poor first man was.

Dr Seguira, you were not given permission to grant this man an interview.

He told me you had given permission, Lieutenant Geddes. That is why I spoke to him.

Mr Shatner ... I would suggest ... misled you into thinking this. I am sure you will allow me to view your tapes, Mr Shatner.

Sure. He didn't let out any state secrets. That's if you have any you're hiding.

There is nothing to hide. You may continue, Dr Seguira. Would you mind pointing your video away from me, Mr Shatner.

49

There seems to be a certain hostility whenever a question is asked on the extent of the plague and the areas affected. We know now that it has hit only the central area, the most heavily populated area in Menaguay. Why it didn't spread further is a question that remains to be answered by the scientists. This is Piers Shatner, Channel 14, New York, Sao Amerigo General Hospital.

Piers lowered his video and began to move away. He was blocked by Geddes standing with an outstretched hand.

'I meant it,' Geddes said. 'I want to see the tape.'

'And I said sure.' Piers punched the rewind. 'You in charge of news censorship as well?'

'There is no censorship,' Geddes said. 'We just do not wish you to ... say ... overdramatize the story. Sensationalize, I believe would be the correct word.'

He took the video and watched a rerun of Dr Seguira's interview. He nodded and returned the video to Piers.

'You could have easily asked me the same questions. I would have answered.'

'You just want to see yourself on television, don't you, Lieutenant? I'm not talent-spotting at the moment.'

Geddes led the way out of the hospital. The soldier walked a few paces to the left of Piers, and from the way he kept his eyes fixed to his back, Piers figured Geddes had ordered the soldier to keep a special watch on him. The hospital driveway was jammed with army trucks ferrying the sick to the hospital and carting away the dead. The dust they churned up made it almost impossible to breathe in spite of the gas masks nearly everyone was wearing. The sun, much lower by now, and cooler, looked blurred behind the haze of dust. It seemed, to Piers, that the bright orange ball was slowly turning an anemic, reddish gray.

Piers was glad to get into their truck. Like the others, he slumped down on the hard, wooden seats. His feet hurt and the left side of his face throbbed. It always did when he was very tired. The dust hadn't helped his eyes, either. They were red and watery, and he rubbed them wearily. Even Geddes had begun to wilt. His uniform was creased, and his back had begun to bend under the pressure of the long day.

'Where to now?' Marion asked. Her voice was strained, and Piers felt sorry for her.

'Back to the hotel,' Geddes said, and a cheer went up. 'You will be in time to transmit your tapes. Some of you, at least.'

Piers wasn't too tired to think as they were driven back to the hotel. Something was worrying him. He had a gut feeling and he wasn't sure whether it was the pain he felt for the devastated country and people or his reporter's instinct trying to shake itself loose. Piers was a man who distrusted emotion, and he tried to smother any feelings he had for the situation. He believed in detachment, and if he trusted his gut feeling, that left his instincts. He could feel tension around him – in Geddes, in Seguira, in O'Brien. It was as if they were all trying to hide something. Piers glanced at Geddes and shook his head. The man was too junior an officer to know what he was doing; he was a man who followed orders, not gave them. Then who gave them? Not O'Brien or Seguira. They were just a couple of clever scientists. The generals? Piers withheld judgment. He didn't particularly believe that generals were intelligent men, and the ones he'd seen that morning resembled gilded, dandified puppets.

All right, Piers thought, forget about who's giving orders. Why the tension? Why were they allowed to interview only the aid people? Why did Geddes have to lean so heavily on him each time he tried to interview the bus driver and Seguira?

Piers shook his head. He was puzzled by the problem. It was a simple and tragic story. Millions had died in the plague, and all he wanted was to pull together a story of the disaster.

'You're looking worried.' Marion leaned over to him. Geddes immediately raised his head and stared at Piers.

'Nothing. Just something bugging me, and I can't figure it out.'

'You've got a story. Give.'

'I'll tell you later. I can feel someone's ears tuning in.'

The truck turned off Avenida Peron and took a side street to the hotel. Piers knew the area vaguely and looked up and around. He was pleased he'd been right. A few blocks down, over the tops of the buildings, he caught a glimpse of the Sao Amerigo cathedral. It was the highest structure in the city and was supposed to be the largest cathedral in the world. It was, as Piers remembered, a delicate weave of arches, stained-glass windows, and soaring spires. He pointed it out to Marion, and as they passed an opening between the buildings, he glanced down at the plaza in front of the cathedral. Piers immediately forgot his exhaustion. He grabbed his video and signaled to Geddes to stop the truck. Geddes shook his head. Piers shrugged, walked to the edge, and jumped down. The truck was moving faster than he'd calculated, or maybe it was his tiredness, but he stumbled and fell on one knee. He winced at the stab of pain as he got to his feet. He flexed his leg as the truck skidded to a halt, and limped toward the cathedral.

He'd wondered why the city had been so empty, and now he knew why. All those who'd survived the plague were outside the great cathedral. Every inch of space was covered with kneeling people, and the bowed heads extended as far as Piers could see through the video. The silence was awesome and almost resembled a visible force that hung in the air over all the heads. Their prayers, their thoughts, their bewilderment, their questions to a God who seemed to have abandoned them, were murmured only in their minds and hearts, for Piers couldn't hear a sound. There was little movement. Here and there a child would raise its head, and a woman, probably the mother, would gently push the head down again. Now and then someone would shift, but otherwise they knelt on the hard stone, seemingly feeling no physical pain. And what pain they did experience was far surpassed by their sadness.

Piers backed away once he'd finished. The silence really did feel physical, and it seemed to be trying to pull him into their sorrow. It was as if the woman he'd seen bend the child's head was reaching out toward him. He shook his head in silent refusal. The other reporters were shooting their pictures, and he could hear their whispered commentary. Geddes caught his eye.

'People should be left alone in their pain,' he whispered angrily. 'Not shown across the world. You have no respect for tragedy.'

'I've been told that before. "Immoral" is the word you want.' He returned to the truck and waited for the others.

At the sound of the truck starting, a man on the edge of the crowd lifted his head and turned to watch. To Lopez it was a welcome distraction from the numbness that he'd felt for so long. He became aware his knees were hurting, and slowly stumbled to his feet. He glanced at his watch. He tried to calculate how long he'd been kneeling, but he couldn't remember when he'd come to join the crowd outside the cathedral. He'd come to sense the people around him, to be a part of the living rather than the dead.

As he walked away from the cathedral, it would have been difficult for anyone who had known him before to have recognized Lopez now. Gone was the immaculate, handsome man. In his place was a scruffy, emaciated figure. The face was unshaven and the eyes were ringed by deep, dark pouches. The clothes were grubby and sweat-stained.

Lopez hesitated on Avenida Peron. He could go home, or . . . He tried to think of an alternative. There was none, and he decided to return to his apartment. He knew it would be empty. It hadn't been when he'd returned, finally, from Fortaleza. He'd dreaded entering that first day, and when he had opened the door, it was as he'd feared. He'd found the body of his mother and of his sister and her husband and their two children. They must have been visiting when the plague had reached them. He was thankful he had no children, for then the pain would have driven him to suicide. In spite of his status, the army had refused him permission to bury his family. They were thrown on the pyre with a thousand other anonymous bodies.

The streets he walked were deserted. Now and then a person would hurry past or a jeep patrol would watch him warily until he turned the corner. Lopez looked up at the clock tower near his apartment. Another hour to curfew. The light had begun to fade, and his shadow was slowly disappearing. He missed the crowd. The feel of someone's breath on the back of his neck, to sense the movement of the person next to him, to smell the warm, sour sweat of their bodies through the stench that pervaded his city. He felt an immense loneliness and tried to pray, but he couldn't. He'd tried before, when he'd been kneeling, but all that had tumbled out his mouth was a mumble. He felt a bewildered rage at what had happened, and there was nothing he could do about it.

Bitterly he thought of his brief vacation.

For the first day and a half, he had felt he was in paradise. Admittedly, there was one minor flaw, Inez, but she was gradually recovering her good humor. He expected that, given another day, she would be her normal, sensual self, but by then, he was sure, he'd have become mad with boredom.

By the nature of his profession he was a very active man. He'd lain in the sun a whole day, fished halfheartedly, spent an hour listening to his favorite composer, Ravel, and sat through two cowboy movies run in the cruiser's salon. The thought of repeating the same routine for another five and a half days appalled him. He was also beginning to worry about his work and his premonitions. Just because he took a holiday, that wouldn't mean his government's enemies would. Somebody, somewhere was always trying to think of a way to overthrow his chairman, Juan Jesus Bolivar, and Lopez passionately enjoyed outwitting them.

By the morning of the second day of his holiday, he had had enough. As soon as he woke, he rang the captain.

'Where are we now?' he asked over the bedside telephone.

'Off Rocas, sir.' It was a small island, and Lopez had thought of doing a day's exploring.

'I've changed my mind. Return to Fortaleza,' he said.

Inez lay asleep beside him. He woke her gently by slipping his fingers between her thighs. She murmured and pushed his hand away. He waited a moment, and then tried again.

Languidly, her legs began to open. When his finger entered her, she moaned and turned toward him. Her hand sleepily stroked his belly and held his cock. He smiled to himself. She was back to normal, and it was about time, too. He didn't waste any more time. He turned her so that her back was to him and held her firm, round breasts as he gently pushed himself into her. He felt he was sliding into a soothing wet fire. The telephone rang. He ignored it; they were moving rhythmically against each other. He squeezed her nipples hard as he felt her come back harder and harder against him. She cried out at the pain and the pleasure, and he knew she was going to come. He raced with her and reached his climax at the same time as she did. They slumped together, dazed and exhausted. There was an irritating noise in the background, and he realized the phone was still ringing.

'What?' he shouted into it. The captain was stammering unintelligibly. 'Calm yourself,' Lopez ordered.

There was a moment's silence. 'Plague . . . in our country . . . reports . . . thousands dying . . .'

Lopez didn't wait. He grabbed his dressing gown and ran up to the radio room. The captain looked shaken as he handed Lopez the mike.

'What is this . . . plague?' Lopez shouted into the mike.

'We don't know what it is,' a voice crackled back. 'The reports are just coming in . . . thousands are dying not only in Sao Amerigo but the whole territory . . .'

'Mother of God.' Lopez wasn't a religious man, but he crossed himself. He had never feared death, but a plague . . . 'How long will it take to return?' he asked the captain.

'Day and a half, sir,' the captain said reluctantly. 'But we must be careful . . .'

'Coward,' Lopez shouted. There was the same fear in him, but he would force himself to return to Sao Amerigo. 'We'll be in port in one and a half days,' he told the man at the other end. 'Have an aircraft standing by to take me to Sao Amerigo.'

'The whole territory is quarantined. No aircraft are flying,' the man replied.

'Charter one.'

'You won't get a pilot to make that journey.'

'I am Colonel Garcia Lopez, chief of SOMIS. I am ordering a pilot—'

'You can be God,' the man said. 'No man wants to die for your sake.'

'I have direct authority from Chairman Bolivar.' He started to shout, and then stopped. He hadn't thought. 'What has happened to him? Is he alive?'

'We've had no news about him. I don't know. But if he is alive, he is no longer the chairman. General Alvaro Peres, chief of the armed forces of Menaguay, declared martial law one hour ago. He also announced that he has appointed himself temporary chairman until the emergency is over.'

Lopez didn't reply. He silently returned the mike to the captain. Inez, in her flimsy nightgown, was standing behind him and crying. But he didn't see her as he made his way out on deck. The cruiser had begun to pick up speed, and it may have been the wind, but Lopez felt tears slipping down his cheeks, and he couldn't stop them.

He thought briefly of Inez as he let himself into the apartment. Like him, she'd rushed to her home, and he wondered whether she'd found the same as he had. He drifted aimlessly through the silent apartment. The dust was thick on the furniture, and the air musty. He couldn't open the windows because of the smell. He wandered into the living room. His mother's knitting lay where it had fallen. He left it where it was. He didn't want to touch anything.

Suddenly he stopped. There was a scrape of sound from the next room. He moved to the desk, quietly opened the drawer, and slid out his automatic. The city was full of looters, and they had no respect for anyone's property. He removed his shoes and moved softly across the room to the door. He waited a moment, tensed himself, and then pulled the door open. He dropped to one knee and aimed. The man sitting in the chair lifted his hands above his head. 'It's me, Santos,' he said quickly.

Lopez lowered the gun and stood up. He crossed the

room, and for a moment the two men stared at each other as if they were seeing ghosts. Then they embraced.

'I heard you were dead,' Santos said. He was a heavy, well-built man. The eyes behind the gold-framed, almost effeminate spectacles were watchful and the mouth tight.

'If only I was,' Lopez said. 'How is Bolivar?' It was a somewhat pointless question. Santos and Bolivar were almost one and the same. As long as he could remember, Santos had been Bolivar's personal bodyguard. Rumor had it they were brothers or cousins, and they were never far from each other. Lopez suddenly smiled wryly to himself. It had just struck him that he now had no job. With the army in charge, SOMIS had been taken over. And he doubted they'd use him in any capacity. He was Bolivar's man.

'He's safe and well,' Santos said. 'We were very lucky. We had just taken off for our eastern visit when we heard about the plague. Bolivar wanted to return immediately, but I wouldn't let him. When we did return three days later, the generals had declared martial law.' Santos paused. 'He wants to see you immediately.'

'What for?'

'We have been checking,' Santos said, 'and we have found that all the generals and all their families have survived this cursed plague. All the wives and children were sent out of the country five days before the plague broke out. The generals were in the mountains, supposedly watching maneuvers. Bolivar knew of this, but he didn't worry then. It's when they maneuver in the main plaza that a man worries.'

Lopez remained silent a full minute. He stared at Santos in the gloom and shivered. The cold wasn't from the outside; it rose from deep inside him. It was as if his bones were cracking with ice.

'What does Bolivar want me to do?' he finally said softly, and his voice was as cold as he felt.

'Come, we must go,' Santos said, and moved to the door. Lopez followed him. 'He will tell you himself, and so can I. You must find out how and why the generals and their families survived. Bolivar knows you can do it. You are still the best hunter in this country.'

'Then I must be allowed to kill them, one by one,' Lopez said as they let themselves out of his apartment.

'No,' Santos said. 'Leave that part to Bolivar. He will push them and everyone connected with them into the same fires our people burn in now.'

4

Printout of journalists in Sao Amerigo, on request of John Darrigan, the Council:

Minor, R.
Towne, K.
Shatner, P.
Hyslop, M.
Schmidt, C.
Harris, R.
Meunier, T.
Martinelli, N.
Medvedev, M.
Valery, F.
Alexeyev, B.
Zakhov, S.
Listing continued ...

'Shatner, P.!' John Darrigan sat back and glared at the monitor. He hit a button, and the names faded. 'Who the hell gave that son of a bitch permission to go there?'

'Why shouldn't he be there?' Charles Mercer asked.

As always, Darrigan ignored him when he thought a question irrelevant. Mercer drummed the table. He was fed up with Darrigan and with Solotov. They were supposed to be equal, which was why they always sat at a circular mahogany table in the council room. Yet whichever way he looked, he always seemed to be trapped in the middle of the other two.

Mercer wished fervently that he could be posted elsewhere than this seat of permanent Europeon representative to the Council, even though he knew it was the most privileged position to be in. With Darrigan and Solotov, he partially controlled the economic life of the Industrial Nations countries. Internal trade, internation trade, industrial growth, fiscal policies, and negotiations with the Third Nations were all within his power. And through controlling the economic systems of the member nations, the Council was gaining control over the political, social, and cultural lives of the people. Ostensibly, every nation had political independence. But every politician knew that he couldn't make a single campaign promise, either to spend or save money, to expand industrial growth or curtail it, without the prior permission of the Council. When the Council was first formed, a few nations did try to flex their political muscle and demand internal independence. England had been one. The Council soon brought her to heel by denying her her quota of scarce raw materials. Within a fortnight the country was on her knees. France had been next, and then Italy. But within a year they all learned their lesson well. Either they survived together or sank together.

Economic equality brought about social conformity. It was a natural progression that had been already building up in the member nations, years before they formed the Council. Mercer remembered sitting in his beloved Paris, on the Champs Elysées, in the fifties and noticing how different the people who strolled along the boulevard were. Gradually, over the years, in the sixties and the seventies, they had begun to look so alike to his eyes. A Frenchman looked like an American, an American like a German, an Englishman like a Swede. They all had the same well-fed, well-dressed, comfortable look. They talked the same way, they thought the same way, and they dressed the same way. They all had the same education, attended the same kind of doctors and lived the same lives. It was one of the necessities of life that they be the same, otherwise the delicate economic balance between the member nations would become upset. An American couldn't be better than a Russian, nor an Italian than a Czech.

Mercer thought of the editorials in the papers. What was it that the *Times* had said: '. . . the Council's economic power is making inroads into the social and cultural lives of all the people. Soon it will interfere with their freedoms . . .' The others had said more or less the same. He didn't blame them for being worried. The Council was getting too powerful, but what was the alternative? How did one deal with OPEC, the Copper cartels, the Coffee Growers Cartel, the Cotton ...? The list was endless. The Third World was organizing itself; it was no longer willing to be the hewers of wood and the drawers of water for the industrialized world. Without the Council to negotiate and fix the pricings of raw materials, there'd be chaos.

He looked out of the window. From the sixteenth floor, he could look across the placid, flat surface of Lake Geneva. It was a nice day, warm, with just a slight breeze. On the far side of the lake he could see the Geneva-Lausanne train. Reflexively, he glanced at his watch. Ten-forty-five. The Swiss never let their trains run late. He didn't like the Swiss; they were too antiseptic for him, and too cold. His glance returned to the room. In front of him were telephones, television monitors, intercoms. He knew he could reach any part of the world – Paris, Washington, Moscow – at a moment's notice, either by voice or by television. On the floor above was the most sophisticated communication setup in the world. Transmitters, receivers, TV studios, coders and decoders, all looked after by dozens of technicians and assistants.

Mercer shifted in his chair and forced his mind to return to his question. I'm sixty-five, fat, white-haired, and responsible. Not only for what we have made of this world but also for what we are doing now. He was so tired. He hadn't slept for a week, and he doubted whether he would ever sleep again. Not the kind of sleep that would allow him to see a peaceful dawn.

'Get me the head of Channel 14, New York,' Darrigan said to the monitor, 'and tell me his name before we speak.' He turned to Solotov and managed to include Mercer with a glance. 'What shall we do about Shatner?'

Solotov seemed to speak without moving his lips. 'Have him expelled or ...' He didn't have to finish.

'What's he done?' Mercer demanded. His voice sounded unnaturally loud in the room. 'All right, he's transmitting reports which are close to the knuckle and asking a few awkward questions. They're not broadcasting him, are they? So I don't see what harm he's doing.'

'Bolivar is still alive, and Shatner knows him,' Darrigan said patiently. 'Those goddamned generals couldn't time their own heartbeats even if they tried.'

'It wasn't their fault that Bolivar was up in a plane when Sao Amerigo was . . .' Darrigan noticed Mercer's hesitation and waited. '. . . affected.'

'If they'd had the brains, they would have sent a fighter up after him. It would have saved any amount of trouble. Now we have Shatner asking his questions and Bolivar alive. If they get together, all hell will break loose.'

'We've already released hell,' Mercer said softly.

Darrigan studied Mercer briefly. The man looked at least ten years older than his age. His skin was a chalky gray and his eyes were ringed by heavy pouches. There was a desperate exhaustion in his face and the way in which he held his body. It was as if he was in a state of physical disintegration. The man was weak, and Darrigan disliked the European even more. It was about time Mercer was retired and a new man sent in his place. The Council was no place for weaklings. Darrigan respected Solotov. They were both very much alike. He chose the word carefully. Practical men. But he had no illusions. They would work with each other for as long as it suited their purposes. And Darrigan was confident that when it came time for them to disagree, he would have the edge. He didn't envisage it happening, however, for quite a long time.

An assistant came up on the monitor screen. 'I have the head of Channel 14, New York, sir. His name is Tom Brauer. He's been head of the station for the last three years. He began—'

'Tell him to hold,' Darrigan said shortly and turned to the other two. 'What shall we do about Shatner?'

'Why this obsession with this man?' Solotov asked softly. 'Whatever he finds out will never be broadcast, so let him play his little games. We have more important things to do.' He opened the folder in front of him, dismissing the problem of Shatner. He studied the papers in front of him. The silence told him that Darrigan was paying attention. 'You have here a figure of ten thousand American personnel who've been sent to Menaguay. How many more are scheduled?'

'In the immediate future, another fifteen. Once the situation has been stabilized, we can discuss how many more people we can send south.'

'These ten?' Solotov raised his head and stared at Darrigan.

'None of them are military personnel,' Darrigan said. 'We agreed on that before. They're all civilians. Engineers, technicians, agriculturists, geologists. I can provide you with a complete list and their exact duties.'

'I would like that,' Solotov said. 'As soon as possible, and it should include information on the others you will be sending over the next few weeks.'

'Naturally, I expect reciprocation from both of you when the time comes,' Darrigan said, and glanced at both of them.

'Naturally,' Solotov said dryly.

Mercer only nodded. Darrigan noticed that the thought seemed to make Mercer even more unhappy, and grayer.

'So far, where have your personnel been deployed?'

'Throughout the country,' Darrigan said. 'They are trying to re-establish the mines, the oil fields, the farms. It will take them another two or three weeks. There is, as you will appreciate, a shortage of manual and semiskilled labor. The generals are promising to shift a labor force from outside the affected area to the locations we specify. We cannot, of course, overpressurize them at the present moment. We must maintain the impression that they are in control. As you understand, this is vital. If Odu or the others, whom I gather are keeping a close eye on the situation, suspect anything, the shit, to use an archaic term, will hit the fan.' He was satisfied with the positive nods of the heads. 'Which is why I believe something should be done about Shatner. If he does find out anything, he could pass the information on to Bolivar. Or Odu. That's the kind of a son of a bitch he is. He's got no patriotism.'

Darrigan had more reason than the other two to know

Shatner. He remembered uneasily how when he was appointed secretary of state and permanent U.S. representative to the Council, Shatner had come to interview him. Shatner had been totally hostile not only to him but also to the appointment, and had somehow unearthed a paper written by him when he was an assistant economics adviser to the president of the United States at the time of the first Arab oil embargo. It had been a brief aide-mémoire advocating that the Industrial Nations take control of all the sources of raw materials necessary for their survival. Darrigan didn't doubt that Shatner would remember that paper in Sao Amerigo. He didn't mention this to the others, as there was some truth in his remark that Shatner was unpatriotic. Shatner didn't have any particular awe for high office. In fact – Darrigan winced – he had made fun of it. It had been a sly little documentary purporting to show how the Council worked. It was only on a second viewing, after it had been broadcast, that Darrigan had realized he and the Council were being made fun of. Darrigan was a man who didn't forgive easily.

'He was the one who did the program on us,' Mercer said, remembering. It had amused him, though the other two hadn't, as usual, agreed with him.

'Ah, that,' Solotov said. 'Have him expelled and finish the matter.' He returned to his folder. 'What I don't understand here is why the figures are only approximately thirty percent casualties in the basin. They should have been higher, shouldn't they?'

'I'm having that checked out,' Darrigan said, 'as I don't understand it either.' He pressed the switch. 'I'll talk to Brauer in a moment.' He looked at Solotov. 'I don't think expelling him will be a good idea. It will arouse Bolivar's suspicions.'

'Then have him killed.'

Darrigan ignored Mercer's sarcasm. 'That will make Bolivar even more suspicious. He must be watched, and if he does find out anything or try to contact Bolivar, then I'll act.'

Solotov shrugged, and Mercer looked out of the window.

'Brauer!' The man staring at him from the monitor straightened.

'Who sent Shatner to Sao Amerigo?'

'Frank Kolok, most probably. He's the news—'

'Kolok, Frank.' Darrigan recorded the name. 'Have copies of Shatner's transmits sent to me as they come. We're not censoring; we'd just like to see what he's reporting. Thank you.' Darrigan pressed the switch before Brauer could reply, and spoke to an aide. 'Get whoever we have with the journalists to keep a very close eye on Shatner. I want to know everything he does.'

Lopez and Santos cautiously stepped out into the street. Curfew had begun half an hour ago, and the street was totally deserted. The half-moon was covered by a thin layer of cloud, and the opaque light gave a sort of semilife to the buildings. None of the streetlights were on because of the need to conserve power, and this was one factor in their favor. It would make it harder for the jeep patrols to spot them.

They waited a few minutes until their eyes had adjusted to the peculiar light and then set off east. It would, Lopez knew, normally take them half an hour to walk to Bolivar's house. With the patrols out, it would take longer. It was a warm night, and there was very little breeze. Occasionally a slight puff of wind would carry the smell of the fires, and he would stop breathing for a minute. He moved quietly behind Santos. A part of him was aware of his surroundings – the silence, the distant sound of a patrol, the need to walk in the deepest shadows. Another part of him was trying to absorb the information Santos had given him. He would shake his head now and then like a fighter trying to regain his consciousness. He felt he was on a seesaw. One moment he would believe what Lopez had told him and he would be fired by an uncontrollable rage, the next he sank down to cold disbelief. It would need Bolivar to convince him.

'Back,' Santos whispered, and pointed. They were on the edge of a plaza and about to cross. Lopez followed the direction. He, like Santos, sensed more than saw the silent jeep parked in the deep shadow. It took them ten minutes to work their way down the side streets to avoid the patrol. They had to make two more detours before they reached the top of the street where Bolivar lived. Outside the gates were two jeep patrols.

'How do we get in?' Lopez asked in a whisper.

'You should know him by now. He always has more than one entrance and exit.' Santos set off down the side street, and cut back toward the house through an alley. Lopez had been to the house only a couple of times to check out the security arrangements. Bolivar seldom used it, for he preferred the chairman's official residence just off the axis. As far as Lopez could remember, there was only one entrance and exit.

Santos stopped at the last house down the alley. It stood fifteen yards back from the wall surrounding Bolivar's house. Santos let himself in with a key, and Lopez followed. He sensed the house was empty, and in fact had never been lived in, as he groped in the darkness after Santos. They moved cautiously down to the basement, crossed it to a door, and entered a tunnel. Santos switched on a light, and Lopez saw the walls curving away toward, he presumed, Bolivar's house.

'Why wasn't I told about this when I was checking security?' His voice was aggrieved.

'Bolivar likes to keep some secrets to himself' – he walked forward – 'and to me.'

The tunnel was about fifty yards long. At the end was a door. Santos passed through it, and Lopez found himself in the basement of Bolivar's house. He looked at the door from the inside and understood why he hadn't noticed it before. It fitted flush with the wall and was the same color.

Bolivar was waiting for them in the study. The book-lined room was heavily curtained and lit by a single desk lamp. Lopez could just see Bolivar behind the pool of light.

Even his flatterers, and there were many, would not have called Bolivar a handsome man. Though he was a *mestizo*, he looked more Indian than Negro or Caucasian. His face was flat and broad, the cheekbones were high, and his lower lip pouted somewhat pink and faintly obscenely. The black eyes were bright as lamps, though half hidden by drooping lids and bushy eyebrows. His nose had a seismic fault in the middle. Myth had it – and his life was half-myth and half-reality – that at one time in a *barrio*, in a jungle village, in the street (it depended who was telling the story) it had been bitten off in a brawl, and a passing doctor, with no time for the poor peasant, had stuck it back on with plaster. His hands, like the body beneath the open-necked shirt, were thick and scarred. Stripped, he would have looked as if he had been carved from flesh-colored granite and that the sculptor had left the job half-finished. The chisel marks were the knife wounds and bullet puckers. The myth, which he fostered, claimed he was the son of a whore and had been fathered by the spirit of the original Bolivar. The reality only he knew, and he never spoke of it. Like the others, Lopez knew only a small part of his origins. He had met Bolivar when he was a union leader in the mines and stayed with him as he rose through the ranks of the Confederacion de los Trabajadores to political power in Menaguay. Lopez had been with him twenty years now, and he always remembered Bolivar's favorite quotation. It was supposed to have been said by Juan Peron. 'By the year 2000, South America will either be one nation or enslaved.' Lopez felt that now, as he stood before Bolivar, there may have been some truth in that old man's prediction. He wondered in which way, though.

Bolivar rose and grasped Lopez' hand tightly. 'I am glad you have survived, my *amigo*,' he said. His voice was surprisingly soft and gentle. 'I have need of you.'

'I am sorry about Madam Bolivar,' Lopez said, and held on to the hand. Bolivar nodded and released his hand.

'You will be surprised to know that the generals and all their families live,' Bolivar said, and saw that Lopez wasn't surprised by the news. 'I suppose Santos has already told you.'

'I am sorry, Chairman—' Santos began. Bolivar waved him silent.

'How did you find out about their families?' Lopez asked.

'The embassies always keep me informed on the movements of ... let's say our more important citizens. I had routine reports of their presence from London, New York, Rome. They all arrived at these cities within a day or two of each other. I didn't give it much thought until now. And now, I don't like it.'

'You are saying that the generals were responsible for ...' Lopez' voice shook, and his hand dropped in a futile gesture. He didn't have the words to express his revulsion.

'I am not sure,' Bolivar said. 'All I have is too many coincidences.' He held up a finger. 'Coincidence one: General Peres, Bardez, and six of the others with chosen units from the army and air force decide to hold maneuvers eight hundred miles north of Sao Amerigo, an area which I now find was not affected by this evil disease. They asked my permission, yes. I gave it. They could do nothing from that distance. Coincidence two: The families of the eight generals just happen to be visiting outside Menaguay at this time. Coincidence three: You are away on your vacation. This was known in advance. Coincidence four: I was supposed to be in Sao Amerigo that day. By chance, I decided to fly north earlier than had been announced. That is all I have. Apart from one solid fact, that is.'

'What is that?'

'I am no longer the chairman and they sit in my place.'

Bolivar sat back and was very still. He seemed really like a statue. Lopez knew he could sit like that for hours without twitching a muscle. He waited a full five minutes and then stood up. The meeting, he suspected, was over. Bolivar moved. He slid two sheets of paper across to Lopez. The first, Lopez saw, was the names of the generals and the locations of their families. The second had dozens of names, and one was circled.

'Shatner?' Lopez raised his eyebrows.

'He interviewed me two years ago,' Bolivar said. 'You may not remember. He was ... *simpatico* toward us. We can make use of him.'

'How?' Lopez asked. 'I don't trust these Americans.'

'I think he is different. He has a good mind and one weakness. He is too partial to the truth. A dangerous flaw, and I can use it. Work with him. He has contacts and may be able to help us.'

'If you say so,' Lopez said sulkily. Bolivar nodded. 'If I find that the generals were responsible, what should I do? Kill them?'

'Leave all that to me,' Bolivar said. 'Odu is willing to help me to regain the chairmanship when the time is right.' Bolivar stood up and shook Lopez' hand. 'Take care, my *amigo*. Generals are very dangerous animals. And these generals may have handlers we cannot see just yet.'

Lopez stopped. 'What does that mean?'

'I cannot say just yet.' Bolivar hesitated. 'Until we find some proof. But be careful. Where is Shatner staying?'

'The Amerigo,' Santos said. 'Room four-nine.'

'Make sure Shatner tapes whatever you find,' Bolivar said. 'We must have evidence to show Odu and maybe the others.'

Santos led Lopez out. Bolivar sat alone. He sensed the emptiness of the house, in himself, in everything that surrounded him. The country outside his house, which had once teemed with his people, was suddenly also empty. For a moment he held himself erect in his chair; then his shoulders slumped. He had been confident in front of Lopez and Santos – were there only two left out of all those millions who'd followed? Maybe there was a handful more rising out of the ashes? But alone now he felt he was grasping at straws. Even if Lopez did find some evidence – and a part of him, as much as he hated the generals, recoiled from believing that they be responsible for what happened – what could he do? His strength lay in his people, and he had no people. While they'd lived, no general had ever dared move against him. Without them, he was reduced to a head without a body. He had no weapons except his hands. Bolivar opened them. They lay still and powerful on his lap. They'd served him well often, but now they were as useless as he was. Odu would, with the other leaders in the Third Nations, try to help him, but he had to have evidence before they would move. Proof. He clenched his fists. Solid proof would be his only weapon, and he would wield it like a sword.

He heard Santos returning and straightened in his chair. He pulled a few papers toward him and bent his head to study them. He thought of his people and his wife. He felt the same toward both. As the door opened, his hands began to shake. He clenched them and forced them to lie still in the pool of light so that from across the room Santos would only see a rocklike immobility.

5

Lopez woke groggy and tired. He sat up in the bed and looked down at himself. He was still dressed in his street clothes. He must have fallen asleep somewhere near dawn. The bedside clock read eight-thirty. Four hours was all he'd had, and he felt it. He thought of the night before. There hadn't been any trouble returning to his apartment. The trouble had come afterward as he'd sat and thought about what Bolivar had told him. It was a nightmare, and he was being asked to solve the problem. Tiredly he picked up the two sheets of paper by his side. They were creased now, and Santos' writing at the best of times was unreadable.

Names! He dropped the list with the journalists. He couldn't see how this man Shatner could be of any help. The other names in his hand belonged to people scattered across the world.

He shook his head. He was hungry, and he hadn't shaved for days. Nor – he touched his shirt – bathed. He moved stiffly to the bathroom. A trickle of water came out of one of the taps. The water supply still wasn't working. He washed his face the best he could and shaved quickly. It cleared his head slightly, and he wandered into the kitchen. Apart from a couple of tins of fruit, there was no food. He opened the tins and finished both of them. He felt slightly better, thought the sweet syrup left a sickly taste in his mouth.

Lopez paused suddenly in the bedroom with a clean shirt in his hands. If someone wanted to leave the country, the person had to have permission from the husband, if a woman; or if a person under eighteen, from the father. And then further permission to leave had to be sought from the ministry of the interior. It would normally take one week to process the exit visa if the person were visiting a South American country; a month or more if he were going to Europe or America, and he or she would have to provide reasons for the visit, final destination, date of return, exchange spent, and half a dozen other bits and pieces of information.

Now, Lopez thought as he slowly and carefully dressed, someone in the ministry must have received all the application forms within a few days of each other. Or maybe even together. And that someone must have noticed the co-incidence of eight generals suddenly deciding to send their families north. That important piece of information had not been passed either to SOMIS or to Bolivar. It was only through the bureaucratic routine of the embassies that Bolivar now knew of the families.

Lopez finished dressing and examined himself in the mirror. He looked somewhat like his former self, neat and well-dressed. Except for his face, which was wan, and the dark circles under his eyes. The eyes themselves, however, were bright and narrowed. He had a reason now to keep going, and nothing would stop him. He picked up his SOMIS credential and dropped it into his pocket. He only hoped that he wouldn't meet someone in authority who would question the validity of his position. He checked the clip in his automatic and slipped it into his waistband.

The ministry of the interior was opposite the assembly hall in the axis. There were soldiers and trucks scattered around the circular plaza and guarding all the entrances to the buildings. Lopez parked his car in the empty parking lot. He climbed the steps to the main entrance steadily and, he hoped, confidently. The three soldiers standing at the door, machine guns in their hands, were watching him approach. When he was ten feet from them, he carefully dipped his hand into his pocket. One of the barrels rose an inch. He pulled out his credential, flipped it open, and kept walking through the door. The soldiers craned to study his picture and the stamp. Lopez kept moving, hoping his show of confidence would lower their guard. It did. Out of the corner of his eyes he saw one of the soldiers – the most senior, he guessed, who no doubt was able to read – nod. The other two relaxed, and he was in.

He reached the stairs and turned around. One of the

soldiers was watching him. Lopez ran up the first flight. He could hear his footsteps echo and realized that the whole building was empty. There were were no busy clerks, no clatter of typewriters, no voices. He stopped on the second floor. The corridor. The corridor stretched out on either side, and there wasn't a soul in sight. Lopez had counted on someone telling him where to find the files for exit visas. Now he had a whole building to search. There was an indicator board beside the elevators. Exit visas could be obtained on the fourth floor. Lopez ran up the next two flights and paused for breath outside the glass-paneled door. He was hopelessly out of condition.

He opened the door cautiously and entered. He found himself in a small waiting room. The usual counter ran along one wall and a row of benches down the opposite one. There was a door diagonally opposite, and Lopez tried it. It was locked. He took a step and kicked the lock twice. The door splintered and swung open. He groaned. He wasn't standing so much in a room as in a hall filled with desks and filing cabinets. There were papers scattered everywhere. On the desks, on the chairs, and on the floor. It was obvious no one had been in here for over a week. One of the windows was open, and the dust was thick on the floor. He glanced at his watch. He wasn't sure how much time he had. Private soldiers were slow thinkers but steady ones, and he had no doubt that one of them would think of reporting his presence.

Lopez didn't know where to start. He picked up a file lying on the nearest desk and flicked through it. It made little sense. He moved to the first of a long row of filing cabinets. It was worse than he'd imagined. Each drawer had numbers and not alphabets. How was he ever going to find the names of the generals' families? He slid open a drawer and pulled out a folder. There was its number on the top, and below, the name and initials of the person. On the top-right-hand corner was a passport-sized photograph. He looked down the row of cabinets. He was sure there were at least a million such folders. It would take him weeks to sift through them. Except, somewhere in the room was a cross-reference book with the names first and the numbers second.

Lopez looked at the number of the drawer. It was the top end: 800–900. He moved slowly and then faster toward the 1–100. If he was lucky, and he briefly prayed he would be, the cross-reference book could be the number-one file. He pulled the drawer open and snatched the file. There was no photograph on the cover. He opened it. The names were alphabetically listed, and opposite them were their numbers.

Lopez ran down the names. P . . . Peres, M. 732/809.

It took Lopez five feverish minutes to gather the eight files together. He quickly cleared a desk by simply sweeping everything onto the floor, and dropped the files on the desk.

He opened the file of General Peres' wife. She had applied to leave the country with her two children on the ninth. Lopez checked a calendar. That was eight days before the plague had broken out. He flicked through her form hurriedly. He stopped. The visa had been granted on the tenth! Someone had had enough influence to reduce a month's wait to a single day. Lopez slowly turned over the last page. The signature was Bison's, the minister of the interior. Lopez looked through the other files. Give or take a day, all the visas had been granted on the tenth, and every one had been personally signed by Bison.

Lopez stacked the files together neatly and tucked them under his arm. He hurried out of the office and took the stairs two at a time. It was urgent that he talk to Eduardo Bison, who was, supposedly, a dear friend of Bolivar's. Lopez only hoped Bison was alive, as he was looking forward to the conversation.

He slowed down as he neared the main doors. There were only two soldiers on guard, and they both turned as they heard him approach. One of them moved to block his path. Lopez was ready for the move. He opened the Peres file and showed it to the soldier.

'General Peres requested me to collect his files. That is his signature. It is confidential business.'

The soldier hesitated and then stepped aside. Lopez saluted him casually and walked to his car. He expected the third soldier to have returned with an officer, but no

74

one tried to stop him as he climbed in and drove away.

Lopez drove straight to Bison's residence in the Santa Maya suburb. It was five blocks away from Bolivar's. He stopped the car and got out. The garden and the house looked empty. Lopez tried the front door. It was locked. He rang the bell. The jangle echoed through the house. He decided to try the back door. It, too, was locked. He looked around. There was no one in sight. He put his elbow against the glass and drove in. It took him a second to undo the latch and climb in.

He glanced around the kitchen. It was spacious and neat. There were no dirty plates in the sink or a tin out of its place. Apart from the usual film of dust, it looked as if the tenants had cleaned up only moments ago. He moved into the dining room. The tabletop was clear, and the glassware on the sideboard shone dully. He picked up a goblet and blew off the dust and tapped it. Pure crystal. The living room reflected the same affluence as the other two rooms he'd passed through. There were a couple of Picassos on one wall and a large Louis de Wet on the other. He admired the de Wet briefly and looked around the room. There wasn't even an ashtray out of place.

He crossed the marble-tiled hall and opened the door. He'd guessed right. It was Bison's study and office. It was obviously a busy man's room. There were a few papers scattered on the desk, and it had a comfortable, lived-in look. He dropped the files from under his arm on the desk and sat down. Carefully he studied all the papers. They were on routine ministry business. He went through the drawers. There was an automatic in the top-right-hand one. He slid out the clip. It hadn't been fired for some time. The other drawers held nothing of interest.

Lopez sat back and studied the room. He tried to remember where Bison had his safe. It was either down here or in the bedroom. His eyes stopped moving at a half-inch crack in the wood paneling opposite. He frowned and moved to it. The covering to the wall safe was open already. He slid it back and tugged at the safe handle. It opened easily.

He reached in and pulled out two bundles of notes and a

velvet-covered case containing a necklace. He dropped them on the floor. There were some papers at the back. He looked through them. They were private papers, and he dropped them too. Someone had cleared out the safe of whatever papers there were. And like him, they hadn't been interested in the money or the jewelry. He bent down to replace the things he'd dropped. The back of his hand brushed the dark carpet as he did so. He pushed the money and the papers and the box back in, and as he closed the safe, he looked at his hand. There were dark stripes on it.

He brought the back of his hand close to his face and then knelt and brushed the carpet gently with the tips of his fingers. They came up with faint black streaks also. Ash! Someone, either Bison or his visitor, had been burning papers in the room. At first he couldn't see the wastebasket, and he had to hunt. He found it behind the rich, black leather settee.

Quite a number of papers had obviously been burned in it. The paint on the outside had blackened, blistered, and peeled. Whoever had burned the papers had done a good job. There seemed to be nothing but fine black ash in the bin. He carefully picked up a handful. It had all been sifted, but he was a methodical man. He took the papers from the desk, spread them out on the carpet, and gently spread the ash over them. He combed with his fingers through the ash very carefully. If there was one piece that was whole, he didn't want to break it. Here and there were bits of charred paper. He peered at each fragment. There was a letter here, a letter there. Nothing complete. Abruptly, his hand shook. A thought crossed his mind. These ashes were so similar to human ashes. He forced himself to continue patiently and slowly.

Suddenly he saw what he wanted. At the edge of the pile was a dark-brown charred scrap about an inch long. He didn't dare pick it up in case it disintegrated. He knelt over it like a man at prayer. There was a gap to the left of the word, and then the word itself. He read it very carefully: *Agua*. After the *a* was a blackened half-circle. It looked as if it could be an *o*.

Lopez sat back on his haunches. *Aguao*. It didn't make sense. The word *agua* was 'water'. The *o*? He shrugged. It didn't seem important at the moment. He wrote the word down exactly as he saw it, and then, taking an envelope from the desk, gently pushed the fragment inside. It didn't appear to break, and he placed it in one of his folders.

He wondered what had happened to Bison. Most probably he died in the plague. No, Lopez thought, he wouldn't have. Bison must have realized something was going to happen. He cursed himself. He should have looked for Bison and his family's exit visa when he was in the ministry. It was a simple matter for Bison to sign his own papers.

Lopez thought of the kitchen and dining room. They were both clean and uncluttered. Yet, in his own place, his mother and sister had been in the middle of breakfast. Bison, Lopez guessed, must have left at the same time as the generals' families. He picked up his files and went out into the hall. He hesitated and then started up the stairs. He opened the first door. It was the master bedroom. He was about to shut the door when he noticed the beds. The covers were rumpled. He stared at the two beds as if they were a puzzle. A woman who had tidied her kitchen and dining room would not have left on a long journey without making up the beds neatly. He crossed to them and pulled back the covers of the right one. The undersheet was almost black and completely stiff with a wide stain of blood. He did the same to the left bed and found the same stain. He looked closely at the cover. Around chest height was a small neat hole. He didn't have to look at the other bed. Bison and his wife had been shot to death while they'd slept.

Lopez opened the closet and found two packed suitcases. Beside them was a briefcase. He snapped it open and took out the passports. Exit visas dated for the tenth had been stamped in both of them. Well, he'd paid for his attempt to betray Bolivar. No doubt his body was as much ash as the papers which would have incriminated him.

Lopez let himself out of the back door. He'd been in the house for over two hours, he realized. He felt satisfied but tired. The lack of sleep was telling on him, and he decided to return to his apartment before trying to figure out his next move. It looked, though, as if he'd reached a dead end. From Bison all he'd found was a pile of cold ashes and *Aguao*.

He fell asleep the moment he lay down, and was woken, impatiently, by Santos three hours later. 'Bolivar is waiting for news, and you sleep,' he said angrily.

'I haven't been sleeping all day,' Lopez said in irritation. He reached for the files and tossed them across.

Santos studied them carefully and looked at the passports. 'The bastard!' Santos spat when he finished reading. He did actually spit at Bison's passport photograph. 'The whore's cunt. If he was alive, I would rip his heart out.' Santos cursed for another minute and then stopped again, his voice was almost gentle. 'So, the generals used Bison to get their families out of the country by the tenth, and then they killed him.' He paused. It seemed as if he was frightened of going further. 'The generals then attend maneuvers while their families are safely visiting abroad. Which means that they knew the plague was to come to the country. It wasn't the curse of God, then, but the curse of man.'

The silence in the room as the two men stared at each other seemed to last for an eternity.

'You should have known about Bison and the generals,' Santos said in angry frustration.

'How?' Lopez asked coldly. 'Bison was friendly with Bolivar right up to the end. I did not receive any information that he had been a betrayer. I cannot tell what a man will do in the future. I only find out what he has done in the past and make sure that his actions catch up with him. Bison's past was flawless. I checked it not once but a hundred times. A factory worker's son who won scholarships to the best universities in the country. He had worked with Bolivar for five years, and he had done nothing to arouse my suspicions.' He didn't add that he'd had a premonition; it was too late.

Santos nodded, reached out and patted his friend's knee. He picked up the envelope, and Lopez took it away from him gently.

'It is a word I found in the ashes,' he said. 'A-g-u-a, and

the last letter looks like an *o*. Do you know what it means?'

Santos brooded and finally shook his head. 'I will ask Bolivar, he may know what it is. Is there anything else you want me to tell him?'

'Nothing. Do you want to show him these folders?'

'No. They are dangerous. Those bastard soldiers walk in and out of the house as if they owned it. If they find these, they will kill him. They are still frightened of him and what he can do. We must not give them an excuse. Keep them safely hidden until he asks for them. But show them to Shatner when you see him.' He noticed Lopez' face tighten. 'Bolivar needs someone like him to communicate the story. See him tonight.'

'All right,' Lopez said with little enthusiasm. 'But I cannot spend much time holding his hand. I have to find out where this ... thing ... started. This plague had an origin, and there must be something there that will give us final proof.'

'Once you have found that, then Bolivar will be armed to face the world.'

'What happens,' Lopez asked softly, 'if the generals are only the dogs, and their handlers are others?'

'Bolivar will know what to do if you find that out.' Santos rose. The two men shook hands and started for the door. Santos stopped and returned to the folders. He looked through them carefully once more and dropped them back on the bed. 'I wanted to remember the dates the families return to this country. They think they have escaped death, but they are mistaken. I will be waiting for each one of them, and I will kill them all.'

Lopez saw Santos to the front door and returned to the bedroom. He picked up the envelope and slid out the scrap of paper. He stared at the word a long time. He was sure it meant something, but what? He hoped Bolivar would be able to solve that.

Piers looked down at the woman underneath him with a sense of detachment. In the dim light of his room, with the shadows masking her face, she looked a total stranger. He moved his head, and the light fell on Marion's face. It still remained distorted. Her mouth was half-open, her eyes closed. She was waiting tensely for the orgasm to envelop her. Piers kept his movements steady, watching the tension increase slowly.

She had come to his room on the first night, as she always had done, for comforting. He needed her body as much as she needed his. He was frustrated. There was nothing happening on the story, and during the night he rid himself of his worrying bafflement in Marion. He increased his thrusting as Marion moaned. For three days now they had been carted around in that truck from one end of the city to the other, and even a hundred-mile journey into the interior. They had been given permission to interview spokesmen from the army, spokesmen from the Industrial Nations, spokesmen ... spokesmen ... spokesmen. Since his interview with the doctor he had not managed to talk with anyone from the country. Geddes now stayed constantly by his side, and this only increased the feeling in Piers' mind that he was deliberately being prevented from finding out anything beyond what he was being told. It nagged him constantly. It seemed as if he was being held behind an invisible barrier and every move he made he was forced back into the center. Yet, try as he might, he couldn't see what there was to hide beyond that barrier. He'd talked it over with Marion endlessly, and even she couldn't see what they were hiding. He trusted her instincts, but yet ...

Marion gave a cry. Her eyes were open, but they saw nothing. Her mouth was slack and damp, and Piers could feel her arching up to meet him greedily. Piers bent his head and pushed his tongue into her mouth. He forced her body down hard on the bed and felt her fingers slipping and sliding over his perspiring back. He could smell the odors of her perfume and sweat as he moved faster and faster. Their bodies fought with and against each other, snatching selfishly at their own needs. Marion came first. She half-screamed and clung tightly to Piers and then relaxed completely as she gave herself to the waves that flooded her body. Piers slammed into her body finally, froze for a long shuddering moment, and then lay limply on top of her.

Piers surfaced first and rolled slowly off Marion. She touched him gently, but didn't move. Only sighed and wriggled against him. Piers looked at her. Her face was totally relaxed

Marion smiled to herself. She felt so relaxed and peaceful. It should last forever. Thoughts, half-formed, drifted through her mind. She wished she were back in her apartment on the East Fifties, by the river, in New York, drowsing and sleeping. She wanted to leave, but ... Piers. He'd stopped thinking of that reporter's paradise. He had a story – what? She shrugged to herself. Piers would find it. He was like a gun dog, and she just followed. Sweet, clever Piers. She wished he wasn't so clever and stubborn. This time was one. She wanted to whisper, 'Let's go home, Piers, let it be.'

'Hey don't fall asleep.' Marion heard Piers' voice from a great distance.

'I won't,' she whispered.

Piers looked at his watch. He'd give her five minutes, and then she could return to her own room. The other two nights he'd allowed her to spend with him, but this night, he was tired. His mind kept going around in circles, trying to solve a problem he couldn't see. And then, he thought, there's New York. Though he wasn't completely sure, he suspected from Harris' remarks that New York wasn't running their transmits. Harris seemed to have a hot line right into Channel 14, and Piers knew that someone was leaning on Kolok. It didn't exactly surprise him, as it had happened too often before. Except this time, he wasn't sure why. They had no revelations that needed to be cut. Some of his footage was pretty hard, and he guessed it could be the reason. But it was only a guess. He could do nothing else from Sao Amerigo. He had talked to Kolok once, and Frank had been colder than usual. But Frank was often like that when he felt that Piers and Marion were overstepping his instructions.

'Time to go.' Piers nudged Marion.

She protested sleepily, and slowly sat up. He cupped one breast. They were round and firm.

81

'You're pretty good, you know,' she said, and kissed him.
'I know.'

'Bastard.' She laughed. She stopped abruptly and added seriously, 'I needed that.'

He nodded. It was a desperate need to feel that you were lucky enough to be alive and able to feel the violent longings of your body and lie with someone warm who would protect you from the menacing fires outside.

She dressed, picked up her shoes, and leaned over and kissed Piers. 'I'll see you in the morning. And Piers,' – he looked up – 'don't keep worrying. Let it be.' She let herself out, and Piers switched off the light.

Lopez saw the woman come out of the room, and pulled back into the shadows of the stairwell. He'd been standing there nearly twenty minutes and had about given up hope of her ever leaving. He'd nearly walked into the room, but just in time he'd heard her noises. He'd felt a deep disgust as he listened. They had no right to make love so passionately, oblivious of the tragedy of his country. He'd reached such a point of self-righteous anger that he'd nearly burst into the room with a drawn gun and shot them. But the wait in the stairwell had cooled him down. It hadn't changed his opinion of Shatner. Where Bolivar had got the idea that this Shatner was *simpatico*, God alone knew. No man who had an ounce of compassion would think of lying with a woman when there were so many countless dead ... murdered, Lopez thought ... in the country. He had, in fairness, tried to think of Inez on the cruiser, and now of the woman as she walked down the corridor. His body felt no reactions. The coldness was still deep in him.

He saw the woman enter her own room, waited a full minute, and then moved slowly down the corridor. He reached Shatner's door, slipped the skeleton key into the lock, and let himself in quickly and silently. He saw the body in the bed struggle to sit up and reach for the light at the same time. Lopez gripped the wrist and felt it twist violently.
'Who the hell are you?'

'Colonel Lopez, SOMIS. Bolivar sent me.'

He felt Shatner relax, and dimly saw the nod.

'I wouldn't have come if it hadn't been for Bolivar, I must add.'

Piers ignored him. 'How is Bolivar?'

'Alive but under guard. God knows how much longer they will allow him to live.'

'I want to see him.'

'Not just yet. Later, maybe. It depends.' Lopez moved across to the window and looked out. The city was dark everywhere except for the flicker of the fires. They were smaller now, and weaker. Like a thought being lost in time. I suppose, Lopez thought, in a few years it will be all forgotten. But not while he was still alive.

'Depends on what?' he heard Shatner ask. Lopez didn't answer. He couldn't quite erase all his doubts. The question was repeated. Finally Shatner said, 'Look, if you came to admire the view, choose another room. I want to sleep.'

Piers was surprised at the speed of the man. In a second he was pushed back in the bed and a gun muzzle shoved into his throat.

'Where do you think you are?' Lopez asked angrily. 'I give the orders.'

Piers choked and began to cough. He reached up carefully and pushed the muzzle out of his throat. 'Then obey the ones you've been given,' he said between coughs. 'Bolivar ordered you to see me. What about?'

Lopez replaced the gun in his waistband and allowed Piers to sit up. Piers caressed his thoat gingerly. He'd repay Lopez when the man wasn't carrying a gun. 'Who's the woman?' Lopez asked coldly.

Piers realized from the tone of his voice that Lopez must have been listening outside the door. He was about to tell him to mind his own business when he remembered the gun. It was best not to keep antagonizing the man, especially as he was the chief of SOMIS. Piers wasn't sure of his power in the present situation, but he'd heard rumors that SOMIS could make men disappear, forever, if it wanted.

'Marion Hyslop. She works with me.'

'What I tell you you must never tell her.'

83

Piers shook his head. 'We're a team. She knows what I know on a story, and vice the versa. I'm sorry.'

Lopez hesitated. Bolivar didn't tell him anything about a team. He bit his lip in thought and then shrugged. Bolivar ordered him to tell Shatner; who Shatner told wasn't his problem. Quickly Lopez recounted what he'd done to date. He kept it terse, as he didn't want to waste too much time with this gringo journalist. What use he was to Bolivar, only Bolivar and God knew. There was a long silence when he finished.

'Oh, my God,' Piers whispered finally. 'It's worse than I expected.'

'Expected?'

Piers told him quickly about his attempts to meet and interview local doctors and ordinary people. He was continually prevented by Geddes.

'I figured that the army was exaggerating the death toll so that they could prolong the emergency and squeeze more aid from the Industrial Nations,' Piers said. 'Or I thought there may be some graft going on. You know, supplies ending up in a general's pocket instead of someone's mouth.' He shook his head and kept shaking it. 'Jesus, but not this. Not in a million years. But it's their own people they've killed.'

'Don't generals always kill their own men?' Lopez said dryly. 'Generals count victories not in the number of lives lost but in the territory gained. And at the moment, they've won this country – one of the richest pieces of land on earth – and gained power. But their victory is going to be short. I will find out how they started this plague, and once Bolivar has that, he will begin to fight. The people who have survived will rise up and tear the generals to pieces, and they will be helped by Odu and Liu and the others.'

'I've got to have that story,' Piers said.

Lopez glanced at him coldly. 'You don't care for anything but your story, do you? Don't you feel any rage, any hatred, any compassion? I don't think you do. It is always the story for a man like you.'

'I'll let you do all the feeling,' Piers said shortly. 'Now, when can I tape those files you have on the generals' families? And interview Bolivar? I better do you now.' He rolled off the bed and took the video out of the case. He checked the tape footage and pointed at Lopez.

Video Report: A frightening discovery has been made by Colonel Lopez, chief of SOMIS, the internal-security organization of the country. On orders from Señor Bolivar, the ex-chairman of Menaguay, who had private information that the present junta may have possibly had some involvement in the plague that has devastated this nation, Colonel Lopez started his investigations.

Colonel Lopez, what exactly made ex-Chairman Bolivar suspicious that this plague was other than natural?

Briefly, there were a number of coincidences. The first being that all the generals in the junta were eight hundred miles north of Sao Amerigo, and out of the central part at the time of the plague. Second, that the families of the generals were out of the country. Third, that I myself was away. Fourth, that Chairman Bolivar should have been in the capital. By chance he was flying north at the time the capital was affected. There was also one fact. That he is no longer chairman.

I think we can ignore the fact that Bolivar was flying at the time. It could have happened under any circumstances. What did you discover about the families?

To leave this country, there are certain formalities to be followed. These take anywhere from a month to six weeks. When I investigated the files of the generals' families, I found that their exit visas had been granted in one day, on the tenth. This was eight days before the plague.

Who had granted those visas, Colonel Lopez?

Eduardo Bison, the minister of the interior. I went to his residence to question him, but he was not to be found.

Did he die in the plague? Isn't it strange that a man who you think was part of this conspiracy should have—?

He didn't die in the plague or escape the country. His and his wife's bedsheets were blood-soaked. I only can presume they'd been murdered.

By the generals?

Who knows?

What will be your next move?

To find out how the plague started, and from where.

Isn't that an impossible job? The area you will have to cover must be thousands of square miles.

The generals no doubt think it will be impossible. But nothing is impossible for me. It started somewhere, and there must be one man who knows this place. I will find him.

Tape pause ...

Piers lowered the video and stared into space. His eyes narrowed as he tried to remember. 'I think I can help you,' he finally said.

Lopez raised an eyebrow. His face showed he didn't believe him.

Piers ignored him and tried to recall the exact words. 'I interviewed Dr O'Brien,' he said. 'He's the American scientist. He said something about the infection not being contagious. I gather it can't be transmitted from person to person after an incubation period. He guessed that the germs were transmitted through the air, and not through the water supply or food.'

'Why through the air?'

'Something about attacking the respiratory system ...'

'Don't you keep a copy of your tapes?'

Piers hesitated momentarily and then lied: 'Never.' The fewer people who knew of his private-studio copy, the better.

'Okay,' Lopez said. 'So it was carried by the wind. Then somewhere along its path they must have released the plague.'

'Check the meteorological office for wind direction.'

'I thought of that,' Lopez said shortly. 'It depends on how wide an area their charts cover. If it's the whole country, it should help us. I'll go tomorrow.'

'Keep in touch,' Piers said. 'I'd come with you, but Geddes keeps an eye on me, and I can't move.'

'Does he watch all of you like that?'

'Only me.'

'Make your peace with him, then, so when the time comes you can move freely.' Lopez smiled suddenly. He seemed pleased. 'If not, I'll have to work alone and tell Bolivar you were unable to help.'

'You don't have to report any fucking thing,' Piers growled. 'Give me twenty-four hours and we'll be buddies.'

'You won't have twenty-four,' Lopez said, and let himself out. He paused in the corridor. He thought he'd heard a sound. It didn't repeat itself, in spite of his standing still for a whole minute. As he reached the stairs, the door to room forty-seven opened a fraction. It swung wide as Lopez disappeared, and Harris stepped into the corridor. He was wearing a shirt, tie, and jacket, but no trousers, and his feet were bare. He studied Piers' door a moment and then returned to his room.

Piers was wide-awake. The tiredness he'd felt earlier had completely gone, and his mind was busy figuring ways to get Geddes off his tail, It was, he knew, going to be tough. Marion! He'd seen Geddes studying her quite often. He would ask her to distract Geddes for a while. It was going to be their biggest exclusive. Momentarily Piers felt a spark of anger against the generals. He smothered it immediately. In his profession, there was little room for emotion.

6

The meteorological office was on the top floor of the Sao Amerigo University science block. Lopez hurried up the steps and entered. There was no sign of the army on the campus, who obviously expected little trouble from this direction. And they were quite right. From what he could see. the student population was almost nonexistent. A fortnight ago it had been the biggest campus in South America, with a student enrollment of 250,000. It was now reduced to pockets of young men and women standing around in silent, dazed groups. He wondered how long they would remain looking so lost if they knew what he knew. During Bolivar's government, Lopez hadn't needed to visit the university too often. Nearly the whole campus firmly supported Bolivar; except, naturally, for a few exceptions. On Bolivar's orders, Lopez had dealt with them as gently as possible. Most of them had been expelled for a year and scattered across the country.

Lopez hurried up the stairs. He hoped there would be someone around to help him. He didn't expect to have the same luck as he'd had in the ministry the day before. Driving to the campus, Lopez had noticed the signs of life returning to the city. A few buses had begun running again, carrying only a handful of people; here and there shops had begun to open; and there were people standing outside offices waiting for someone to let them in. Lopez had felt very proud at the resilience of his people. This pride, in turn, only made him more determined to find the proof Bolivar wanted.

He entered the meteorological laboratory. His heart sank. There wasn't a sound to be heard. The computers on his left were lifeless and the row of desks empty.

'Anybody here?' he called. There was no answer. He

moved to a wall chart of the country and studied it for a moment. It was covered with lines and calculations and didn't make even the remotest sense to him. He flicked through a sheaf of tables lying on a desk and dropped them. He knew nothing about the subject and couldn't even start looking for what he wanted.

'What do you want?'

Lopez started. Even as he began to turn to face the unexpectedly loud voice behind him, his hand was reaching for his automatic. It was halfway out before he saw who it was. A plump, middle-aged woman with sad, red-rimmed eyes. He saw her glance down at his hand, and he sheepishly pushed the automatic back into the waistband.

'Who are you?' she asked.

'Colonel Lopez, SOMIS.' He flipped open the credential. She didn't even look at it. 'I wanted some help.'

'There's only me here, so don't expect too much. The others . . .' Her voice broke, and she began to sniffle. Lopez stood awkwardly until she had controlled herself.

'Any help you give will be invaluable. I want to find out the wind directions in the basin territory on the sixteenth and seventeenth of last month. The more details you can give me, the better.'

'That's the day before and the day on which the plague came to Sao Amerigo.' She studied him carefully. 'Is SOMIS going to try to make the winds talk? I know you people have ways, but—'

'I just want to know the wind directions,' he said patiently.

She moved to a filing cabinet and pulled open a drawer. From the folder she took out a sheaf of charts. She flicked through them and finally shook her head. 'I can't help you. The reports aren't here.'

'Have they been stolen?'

She laughed at his suspicion. 'Who'd steal weather reports? No. The charts are usually completed the morning after. By that time we would have received and analyzed all the information that had come in on the previous day's weather conditions. It's then filled onto one chart like this.'

She handed him a relief map covered with wind movements, cloud formations, and temperatures. It covered only a few hundred square miles around Sao Amerigo.

'It doesn't cover the whole country?'

'No. That report you have is for the fifteenth. I'd guess the information for the sixteenth is still in there.' She nodded toward the computers.

Lopez studied the chart in his hands. He'd expected too much. However, even if he had a possible idea in which direction the wind had been moving that day over a few hundred square miles, he could narrow his search down.

'Can you get the information out of the computer?'

'I could,' the woman said, 'but I can't.' She saw his eyes narrow. 'They're not working, they're all burned out. On the sixteenth there was no one here to take care of them. I came in yesterday and tried to work. To get my mind off . . .' She gestured vaguely.

Lopez nodded sympathetically and thanked her. When he left, she was sitting at one of the desks, forlornly alone, staring at the computers. Sometimes, one found oneself in a useless job in which nothing could be done. Lopez understood how the woman felt, because he had the same useless feeling in the pit of his belly. He was at a dead end again and didn't know which way to turn.

He didn't return immediately to his car. Instead he moved across to a bench under the shade of a tree and sat down. It felt slightly cooler, and he shut his eyes to cut out the glare and think. He let his mind drift over all the information he'd gathered so far. Half an hour later he returned to the same dead end. How to find out the exact location where the plague started?

He opened his eyes and stared out across the campus. It was so peaceful and quiet, and he wished he could sit under the tree all day and forget his problems. He stirred restlessly. He couldn't just give up and lie down under a tree. He took a sheet of paper out of his pocket and absentmindedly sketched a map of the central territory. It was a roughly shaped oval. He drew a vertical line through the center and then a horizontal line. The oval was now divided into four parts. He sat up straighter. Carefully he drew four more vertical lines to the left of his original one, and then four to the right of it. He did the same thing with his horizontal lines. He had a grid pattern on the oval. In the center of the oval, in a square, he carefully wrote eight to nine A.M. at S.A. That was a start. If he could find out the times of the plague in the other squares, he could build up his own wind map.

The only way he could do that was to contact the SOMIS agents located in each square and get them to tell him the times the plague reached their area. That was, if they were still alive. If he could reach even fifty percent of them, he would have some idea as to where to look. The numbers and code names of his SOMIS agents were in his book.

He hurried back to his car and got in. It took him fifteen minutes to return to his apartment. He went directly to the wall safe in his bedroom and opened it. He riffled through the papers, at first calmly and then feverishly. The book was missing. He set the papers down on the table and methodically went through them for the third time. It was definitely not among them.

He sat back and tried to think. If the book had been stolen, the life of every one of his agents was in jeopardy. No. He shook his head. If the book had been stolen, the other papers would also have been taken. One of them was a confidential report to Bolivar which he'd been working on before he'd left for his vacation. Vacation! The book was in SOMIS headquarters, he suddenly remembered. He'd left it in his office safe the night before he'd left. He was the only one who knew the location of that safe and its combination, and he'd calculated it would be the most secure place for the book. He hoped to God he was right.

He ran down the stairs and across to his car. The SOMIS headquarters was on the Calle Trabajadores. It was a small, inconspicuous building tucked away in a small, inconspicuous street. He pulled up a hundred yards short of the discreet entrance. He didn't get out immediately but studied the two-story building. It seemed quiet and peaceful and deserted. He waited. Twenty minutes later a soldier stepped through the door, stretched his legs, and returned. Lopez straightened. If only one soldier was guarding it, he could ... He stopped. A jeep pulled up, and two officers entered. He started the car and drove slowly away. He had to get to that safe before the army did. If not, he and Bolivar and hundreds of others were as good as dead. The only chance was going to be that night.

'Oh, my God ... oh, my God ...' Marion covered her face with both hands and gently rocked herself. For a moment she looked like an old peasant woman in mourning. Piers kept silent, waiting for her to pull herself together. 'Are you sure? I mean, he could be setting you up ...'

'I don't think he was,' Piers said. 'He's still digging anyway, and Bolivar wants me to work with him. I'll find out soon enough how authentic his material is. We're on the biggest story in our life.'

'How can you say that so enthusiastically?' Marion said angrily. 'I feel sick ... and I don't know what to think.'

'We must find out the truth.' Piers leaned across the breakfast table and held her hand. Her food was untouched, like his. Neither felt they would ever eat again.

'I don't know,' Marion said. She saw Piers blink in surprise at her hesitation. 'I wanted us to leave the country yesterday,' she confessed.'Let it be, Piers, please.'

'No, we can't. We've got to dig it out.' He was too keyed up to think anymore about her hesitation. 'I need you to distract Geddes. Just get him off my back, so that I can work with Lopez.'

Marion nodded without saying anything. It was too late. Piers would never let go the story now, and, as always, she'd follow. She saw Piers smile cheerfully up at Geddes.

The lieutenant looked at him suspiciously. 'Why are you pleased at seeing me this morning?'

'I need your help,' Piers said. 'I want to interview Dr O'Brien. These are the questions. I know you'll be with me, and I promise I won't do anything stupid.'

He gave a sheet of paper to Geddes, who read over the

questions carefully. Finally he nodded. 'I'll arrange it for this morning,' he said. 'Does anyone else want to ask O'Brien questions?'

'Ask around,' Piers said, and hoped not too many of the others would want to come.

He watched Geddes move around the tables and jot down the names. Harris, it seemed, was one, and the French woman, Meunier, was another. The others looked too exhausted to stir. They were obviously wanting to spend a quiet day in the hotel playing cards or transmitting roundup stories on the situation. Geddes nodded to a soldier who at once became more alert, and left the room. He was back in ten minutes.

'Dr O'Brien says he will spare you a few minutes. We must leave at once.' He moved to Harris and Meunier, and the four of them followed Geddes to the truck.

O'Brien, Piers noticed the moment they walked into his makeshift office, looked older. His face was paler and thinner. His nostrils were pinched, and the superior jut in his jaw now looked indecisive. He shuffled his papers nervously as he waited for the journalists to settle themselves. My God, Piers thought, he's aged a decade in a few days. There was something else, but Piers couldn't put his finger on it immediately.

Video Report: *As I told Lieutenant Geddes over the phone earlier, I have nothing new to report. There has been no progress made in our investigation of the cause of the plague. However, there are, I gather, some points to be clarified. I would appreciate it if you kept your questions brief.*

Shatner, Channel 14, New York: In your press conference you stated that the plague had been transmitted through the air. Would it be correct to assume that by this you meant that the wind carried this virus, or whatever, across the basin territory?

I . . . I . . . I'm not able to answer that question until we've done further research into the nature of the disease.

But you said it had entered the body through the

respiratory system and caused clotting in the lungs. Have you changed your opinion?

I was only advancing a preliminary theory at the press conference.

But you seemed definite.

I am sorry I gave that impression.

Doctor, can you tell me what causes paralysis?

I told you just now, what I said earlier was only a preliminary theory.

Yes, I realize that. But for my own benefit could you explain what exactly happens in the body to make a person paralyzed?

Well . . . as long as you understand that this has nothing to do with the virus, I can tell you. If a key enzyme in the human system, called acetylcholinesterase, is affected in any way, paralysis can occur.

How does this acet . . . work?

In layman's terms, there are millions of junctions in the nervous system. At these junctions a body-produced chemical called acetylcholine transmits the nerve signals. On receiving a signal from the brain, acetylcholine jumps across these junctions and activates the muscles or the nerve cells on the other side. When sufficient activity has taken place in the nerve cell, the body produces acetylcholinesterase to neutralize or destroy the surplus amount of acetycholine. If this process is in any way interfered with, paralysis will occur in the human body. This does not necessarily mean it will cause death. You do understand this, don't you?

Of course, Dr O'Brien. Thank you.

Hyslop, Channel 14, New York: Could you give an estimate of the casualties in the country? Would twenty-five to thirty percent be accurate? Or less?

You'll have to ask Lieutenant Geddes that question.

Harris, TTN, London: How effective has the British role been in the caring for the people of this country?

The help your country has given is incalculable. I must . . .

Piers switched off his video and sat down. He didn't expect either Harris or Meunier to ask any revealing questions. Out of the corner of his eyes he saw Geddes bearing down on Marion. The lieutenant looked very disturbed.

'What do you mean "less"?' Geddes demanded.

'What do you think it means?' Marion said. 'You could be exaggerating the figures.'

Piers closed his eyes. He was thankful that he had her to help him. She had Geddes' total attention, and would continue to have it until he could prove that the army wasn't lying. It seemed, as he spluttered, as if his whole integrity and honor were at stake. Studying his genuine indignation, Piers realized that Geddes and most probably a large section of the army had no idea what the generals had done.

'I will prove to you that the army has issued accurate figures,' Geddes was saying. 'You will come with me to army headquarters and meet General Orantes, who is in overall command of the rehabilitation operation. He will show you the reports.'

'All right,' Marion said, and stood up.

Geddes glanced at Piers. He hesitated. 'After we have left the others in the hotel.'

Piers' attention returned to Dr O'Brien. Though the questions he was being asked by Meunier were harmless, the man was beginning to sweat. He was, Piers realized, on the verge of a breakdown. That's it, Piers thought, he knows something. Somewhere along the line he's found out about the plague, and he's running scared.

Abruptly Dr O'Brien stood up, scattering his papers over the floor. He seemed to be on the point of saying something but changed his mind. He turned and hurried out of the room.

'He's tired,' Geddes explained quickly. 'They've all been working too hard.'

The alley running off Calle Trabajadores, a building away from the SOMIS headquarters, was pitch black. Lopez felt his way to the end, groped for the rear entrance door of the building, and slid the thin steel skeleton key into the lock.

He gave it a twist, and the door opened. He didn't hesitate but hurried up the stairs and let himself out onto the roof. He walked to the edge. There was a ten-foot gap between him and the SOMIS roof. In daylight it was an easy jump, but at night, with a soldier guarding the entrance below, it was going to be difficult. He peered across the space. He would have to fall well clear of the edge, as there was no ledge to hang on to. He didn't have time to waste. He moved back a dozen feet and then ran forward and jumped. He hit the roof opposite heavily, and for a minute lay winded. He pushed himself up and winced. He'd scraped his right elbow and could feel the blood trickling down his arm.

He opened the roof door. There was no one guarding the stairs. The army, he guessed, didn't expect anyone to break in to SOMIS headquarters. Break out, yes, but not in. He stopped at the top of the stairs leading to the ground floor. Two soldiers were sitting near the door playing cards. He would have to use the rear stairs to get to the basement. He passed his office and felt a moment of longing. It was a comfortable room, carefully furnished by him with the things he liked. Next to it was a bedroom and bathroom. He had formed the habit of working very late at night, quite often not leaving the office for forty-eight hours at a time.

He crept softly down the stairs to the ground floor. If the soldiers decided to look up at that moment, he was dead. He pressed himself against the door leading to the basement, and slowly turned the knob. He watched the soldiers laugh over their cards and sit back before the next hand. He prayed neither would decide to check the corridor. He broke out in a sweat. The knob had stopped. The door was locked. He twisted harder. It was only stuck. He opened the door and quickly slid in.

He switched on the light. The basement was deceptive from the outside. It was, in reality, twice the size of the other floors, and there was a complex of rooms below the street. It was also soundproof and filled with the most modern interrogation equipment. Lopez, as chief of SOMIS, didn't believe in hurting a man's body. He worked on the psyche of a man, and the medical equipment and special rooms could extract most information he wanted painlessly. He had no illusions about his work. It was to try to read the minds of men, unravel the puzzles they had created, and protect the state he served. He believed he had failed in that job, temporarily at least.

He hurried down the steps. As he'd expected, the rooms on either side of the corridor he moved down were empty. Coup d'etats were, in his business, a game of musical chairs. Those who were imprisoned were freed, and those who were free took their places.

He entered a cell at the end of the corridor. It looked no different from the others. It was comfortably furnished and seemed most ordinary. He knew, however, that it was a complex piece of electronic gadgetry. Videos covered every square inch of the cell, the walls and ceilings could be used as screens for the hidden projectors, there were speakers and microphones in the walls, even the landscape outside the window was a carefully controlled illusion. He turned to the light switch and spoke: 'It is Garcia Lopez.'

He waited a moment, and then one of the blocks in the floor slid smoothly back. He knelt and repeated: 'It is Garcia Lopez.' The wait was a bit longer as the machine matched his voice patterns with its memory. He heard the tumblers click, and reached into the opening and lifted the safe door.

The book was there. It was a drab green color and the size of a small diary. He checked to make sure it was the one he wanted, and closed the door of the safe. He remained kneeling for a moment. There were important papers left inside the safe. The army may never find it, but that was a chance he couldn't afford to take.

'Destroy.'

He bent his head and listened. There was the faintest of clicks. The acid had been released. In a minute there'd be nothing inside except ashes and fumes.

Tucking the book into his pocket, he left the cell. At the basement door, he peered down the corridor. Only one of the soldiers was sitting at the card table. Lopez guessed the other had gone to relieve himself. He ran up the flight to the second floor and flung open the door. He stepped straight into the missing soldier. They were both equally surprised. The difference was that Lopez recovered a fraction of a second quicker than the soldier. As the man began to lift the barrel of his machine gun, Lopez pressed his automatic into the man's belly and pulled the trigger.

The 'thuck' seemed unnaturally loud, but Lopez knew it wouldn't carry more than a few feet. He felt the blood spurt onto his fist, and in a moment his whole arm was stained. He pulled the dying soldier to him and dragged the man into a side room and locked the door. It would take a few minutes for him to be found, and with luck Lopez would be back on the street.

He hurried up to the roof, wiping his arm against his shirt front. He would have liked to wash, for if a jeep patrol caught him, he wouldn't be lucky enough to be shot. No doubt he'd end up either in the barracks or one of his own cells.

The street was reached safely, and the soldier was no longer outside the SOMIS door. He'd been called in to search for his comrade, and soon the search would spread to the streets. Lopez started back to his apartment at a jog. He would have liked to run, but he knew that in his panic he would have run straight into a patrol.

He was pouring with sweat by the time he let himself into his apartment. He washed and changed quickly and sat down at a telephone. It was one in the morning, and it was going to be a long night. He opened the book, took out his rough sketch of the basin territory with its grid markings, and picked up the phone. He hesitated and slowly put it down. When you tapped phones you became suspicious of every instrument. He had to be positive no one was listening to him. It was the first time he was going to make voice contact with his agents and reveal their identity.

He left his apartment and went up two flights. He moved slowly down the corridor, stopping to listen at doors. He had to take a chance. He slipped his 'key' into the lock and jiggled it around, and opened the door. The apartment smelled musty and abandoned. He checked the rooms to make sure, and then moved to the phone. He made himself as comfortable as possible, picked up the phone, and began dialing.

By the time he finished, it was nine-thirty in the morning. He blinked in surprise at the bright sunlight outside as he slumped back in his chair. His mouth was dry from talking and explaining and questioning, and his head ached from sheer exhaustion. But he felt satisfied. He hadn't been able to contact thirty-six of his agents, and he presumed them to have died in the plague. Those he talked to had told him exactly what he wanted to know. He looked at the map in front of him and studied it for a long time. He had marked the approximate times his agents reported the plague to have reached their area, written 'No' in those squares which had not been affected, and shaded those squares from which he could not make any contact. He now had a map on the variations, both direction and timings, of the wind across the basin territory. Some of his 'Nos' were right in the center of affected areas. At first he'd been puzzled. Now he realized that by some freak of fate the wind had changed its direction and left the people living there totally unharmed. He drew an arrow at the bottom of the map and slowly drew a head on it. The wind direction was northeast. He brooded over the two southernmost shaded blocks. It had started somewhere within those squares. If he could find the timings in those two blocks, his search would narrow itself down even further. As it was, he now had only a few hundred square miles to cover. It was better than the thousands he'd had when Bolivar had issued the order.

He could cut the area down even further. If the wind was moving northeast, it would have first passed through the lower of the two squares. That was as much as he could do for the moment. He would now have to go down to his square and search it, foot by foot if necessary, to find whatever there was to be found. He stopped. But that would take time, and he had none. He thought for a while and then made a few more calls.

99

When he finished, he was satisfied. He gathered up his book and map and left the apartment. He wondered vaguely who had once lived there. Maybe he'd met them on the stairs daily and wished them good morning as he'd passed. He was bone-weary and went straight to bed and fell asleep.

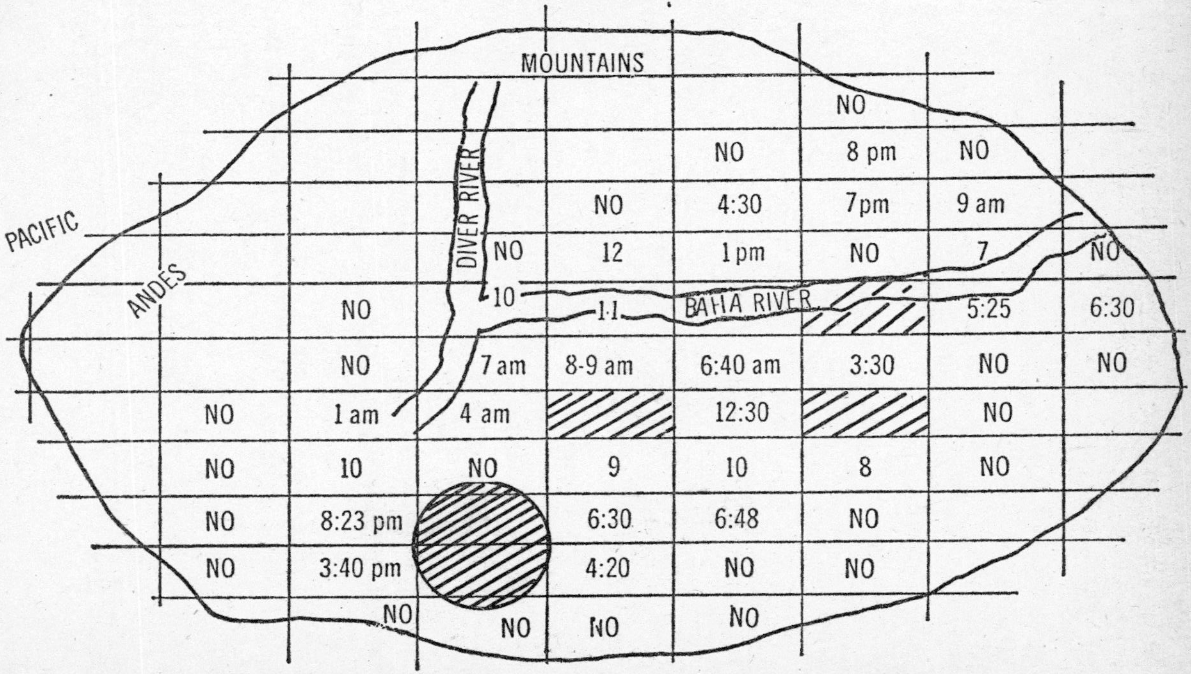
MOUNTAINS
PACIFIC
ANDES
DIVER RIVER
BAHA RIVER
NO
NO
8 pm
NO
NO
4:30
7pm
9 am
NO
12
1 pm
NO
7
NO
10
11
NO
5:25
6:30
NO
7 am
8-9 am
6:40 am
3:30
NO
NO
NO
1 am
4 am
12:30
NO
NO
10
NO
9
10
8
NO
NO
8:23 pm
6:30
6:48
NO
NO
3:40 pm
4:20
NO
NO
NO
NO
NO
NO

7

Mercer settled back in his chair and stared at the blank monitor. Darrigan and Solotov were doing the same. The silence was vacant as they waited. Darrigan impatiently pressed a button.

'We're ready. Run it.'

On command, the monitor lit up.

Video replay of Shatner-O'Brien exchange. Recorded 11/7 at 11.30 hours, Sao Amerigo General Hospital . . .

As I told Lieutenant Geddes over the phone earlier, I have nothing new to report. There has been no progress made in our investigation of the cause of the plague. However, there are, I gather, some points to be clarified. I would appreciate it if you kept your questions brief.

Shatner, Channel 14, New York: In your press conference you stated that the plague had been transmitted through the air. Would it be correct to assume that by this you meant that the wind carried this virus, or whatever, across the basin territory?

I . . . I . . . I'm not able to answer that question until we've done further research into the nature of the disease.

But you said it had entered the body through the respiratory system and caused clotting in the lungs. Have you changed your opinion?

I was only advancing a preliminary theory at the press conference.

But you seemed definite.

I am sorry I gave that impression.

Doctor, can you tell me what causes paralysis?

I told you just now, what I said earlier was only a preliminary theory.

Yes, I realize that. But for my own benefit could you

explain what exactly happens in the body to make a person paralyzed?

Well . . . as long as you understand that this has nothing to do with the virus. I can tell you. If a key enzyme in the human system, called acetylcholinesterase, is affected in any way, paralysis can occur.

How does this acet . . . work?

In layman's terms, there are millions of junctions in the nervous system. At these junctions a body-produced chemical called acetylcholine transmits the nerve signals. On . . .

'That son of a bitch knows something.' Darrigan banged the table. 'And he's playing O'Brien for a sucker.'

'I can't see anything wrong,' Mercer said. 'He's basing his questions only on what O'Brien had told him at the first press conference.' He looked across to Solotov for confirmation. The eyes that met his were bleak and unresponsive. They flicked toward Darrigan.

'He does know something,' Solotov said. 'His questions are specific. They're not fishing, they're only trying to confirm.'

'Now, watch his face while the others are asking questions.' Darrigan pushed his button. The screen went blurred for a few seconds; then the picture returned to focus.

It was a tight close-up of Shatner's face. The eyes were watchful, and Mercer felt he could actually see the man thinking. Quite suddenly Shatner's eyes narrowed, and then his features relaxed. It was as if he'd seen something that had answered his questions. The picture blurred again as the video jerked. It caught O'Brien hurriedly leaving the room. The screen went blank

'O'Brien also knows,' Mercer said, and tried to keep the sly satisfaction out of his voice. He felt an almost masochistic pleasure in seeing Darrigan glare at him.

'We'll have to recall O'Brien and place him under observation.' Darrigan glanced at Solotov, who nodded. He pushed his button, and an aide appeared on the monitor. 'Recall O'Brien and place him under surveillance. And' – he looked this time at both Mercer and Solotov as he spoke

– 'have Shatner expelled from the country. Make sure that the charge for expulsion is legitimate, though not necessarily factual. I'm sure he's given more than enough reason for the generals to have him thrown out.' The screen went blank before the aide could acknowledge the instructions.

He enjoys his bloody little buttons, Mercer thought. He can make people appear and disappear at his whim. In real life, however, he and the other two could only keep them disappeared. Resurrection was beyond even the powers of the Council. He saw Solotov open the folder in front of him and pick up the papers. He must have been trained in some ancient college of bureaucracy, Mercer thought. He fondles those sheets as if he were caressing his penis. Only a bureaucrat could love paper that much. Mercer only touched his file; he didn't open it. Just staring at it was enough to make him feel ill.

'The researchers report that their figures are one hundred percent accurate,' Solotov said in his monotone. 'Before we extend the operation area, we must discover why the casualty figures in Menaguay were below the projected figures. We can't take any chances.'

'Do we have to extend?' Mercer asked miserably. 'I would prefer to defer—'

'No time,' Darrigan said shortly, and turned to Solotov. 'The discrepancy between the projected figures and the actual figures is between fifty and sixty-five percent. Given the fallibility of our scientists, this means only half the projected potential has been realized.'

'Why don't you use the word "flask", for God's sake,' Mercer said angrily. 'One flask only was released. So there's another flask with virus still in it. Intact. Lying somewhere out in that poor, godforsaken country.'

'You're getting hysterical,' Darrigan said coldly. 'and that's not going to be of any help at all. You were a part of the decision-making process, and your negative attitude is beginning to grate.'

'I voted against it, if you remember,' Mercer said loudly.

'We are aware of that,' Solotov said. 'That's in the past. We must retrieve that flask. If somebody else should find it

. . .' He didn't finish, but pressed the button in front of him. He did this fastidiously and stared for a long time at the aide who appeared on the monitor. The young man began to look nervous. It seemed as if Solotov was composing a speech mentally. 'Send instructions to Sao Amerigo. One flask intact. Imperative to retrieve immediately.'

'Yes, sir,' the aide said, and went off the screen.

Solotov nodded in reply and sat back satisfied with his performance.

Piers lay fully dressed on the bed with his combat boots on. The video was by his side, and his arms were folded across his chest. He had the air of a man who was waiting, as patiently as he could, for something to happen. Though he didn't have the lights on, he could clearly distinguish the details of the room. It always surprised him how bright and clear the moonlight in this part of the world was. He could almost read by it. At the thought of that, he picked up the scrap of paper lying on the bedside table and read it. 'Tonight, ten. L.' Piers sighed and looked at his watch; it was 10.30. Punctuality, he guessed, wasn't Lopez' habit. He picked up the video and scanned the room. The night lens and filter made it all as bright as day.

He sat up. There was a scrape on the door. He moved and hoped it wasn't Marion. He had told her he was exhausted and needed sleep.

'Who's that?'

'Lopez.'

Piers opened the door and stood aside, but Lopez didn't enter.

'You had my note?'

'Yes, what have you found out?' It had been lying on his pillow.

'We must go.' Lopez turned and hurried down the corridor.

Piers picked up his video and followed him. 'Where are we going?' he asked breathlessly as they ran down the stairs.

'Later,' Lopez said, and opened the exit door carefully. 'We must be careful of patrol. Follow and do exactly what I do.'

It was 10.40, and the curfew had been in force for the last three and a half hours. The streets were totally deserted and looked as if they'd been abandoned to the puffs of dust and garbage that rolled across them. There was a full moon, and the shadows they threw were sharp and long. Piers walked two steps behind Lopez and imitated him the best he could. He wished he knew where he was going. Suddenly Lopez stopped and listened. It took a moment for Piers to also hear the jeep patrol approaching them. They ducked into an alley and pressed against a door. The patrol, four soldiers all carrying ancient automatic rifles, roared past. They waited a minute and then stepped back onto the road.

'Where are we going?' Piers asked impatiently after ten minutes of silence.

'To the outskirts of the city. It's a long walk, so save your breath.'

It was a very long walk, and they finally reached the end of the suburbs after forty-five minutes. Piers was covered with sweat and dust. A couple of patrols had interrupted the walk, but they'd had no trouble. They turned off the main road and onto a side street and kept going until they reached an open field. Lopez pointed to a clump of trees one hundred yards across the field. They'd have to run, and pray as the moonlight silhouetted them clearly. They both crouched as low as possible, and Lopez set off first, ducking and dodging. When he'd made thirty yards, Piers followed him, his back tense for the impact of a bullet. Nothing happened, and they made the trees, out of breath but safe. There was a car waiting for them, with a young boy for a driver. Lopez jumped in and slumped back in his seat. Piers joined him as the car started off with a jerk and then accelerated wildly.

'Now will you tell me where we're headed?'

'About three hundred miles south,' Lopez said.

'In this?' The young driver had more enthusiasm than skill.

'No.' Lopez laughed. 'We're flying in Bolivar's private jet.'

'What are we going to find?'

'I told you that nothing was impossible for Colonel Lopez. I think I've found where the plague started. My agents – those who survived – gave me the times the plague reached their area. From that I narrowed down the search to a few hundred square miles. By the time we reach the general location, it should be down to a few square miles. I ordered all my agents to concentrate their search.'

'Any idea what you're going to find?'

Lopez shrugged. The car was racing across a clearing, and Piers could see a well-camouflaged hangar at the far end. As they neared it, a jet whined and roared to life. It was a Harrier VTOL. There was just enough space for Piers and Lopez to squeeze into before the pilot, who had obviously already been briefed, lifted off.

'It'll only take forty minutes,' Lopez shouted in Pier's ear as the plane began to accelerate.

'Won't the army spot us?' Piers shouted back.

'We'll be flying very low. I only hope those on the ground who see us will think we're the army.'

Piers hoped Lopez was right. In this moonlight an observer would have to be blind not to be able to distinguish the nonmilitary markings on the aircraft. That was, of course, if they didn't crash first. They were flying so low that Piers sometimes felt the trees were higher than the aircraft, and when he looked down, he could see skid marks on the roads they flew over. He shut his eyes and held on.

He opened them when the aircraft began to hover. He peered at his watch; forty minutes had passed since they'd lifted off. The aircraft banked, and Piers saw two men sheltering behind a tree. As soon as the Harrier landed, the men ran toward it. Colonel Lopez jumped out, crouched, and ran to meet them halfway. The three of them huddled and gesticulated, and Piers, looking around at the open field, wondered where they were. He'd seen a largish town ten minutes back but, as he'd never been to this part of the country, couldn't recognize it.

Lopez ran back to him and climbed in. He spoke quickly into the intercom to the pilot, and the aircraft rose once more off the ground.

'We have to head farther south,' Lopez shouted to Piers.

'One of my men found an old Indian vaquero who says he saw something. I want to question that man.'

'Where is he?'

'About thirty miles from a town called Rio Branco.' Lopez smiled triumphantly. 'I knew I'd find one man who knew something. My men have been working all day questioning everyone in this area. Two of them went to one of the big ranches west of Rio Branco, where they heard about this Indian who kept saying he'd seen something. No one believed him. He is old and dreams of his past and believes it is God punishing the people. Also, no one wanted to visit the place, for they think it is cursed. The Indian and my agents are waiting near a village called Cochos.'

It took them ten minutes to reach their destination. As the aircraft hovered and then slowly began to descend, Piers could see the village. There were about nine small shacks on either side of a narrow, dusty road that ran east to west; there was a *cantina* and a bus stop. It looked ghostly in the moonlight, and nothing moved as the aircraft dropped lower. The dark shapes Piers had seen from a hundred and fifty feet up turned out to be dogs and chickens and goats, and they never moved. As soon as the aircraft settled, Piers saw three men coming toward them. The one in the center moved slowly and cautiously. He was being held by one of the men, and seemed afraid. The pilot cut the engines, and the silence was sudden and unnatural, and for a moment Piers could hear nothing. Gradually the sounds of the night came drifting gently to him. Crickets, frogs, the wind, the crunch of gravel underfoot.

He lifted the video to his eye as Lopez jumped out and met the ancient Indian. The Indian pointed east, and Piers jumped out and followed the three men a few paces behind. The vast landscape was totally deserted except for the three in front of him. He felt a loneliness as he thought that they were the only living creatures for many square miles. It could have been an illusion, but he felt that after only a few days of neglect, the great primeval jungle that had dominated this part of the world for millions of years was slowly beginning to rise out of the earth and reclaim its rights.

The men in front of him came to a group of bodies. They lay sprawled on the road with their farming tools around them. The stench made it obvious they'd been here for the week, and the buzzing of flies sounded like a thousand jets in the stillness.

'Why haven't they been buried or burned?' Piers asked.

'People are frightened to approach them,' one of the agents, the shorter man, said. He pointed. 'Just down the road is the car the Indian saw.'

'Why wasn't he killed?'

'The wind,' Lopez said. 'Your scientist must have guessed right. The Indian was up there on the slope and upwind from the man in the car . . .'

The Indian, as if on cue, stopped and squatted on the road. It was as far as he would go; fifty yards ahead was the car. Cautiously Lopez and his agents moved toward it.

Piers passed the Indian and then stopped. He shut his eyes momentarily. When he looked back at the Indian, he saw that the man was looking at nothing. His eyes were open, but they stared at something that was too far away for Piers' video to capture.

It was then that Piers knew he'd made a mistake. The Indian marked a boundary line. If he stepped any farther, all the protection he'd built around him would crumble and break; he would no longer be able to retain his detachment if he knew what was in the car. He shifted uneasily. He'd kept the pain of other people at a clinical distance, always separated by the narrow tunnel of his video's viewer. It seemed now as if the lens was slowly splintering and that he was being sucked into the tunnel. Once that happened and he found himself on the other side, he would become a part of all the pain he'd ever seen. And there'd be no way of returning back up the tunnel.

Piers was frightened of the car and of the landscape that filled him with awe. He was an urban man, used to crowds and dusty streets and buildings, and here there was no shelter or protection.

'Come and see, reporter,' Lopez said softly.

Piers took a deep breath and stepped forward slowly with

the video up to his face. He could see the man behind the wheel of the crashed car. The man's eyes stared up at the roof of the car, his face forever frozen in what seemed surprise. It looked as if he hadn't expected death. His body was in the same state as the peasants up the road, and the agents shooed the flies away while they held handkerchiefs to their noses.

Colonel Lopez began to gingerly search the man, while his agents searched the surrounding area. Piers remained at a distance with his video covering all the actions.

Lopez grunted and carefully extracted a sheet of paper from one of the dead man's pockets. Piers stepped nearer as Lopez read the paper. He could see Lopez' face grow cold and angry.

'What is it?' Piers asked.

'Rental carbon for the car. The man's name is Charles Whitlam, and his address, according to this, is 245 East Thirty-fifth Street, New York. The car was rented from the Carlton Hotel on the day the plague broke out.'

Lopez silently held out the thin sheet of paper to Piers. His face was a mask, but Piers could see the tension in his body. The hand holding the paper was shivering as if it were touching something cold and evil.

'Oh, my God,' Piers whispered.

Lopez turned back to the body, and Piers moved closer. On the dead man's left thigh was a four-inch narrow charred patch. Clinging to the edges of the patch were tiny flakes of gray ash.

'That's a cigarette burn,' Piers said. 'He must have lit it a few seconds before he died. He couldn't have known it was going to happen.'

'Why not?' Lopez asked. 'A last cigarette, isn't that the cliché of executions and suicides?'

'But there's still no proof he was responsible.'

'Colonel!' one of the agents called urgently.

He was standing in a ditch pointing to his feet. Lopez and Piers hurried across and saw, half-hidden in the grass, an object that looked like a small cylinder. It was dull silver in color, and open at one end. Piers felt the cold touch him as

Lopez wrapped his hand in a handkerchief and picked it up. Very, very slowly Lopez brought the open end of the cylinder to his nose; he was tense and ready to drop it. He sniffed, and then grew surer. There was nothing. He looked at Piers; his eyes were moist, as if he were about to cry.

There was a long silence as Lopez stared into the camera. It seemed as if now that he'd reached his goal, he found to his surprise that he'd been beaten.

'Colonel!' It was the other agent calling, and the three of them moved slowly and heavily to him. There was no escape now. They knew, almost mesmerically, that this was going to be the last part of the proof they needed.

The agent had what looked like the cap for the cylinder in one hand, and in the other the empty shell of a can of deodorant.

Lopez fitted the cap and then slid the cylinder into the hollow can. He was crying and wiping his face as he did so; and held the can out to Piers as if it were a destroyed child.

'My people . . . my mother . . . my people . . .' He stopped and couldn't continue. There was too much rage and pain in him.

At another time, Piers would have watched him through the video and recorded every last moment of the tragedy; but it seemed impossible now. He lowered the camera from his eye, and then, as if in a dream, he unscrewed the circular plate in the base of the camera and slid out the telescopic legs. They adjusted their height automatically so that the picture would remain perfectly horizontal. Piers unclipped the microphone, pinned it to his shirt front, and switched the camera to automatic. From now on it could tape and keep him constantly in focus.

Piers moved toward Lopez. It felt as if he were stepping into a cold, alien world, one filled with black despair, in which there was no longer any protection for him. Even if he didn't feel the same pain, he was touched by Lopez' rage and bewilderment at the enormity of what they'd discovered. He looked at the can Lopez cradled in his hand and shook his head. What kind of man was capable of killing so many people?

Lopez began to swear obscenely. It began in a mutter and then became louder and louder until it ended in a scream at the sky.

Neither of them noticed the agent standing nearby with the briefcase in his hand. He waited until Lopez had finished and then showed him the case. There was a can of deodorant, similar to the dummy Lopez held, in it. It took Lopez a second to wrench off the cap and slide the same silver cylinder out of the can.

'You think they are the same?' Piers asked.

'They look the same. We'll have to run tests on it.' Lopez weighed it in his hand. He had control over himself now, and the mask of the professional hunter had been replaced. 'If this man was carrying two flasks, he meant to use both. The casualties would then have been double. Why didn't he use both, and complete the job?'

'Maybe he wanted to use it in another location?'

'A dead man can't drive,' Lopez said. 'Who cares now? I have fulfilled Bolivar's command. In my left hand is the proof, in my right the loaded weapon. How I hate this Whitlam.'

Coldly Lopez pulled out his automatic and moved to the body. He pointed and emptied the magazine into the decomposing flesh. The explosions made them start, and the skin on the body shred like cotton as it slammed across the seat.

'Hai!' the Indian called out, and one of the agents ran to him. They whispered, and the agent called them.

'He can hear a truck approaching. It will be here in fifteen minutes, he guesses.'

Colonel Lopez stuffed the two cans into the briefcase and sprinted for the aircraft. Piers grabbed his video and followed him in. As the aircraft began to lift, he could see the agents and the Indian hurrying across the fields.

'Who's in the truck?' Piers shouted.

'A patrol,' Lopez said. He hugged the case to his chest.

Neither spoke on the flight back. Piers tried desperately to think, but his thoughts couldn't slide past the massive boulders of Whitlam and the two flasks. They filled his whole mind, suffocating him. He shivered, and it wasn't from the chill in the aircraft. He was frightened. He had expected, if anything, to find a soldier responsible for the plague. But not a Charles Whitlam, whoever the poor son of a bitch was, an American. If the Industrial Nations were involved ... Piers could go no further. He broke out into a sweat and turned to look at Lopez. He was fast asleep. The handsome face, profiled against the lightening sky outside the oval window, looked peaceful. Like a hunting animal that had made its kill and was fully sated. Piers glanced down. The briefcase was on Lopez' lap. His right hand was resting on the case and was gently curled around the butt of the automatic. Bolivar might trust him, but Piers knew that Lopez never would.

By the time they reached the outskirts of Sao Amerigo, it was five-thirty in the morning. It was pleasantly cool, and though the lack of sleep was beginning to slow him down, Piers wasn't feeling tired. The tension in his guts had become a physical pain. In contrast, Lopez still looked calm. He had done his job, and now all he had to do was get the information to Bolivar. Bolivar would decide what to do next, and that was what frightened Piers.

It was easier returning to the hotel. The curfew had been lifted at five, and though there weren't all that many people about – a few farmers bringing in a supply of fresh vegetables, street cleaners lethargically sweeping the roads – it made movement much easier. The patrols were still scattered around the city, but the soldiers mostly dozed in the jeeps.

'I'm going to the Carlton to find out more about this man Whitlam,' Lopez said as they neared the Amerigo. 'Do you wish to come?'

Piers wanted to refuse. He dreaded to think what they'd find out about Whitlam. But he knew he would have to face whatever it was, and he nodded. The pain in his gut only increased as they entered the Carlton's lobby.

There was no one on reception, and they moved quickly to the stairs. By the time they reached the seventh story they were both breathing hard. Piers stopped to catch his breath, but Lopez kept going. He stopped at a door, 708, and slid his skeleton key into the lock. In a second he was inside. Piers moved slowly, and when he reached the door, he took a deep breath, lifted the video to his eye, and entered.

Video Report ... Tape continued ...

This is Charles Whitlam's room at the Carlton Hotel in Sao Amerigo. Colonel Lopez methodically starts searching the room to find out more about Whitlam. Who was he? Where did he come from? Is he really from America? At the end of ten minutes, Colonel Lopez has found absolutely nothing. The closets are bare, the drawers empty, and the bathroom doesn't even contain an inch of dental floss. Colonel Lopez' disappointment is obvious, but he doesn't give up. He starts again. This time he searches the more secret places. Under drawers and tops of cupboards. He flicks up the bedspread, peers underneath, and then goes down on his belly. He pulls out a rolled ball of paper. He carefully smooths out the ball. There are two sheets, which he places on the table. One has some print on it; the other looks like a graph of some sort.

In summation, we believe that it is imperative that we immediately put into effect our project for C.P.G. over as wide an area as possible. If this is not done with the use of the I.R.S. system, mankind will face O.T. within five years. Once O.T. occurs, the situation will be hopelessly irretrievable.

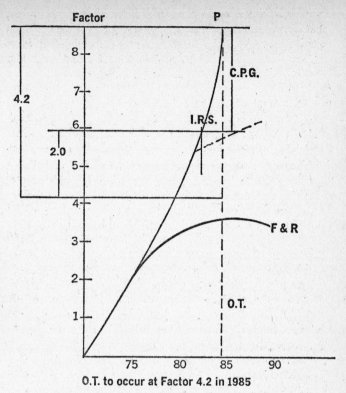

O.T. to occur at Factor 4.2 in 1985

Colonel Lopez, what do you think the papers mean?

It is difficult to tell with the graph unless one knows what this O.T., IRS, and CPG mean. But the print, what do you think as wide an area as possible means?

It could be referring to the territory.

Or to other parts of the world, my friend.

If Colonel Lopez is right, then Whitlam and what has happened here in Menaguay is only the tip of the iceberg. But there is still doubt as to who exactly Whitlam is. He could be a paid employee of the generals, a scapegoat who had no use apart from releasing the virus. He still has no other identification than a name and address on a rental carbon.

We'll rectify that immediately. When you check into a hotel in this country, you have to surrender your passport. Come, we'll ask the manager.

Tape pause . . .

Tape continued . . .

The manager who was in charge when Whitlam checked in is no longer alive. Nor is most of the hotel staff. The young man temporarily in charge of the hotel nervously shows Colonel Lopez his register. There is no Charles Whitlam registered at all. Nor, Colonel Lopez discovers, is any passport being held by the hotel in his name. At the car-rental counter, Colonel Lopez tries to match the carbon he found on Whitlam with the originals held by the company. For some strange reason, there is no original to the carbon. And there is no one to question. The temporary manager of the hotel says that the car-rental firm has been unmanned since the plague. The mystery surrounding Charles Whitlam gets deeper. He exists as a corpse, but in life, there seems to be no trace of him at all. For all we know, his name may not even be Charles Whitlam, and the address a false one. In which case, this rental carbon, our only evidence that he existed, could be another thread that leads to nowhere. This is Piers Shatner, Channel 14, New York, in Sao Amerigo, with Colonel Lopez.

Lopez no longer looked calm. He was frustrated and angry at the dead end he'd reached. If the carbon hadn't been the only evidence that Whitlam existed, he would have torn it to shreds and stamped on it. He made an effort and controlled himself. He folded the carbon neatly and tucked it into the briefcase. Piers caught a brief glimpse of the flasks. In the sunlight, the dull silver of the night now seemed to shine malignantly.

'Maybe he didn't stay in the hotel,' Piers suggested.

Lopez shook his head. 'I feel inside he did. That graph and that print just . . .' He hesitated and then said stubbornly, 'They belonged to him. I feel it. I will get a man to

116

check the prints in the room. I bet they'll match the ones on the flask.'

'Okay, so he stayed in the Carlton. But who is he?' Lopez grimaced at the question.

'As far as I can figure, this is how it worked out. He throws a flask out of the window, starts driving, and lights up a cigarette. If he knew what was in the flask, then his actions just don't correlate. If he didn't know, then I'd guess there was supposed to be something else in that flask. And maybe the intact one as well.'

'He could have been mad,' Lopez said in frustration.

'In which case he would sit on the roadside and wait for his death.'

Lopez shrugged eloquently and hopelessly. He would have liked to dismiss the identity and the mental condition of Whitlam as unimportant. He had all the evidence that Bolivar wanted, but he knew that Whitlam, in a strange frustrating way, was the heart of the puzzle. He is, in fact, Lopez thought, the bull's-eye in a target. Whose head does Bolivar point his gun at? The generals?' Or those who sent Whitlam on his journey to Cochos with two flasks? Maybe it was the generals? Whitlam? Whitlam? Whitlam? Who sent you there? Lopez wanted to scream out. 'Maybe Bolivar will be able to solve the problem,' he said finally. He was, he knew, giving up on Whitlam. He put out his hand to Piers. 'Please give me all the tape you used so far.'

Piers looked at Lopez in surprise. 'Why don't you drop ...' He looked down at Lopez' automatic pointing at his belly. By now, he wearily thought, I should be able to recognize that damned gun anywhere. '... dead? ...' He rewound the tape, took it out, and handed it over to Lopez.

'I will return it to you tonight,' Lopez said as he dropped it in the briefcase. 'We will see Bolivar, and you will show him this tape. It's partly for your safety and mine. If Geddes finds you have been missing all night, the first thing he'll check will be your tapes. And if he sees what we've found, we're both ...' He gestured with a finger across his throat.

117

'What time tonight? And Bolivar will give me an interview?'

'Yes. And I will meet you outside the hotel at ten-thirty. Make sure you're not being followed.'

Lopez hurried out of the rear exit. Piers walked slowly back to the Amerigo Hotel. The adrenaline that had kept him going all night was draining out of him, and he could feel exhaustion pleasantly enveloping his body. He hoped Geddes didn't have any plans for him that day. But most of all he prayed his absence hadn't been noticed. He slipped into the hotel and ran up the stairs. It was still early and there wasn't anyone in the corridor. As he reached his door, he heard another one open behind him. He turned. Harris was standing outside his room with his face half-shaved.

'I went for a walk,' Piers said in explanation.

'Must have been a long one,' Harris said sarcastically. 'I came to borrow some tape at midnight for my transmit to London, and you weren't in your room. What the hell are you playing at, Shatner?' He waddled across the corridor. 'You've got something, and I want to know what. Or . . .'

'You'll tell Geddes.'

'Could be.'

Piers stalled for time. 'I'm tired now. When I wake up, I'll tell you what I found.' By that time, he hoped he could make up a story. He was thankful now that Lopez had taken the tape. Even if Harris did call Geddes, there was nothing incriminating to be found on him.

'You better,' Harris threatened.

Piers drew the curtains in his room, pulled his boots off, and lay down. He felt drowsy and closed his eyes. He opened them briefly and sniffed. Perfume. Very slight but recognizable. Marion had also been looking for him. He would have liked to have her beside him now. Not to make love to, but to be comforted. Under the layers of exhaustion there was the fear of what Bolivar would do with the unused flask.

8

Video Replay: General Costa Goncalves. Recorded 13/7 at 0415 hours at drop zone. Report to General Peres, chairman of Menaguay.

I and my men arrived here at 0408 hours. At approximately 0350 hours, on our way to the drop zone, we heard an aircraft. We could not get a visual sighting, but I have requested that all military aircraft who were in the general vicinity of the area at 0350 hours report to me at once. We have not, repeat not, been able to recover the flasks. A general examination has revealed that three or four men were here shortly before our arrival. It is possible that they have the flasks and that the aircraft was theirs. At first summation, I had thought that some of the local people had been involved in the removal of the flasks. This has now been proved incorrect. As you can see, the dead body of this man has been shot at least four times. I am leaving my men to guard the drop zone. In the morning a more thorough investigation will be carried out. In the meantime I am returning to base to send in this report and await your orders.

The monitor went blank. Darrigan, Solotov, and Mercer glanced quickly at each other and then avoided looking at anything more disturbing than the spot on the table in front of them. In the silence, Mercer could hear Darrigan's fingers drumming impatiently. Each second they grew louder and louder, until they seemed to fill his head and he couldn't think. Watching the monitor, he'd felt a slight, and dangerous, elation. Somebody in this world was one jump ahead of the all-powerful Council and was about to give them a run for their money. It could only be Bolivar, and Mercer vaguely wondered how far he'd get. If he went all the way,

Mercer knew it was the end. But he wasn't about to place any bets on the man. The odds were always in favor of the Council. Like night following day, Mercer thought in irritation.

'Will you please stop that,' Mercer said. The fingers stopped drumming and then started again softly.

'Bolivar,' Darrigan said to the room. Solotov nodded. At the touch of Darrigan's finger, the monitor came on again.

'Report on Bolivar,' Darrigan ordered the aide who appeared.

'Yes, sir, and . . .' the aide said quickly, before he was wiped off, 'there is also a short report from Sao Amerigo which has just come in.' Darrigan nodded.

Video Replay: Major Vasco Soares, commanding the guard duty on Bolivar. Recorded 13/7 at 0800 hours.

Within the last twenty-four-hour period, Señor Bolivar has not left his residence. Hourly checks have been made on him as per the orders. His companion, Santos, has also not left the residence. No calls, either incoming or outgoing, have been made within the twenty-four-hour period. End of . . .

'It's the same goddamned report day after day,' Darrigan said angrily.

'They can't vary it for your sake,' Mercer said. 'He hasn't moved out of there for three weeks. Not that he could, with all those soldiers around him.'

'Bolivar doesn't have to move to cause trouble. He's got his aides, and he's getting word to them somehow. And those dumb soldiers are too lazy to find out how.'

'What is the other report?' Solotov asked.

Video Replay: General Alvaro Peres to the Council. Recorded 13/7 at 0930 hours.

As you know, we have not as yet been able to recover the intact flask. I and my cabinet would deeply appreciate it if the Council could give us an assurance that none of their agents now have the flask in their possession. We expect a reply within the hour. Otherwise, we will have to take appropriate action.

The silence was broken by Mercer's humorless chuckle. 'He thinks we've got it and are about to let it off under that fat nose of his.'

Darrigan and Solotov ignored him.

'I suppose that possibility was always on the minds of our general friend,' Solotov said quietly. 'It is good to keep him nervous, but I think we must assure him immediately that we don't have the flask.' He pressed the button.

Video Record: Solotov to General Alvaro Peres. Recorded 13/7 at 1000 hours.

I and the Council can totally assure the general and his cabinet that none of our agents nor this organization has possession of the flask. We would like to take this opportunity to renew our pledge that the Council only wishes Menaguay peace and prosperity and that the Council will work only toward this end. It was to show our belief in the general and his cabinet that we sent our information to him in regards to the intact flask. I and the Council would suggest that you double your efforts to recover the flask. In the wrong hands it could work against our joint efforts to attain friendship and cooperation between our two peoples.

'That was our big mistake,' Darrigan said sourly, 'asking them to get it back.' He pressed the button. 'Make contact with our agents in Sao Amerigo,' he told the aide, 'and tell them it's imperative to help the generals recover the flask. If they do recover it by themselves, they must, repeat must, tell the generals.' He released the button.

Darrigan studied his finger for a moment, then chewed delicately on it.

'I think,' Darrigan said slowly, 'we should delay any further expansion of the area. Postpone, I would say, until we have recovered that flask.'

'Yes,' Mercer said quickly, and didn't hide the relief in his voice. 'It would be dangerous if it were found later and used . . .' He trailed off.

They waited for Solotov to answer. He looked at both of them. His face was unreadable. Finally he shook his head. 'No.' He said it very firmly. 'Any delay would give you an advantage. I represent the people of the USSR . . .' He turned to face Mercer. '. . . and it is vital that we keep pace with your economic development.'

Mercer made his face go blank. He knew he was in for a long speech from Solotov. Next, he'd get one from Darrigan. The Council had to have a majority decision, and if they could persuade him to join one side or the other, it would give them a temporary advantage over the other.

'I said I agreed with Darrigan,' Mercer said loudly, and cut Solotov in mid-oratory. 'We must delay the further expansion of the area.'

Darrigan tried not to look pleased, but though his face remained poker, his eyes reflected his satisfaction. Solotov blinked at Mercer, and Mercer shifted uneasily. You would, he thought, expect the man to get angry, like Darrigan would, but he reveals nothing. Just blinks owlishly.

'I will suggest a compromise,' Solotov said smoothly. 'A delay of twenty-four hours will give more than enough time for the flask to be recovered. We know Bolivar has it.'

Darrigan nodded. 'Okay, twenty-four hours. What do you think Bolivar will do with it?'

Mercer suddenly felt that he'd lost the initiative. They'd agreed to do something above his head, and he was no longer necessary for the consultations.

'He won't release it,' Solotov said. 'Most probably he'll take it to Odu and Liu and others to show them what happened.'

'We've got to be sure he never gets to see Odu. Or anyone else.'

She came to him in the middle of a restless, sweating nightmare. It wasn't frightening; it was black and numbing and like a viscous treacle was inexorably pulling him deeper and deeper into its suffocating center. He felt her beside him.

Warm, perfumed, calling to him. He touched her and woke. The room was hidden in shadows, and for a few seconds he thought he was still in his dream.

'You okay?'

He nodded. Through a small gap in the curtains he could see the bright sun outside. He turned on his side to face her. She looked worried and concerned; and it seemed to add a greater depth to her beauty. He touched her face and let his hand slowly move down her breasts and belly and thighs. He wanted her only to hold and comfort him. He bent his head and buried it between her breasts. She cradled his head. 'Just a dream,' he whispered.

'Tell me. I'm here.'

For a long while Piers didn't answer her, and she didn't repeat herself. They lay together in the silence, comforted by each other's presence. Piers was frightened, and he didn't want to contaminate Marion as well. But he had to talk to someone. Slowly, haltingly, he whispered the details about Whitlam and the flasks.

Marion listened, staring up at the ceiling, sometimes hearing him, sometimes not. She felt as if each word he spoke was another tiny, numbing cut of death; that she was being frozen piece by piece so that when the time came she wouldn't feel the pain of the knife.

She gradually realized that he'd stopped talking and was asking her a question.

'Well . . .?' he repeated himself.

Marion shook her head. 'Nothing,' she said softly. 'I can't think anymore.' She felt it was already too late, but she had to try. 'Piers. Let's leave here; forget everything.'

She felt him shake his head. He was like a toy, wound up to keep running until either someone broke the spring or he found the end of his story. She knew him too well.

'I can't,' he whispered. 'Whether it's one person or fifteen million . . . someone has to account for it; someone has to answer.'

Marion felt a brief spurt of anger. 'You sound like a judge. Putting fifteen million on one scale, and yourself on another. It's not going to balance, Piers. You'll only become fifteen million and one. They will do everything to kill you.'

'I know.' He said it with finality. 'That's why you've got to stay clear.'

'I can't,' Marion said. 'We're Shatner and Hyslop.'

He turned and kissed her on the cheek, but she didn't respond. They lay silently, trapped and held by what they knew. Marion listened. Piers' breathing gradually became steady. She waited a minute and then slowly sat up and looked down at him. He looked a boy in the faint light filtering into the room. And me, Marion thought bitterly, I'm the ageless mother. They never change, their faces retain the stamp of their childhood right up to death. We do. We lose our prettiness, we lose our shape, we change so much that the child and the old woman are not the same.

She touched him gently on the mouth with her finger and slid quietly off the bed. In her own room, she lit a cigar and sat crouched on the bed, staring out at the sunlight. Piers, Piers, Piers, she said to herself. It didn't help. She knew she could see the end; they were racing toward each other like express trains on the same track. In the collision they could both live, or die; whoever survived would carry the scars to the end of life. She had tried to tell him, but he didn't hear. He was no longer human. He couldn't see or hear or feel or sense. He would keep moving until they met, and then . . .? She could leave for New York by herself, but that wouldn't help him or her.

The telephone rang. She let it ring three times before she picked it up and listened. She knew what she was going to say. 'Nothing,' she said abruptly, and replaced the phone. She stubbed out the cigar and lay back on the bed.

When Piers woke, it was late afternoon. He reached out beside him, but she'd gone. It was like a dream, and he wondered whether she had really come to him, or whether it had been an interlude in his nightmare. He was still feeling exhausted, but he knew by ten that night all tiredness would have left him. He was going to see Bolivar, and it was important that Geddes be kept off his back. He dialed Marion's room. She answered warily.

'Can you keep Geddes preoccupied for the day?' he asked.

Marion answered abruptly that she would and put the phone down on him. He looked at his phone in puzzlement and shrugged. She was most probably frightened for him.

Piers showered and shaved and went down to an early dinner. In the lobby he saw Marion talking with Geddes, and she nodded at him over the lieutenant's shoulder. He was grateful to her and blew her a kiss. He didn't see Harris, and though he was thankful, the man worried him. He had no doubt Harris would drop a word or two to Geddes.

He finished his dinner quickly and returned to his room. He had two hours to wait, and he lay down and stared at the ceiling. He knew it would be spent worrying. He thought of the intact flask that Lopez was carrying. It had looked so innocent and harmless when he'd first seen it, but now, with each second passing it loomed larger and more evil. It was the weapon that Bolivar wanted, Lopez had said, and Piers began to sweat. What was Bolivar going to do with it? Open it? It would kill not only the generals but also the rest of his people. Bolivar would never do that. It was a weapon that couldn't be controlled once it was released. Yet, he knew, Bolivar would use it to take his revenge. But how? Only Bolivar would be able to answer that question, and he would have to ask it tonight.

Piers shifted uneasily as he thought about the dead man Whitlam. Charles Whitlam. It was such an innocuous name. It felt ... made up. Who the hell was he? A dying man would not be able to feign surprise, and it was surprise that he'd seen on the features of Whitlam. He was sure of that. He tried to figure it out, but Whitlam, at the moment, was too one-dimensional, and everything would only be sheer guesswork.

Like trying to understand why the generals should take such drastic measures to overthrow Bolivar. Killing millions in order to unseat one man seemed so illogical. It would only have been a matter of time before Bolivar's grip would have slipped. Then a quick coup with the deaths of a few soldiers on either side would have settled the matter. Piers shuddered in distaste. But millions? Unless, of course, Bolivar had been plotting something and the generals no longer had the time to wait. It was another question for Bolivar.

Piers rolled off the bed and picked up his video. At times the feel of its worn, smooth sides comforted him. This time it didn't; and he knew why. He had violated it. He had slipped through the tunnel, and it was no longer his protection against the pain in the world. By going to comfort Lopez he had become part of the pain, and there was no chance of returning to the other side. It was, he knew, a one-way tunnel. The machine he held in his hand no longer felt familiar, and he fumbled as he checked the new tape and shot a couple of feet. It was as if, in its own way, it was withdrawing from him.

Piers looked at his watch. It was time to move. He peered into the corridor; there was no one around. He hurried to the emergency stairs, and before running down, looked back. The corridor remained empty. Before letting himself out, he carefully jammed the exit door open. There was no moon this night, and the whole world was in utter darkness. He lifted the video and scanned the street with his night lens. He jumped when Lopez touched him.

'You are late,' he whispered. 'We must hurry.' He gestured to the video. 'Can you see at night with that?'

'Yes, and film.'

'It will be useful. Without the moon we will not be able to see the patrols.'

Piers noticed Lopez holding tightly to the briefcase as they set off. They moved in silence, and warily. At each corner, Lopez would gesture, and Piers would scan the street ahead. It was lucky they took this precaution, for on Calle Cunhal, Piers spotted a patrol. The jeep was parked in the darkest shadow, and the soldiers were as still as collective spiders waiting for a fly. Lopez and Piers wasted five minutes backtracking to skirt the jeep. As they were about to cross Avenida Esta, Piers had given the all-clear. Lopez stopped.

'There's nothing ahead,' Piers whispered.

Lopez only turned and pointed back. Piers scanned the street. 'I heard a sound behind us,' Lopez said.

'I can't see anything,' Piers said.

Lopez wouldn't move for a whole minute in spite of the assurance. When they started off again, he kept glancing back.

'I'm positive I heard something,' Lopez said. 'You weren't followed from the hotel?'

'Positive.'

'And you told no one about our journey.'

'Yes,' Piers whispered loudly in exasperation. 'How long to Bolivar's place?'

'We are not going to see him just yet.'

'You promised.'

'There is something else we have to investigate. In Bison's house, I found the remains of one word – a-g-u-a – and the final letter looked like an *o*. I heard from Bolivar that it wasn't an *o* but a *d*. The word is Aguada.'

'What's Aguada?'

'It is a military air base located an hour from the city. I want to see what is happening there. We must hurry.'

They reached the outskirts of the city in half an hour, but as far as Piers could see, it didn't look like the same spot as the night before. He calculated, the best he could, that they were west of the previous rendezvous.

'Wait here,' Lopez whispered, and returned the way they'd come. He returned in five minutes shaking his head. He seemed particularly jumpy as he led Piers to the waiting car. It was the same driver, the boy, and his driving was, if it could have been, worse. He seemed to steer the vehicle by blind instinct, for because he couldn't use the lights, there was nothing to see ahead of them. Piers guessed as they took the corner wildly that the boy must have inbuilt night sight.

It took them two hours to reach Aguada, and it was visible for miles around. Every light on the air base seemed to be on, and jeep patrols constantly circled the narrow strip of road around the perimeter. Lopez stopped the car short of the light glow, and he and Piers moved slowly forward by foot. The brightness increased as they neared, and Piers saw the reason why. The base was beside the river, and the waters reflected the lights like a mirror. They had to worry only about not being seen, for the noise from the base was awesome. It was as busy as JFK at noon. There were transport planes landing and taking off, and it seemed as if the base was running a round-the-clock shuttle. There were lines of soldiers unloading supplies, and Piers adjusted the zoom lens carefully on the civilians disembarking.

Lopez snatched the video from Piers, but Piers seemed not to notice. He stared, frozen by what he'd seen, at the blurred figures moving toward the terminal. He had recognized the markings of the aircraft and the people who were pouring into the country. He closed his eyes. If it was a round-the-clock operation, there must be thousands of Americans and Europeans in the country; yet all that he'd seen were the scattered medical teams and technicians.

'What do you make of it?' Piers whispered.

Lopez didn't answer. He continued to study the air base, and when he did finally lower the video, Piers could just see the rigid coldness in his face.

'The generals are bringing in thousands of people to run the industries in the country.' He spat. 'What else do you think it means?'

'Maybe it's only a temporary measure, until your country gets back on its feet.' Even to his own ears his voice sounded flat and hopeless.

Lopez stood up, ducked, and moved back to the car. Piers followed him, clutching his video to his stomach.

'Is that what you really think?' Lopez asked softly. 'If you do, you're lying to yourself. Why weren't we told they were coming, answer me?'

Piers shook his head. 'Maybe they'll announce it soon.'

'That's not soon enough for me,' Lopez said as he climbed into the car. 'They're here for good; those fucking generals must have made a deal of some kind with the Industrial Nations. I swear by God I'll kill them all, whether Bolivar orders it or not.'

Neither spoke on the journey back to the city. Piers didn't even notice or care how fast the car went. Now and then he glanced at Lopez; the man looked brooding and violent. Piers himself felt numb. He tried to goad his mind to think, but it balked. It didn't want to face the reality of what he'd seen. First the plague and then the people coming in. The puzzle was beginning to fit; almost too perfectly.

It took them both a moment to realize the car had stopped and that they'd reached the outskirts of the city. Again it was a different location, and Piers felt totally lost. They climbed out, and both felt the urge to hurry, to run to Bolivar, who could interpret what they'd seen.

It took them ten minutes to reach the top of the road where Bolivar lived. Piers scanned the street; half a dozen soldiers were lounging outside the gates. Lopez cut down a side street and let himself into a house. Piers followed him down to the basement and through the tunnel that led to Bolivar's study.

Santos was there to greet them, and he insisted on patting Piers down for concealed weapons. Piers didn't like Santos very much; they'd met when he'd done the interview on Bolivar a few years back; and he knew Santos reciprocated the feeling. In Piers' opinion, Santos was only a bodyguard for Bolivar; he would kill anyone, on Bolivar's orders, without compunction.

They followed him to the study, and Piers saw Bolivar in exactly the same way Lopez had first seen him, sitting still behind the desk with only the table lamp on. He waited until Piers reached the edge of the desk and then half-rose. He reached Piers' shoulder. 'How are you, Piers?' he said softly.

'Well, sir. I am sorry for what has happened to your country.'

Bolivar waved him to sit. 'If by saying "sorry" I thought you could raise my people, I would make you say it a million times. It is too late for that now. I must do things.' He turned to Santos. 'Keep a watch on those soldiers while I find out what Lopez and Piers have been doing.'

Santos left reluctantly as Colonel Lopez placed the briefcase on Bolivar's desk. Bolivar snapped it open and flicked through the files taken from the ministry of the interior and dropped them on the desk. His face revealed nothing; every feature looked as if it were carved from brown granite. Bison had been a close friend of his, and the betrayal had been enormous. Next, Bolivar looked at the carbon of the rented car and gently placed that on top of the files. He sighed when he saw the flask; it was the first sound in the room. He picked it up; in his fist it looked small and fragile. His touch seemed gentle at first, and then slowly the grip on it tightened until the knuckles whitened and the veins on his forehead bulged and seemed near bursting point. He was shaking with his own strength and hatred, but the metal of the flask was beyond even him. He dropped it on the table and caught his breath. There were beads of sweat on his forehead and on his upper lip. He pulled open the top-right-hand drawer and took out a hunting knife and stabbed at the flask, but the point slid off harmlessly and dug deep into the desk. He tugged at it, and the blade snapped. He picked up the flask and stared at it; he was holding it as if it were a grenade.

'What do you think it is made of, Piers?' he asked without lifting his eyes.

'Maybe a titanium alloy of some kind. It's light but very strong. For a moment I thought you'd crush it.'

'If you only knew my hate. There is enough in me to break a man's body as if it were a matchstick.' He tossed the empty can aside and picked up its companion. He held it gingerly. 'This one fascinates me. I want to open it up and see what this ... thing ... inside is. This destroyer of my people. What is it? Worms? Smoke? A liquid? It doesn't rattle. It's like a Pandora's box. I have the urge to open it and push my face in. But I won't. There will be a time and place for this little toy ... and then ... millions will die in the same way as my people died.'

He placed the cylinder to one side and studied the crumpled sheets of paper found in Whitlam's bedroom. He spent a long time on them and then sat back as if he understood the puzzle.

Video Report: *I can tell you the meaning of OT. Opti-*

mums Terminated. It is the most menacing word in history. You've never heard of it, have you?

No, Señor Bolívar.

In layman's terms, it means the point of no return. At OT the Industrial Nations, given the known available resources and food supplies, will plunge to the economic level of the Third Nations. And the Third Nations will be forced even further down to a subsistence level. These are the calculations of western scientists. Within five years of OT having occurred, according to the same calculations, the people of the south will begin a massive migration northward. History always repeats herself, Piers. We will need to graze our goats and cows and hunt for whatever food we can find. And like those ancient nomadic hordes, we will sweep through the north countries. As I said, I was aware of this OT about three months ago and had taken steps to prevent the Third Nations from being pushed down further. I believe by my actions I precipitated OT for the Industrial Nations by five years.

What were these actions, Señor Bolívar?

In order to protect ourselves and prolong our own survival, the Third Nations convened the Cape Town Conference. The conference was only a formality. We had agreed in principle to all my suggestions.

Which were?

To embargo all food supplies, all fuel supplies, and all raw materials. All trade between the West and the Third Nations was to stop immediately. In the short term, we would have been affected, but in the long term, by conserving our resources, we could have expanded our economies.

I never heard of the Cape Town Conference.

You wouldn't have, but the Council must have. It was scheduled for a fortnight ago. I couldn't attend because of this disaster, and the other leaders decided to wait for me. I will be with them tomorrow, and I will have a lot more to show them.

If you had brought about this embargo, Señor

131

Bolivar, how would you have defended it? As you say, it would have brought OT closer for the Industrial Nations, and surely you must have expected some reaction.

Señor Bolivar, instead of answering, rises to his feet and crosses to a wall. He presses a button, and a panel slides back to reveal a map of the world.

There are only six maps like this in the world. Three in the north and three in the south. Those pins you can see are missile bases, and you will notice there are about five times as many in the north as in the south. What do you think happened once détente was achieved? Do you think America and Russia and Europe destroyed all their missiles? Of course not. They turned some of them ninety degrees; they now face south, instead of east-west. We would have been able to retaliate against a missile attack, though not inflict the same damage. I hadn't expected what has happened to my country. And even if I had, it would have been impossible to defend ourselves.

You are accusing the Industrial Nations, Señor Bolivar, of having taken preemptive action in order to prevent this Cape Town Conference formalizing the embargo.

No. I think they've taken preemptive action to postpone OT indefinitely. If you look at that graph, you will see that IRS, whatever that is, maybe the contents of this flask, deflects the population curve. I would like to see your tapes now, Piers.

Tape pause ...

Piers rewound his tape, fitted in the one Lopez had taken from him, and handed the video to Bolivar. He fitted the earpiece for Bolivar and sat down. While Bolivar studied the tapes, he tried to think. It was all far worse than he'd imagined. He wanted to argue and defend the Western people. Try and explain to Bolivar that they had nothing to do with what had happened, and once they found out – and Piers vowed here that if it was the last thing he ever did, they would know what had happened – they would be filled with the same numb horror as he was. He shook his head. It wouldn't deflect Bolivar an inch. Once he showed all the evidence to the other Third Nation leaders, they would definitely take retaliatory action. It would be in their interest, for there was little doubt now that they were next on the OT list. Piers knew once Bolivar reached them, all hell would break loose. When did he say? Tomorrow, Piers remembered, and there was nothing he could do or say to stop Bolivar.

Yet, Piers thought, if I could stop him, would I? If I don't, I will be responsible for the deaths of millions more people in other parts of the world. I could not bear the agony of that responsibility. If I allow him to reach Odu, the retaliatory action that the Third Nations will take will destroy the world.

Piers glanced at Bolivar. He was totally absorbed in watching the tapes. Lopez was about ten feet away, and like a faithful dog, had eyes only for Bolivar. Piers could just catch a glimpse of the automatic in his waistband. It would take only a second to cross the space and grab the gun. It would take another second to pull the trigger and kill Bolivar. But would he be able to? No. He would hold him prisoner? Piers tensed. He wasn't sure what he wanted to do. His mind seemed to have ceased working.

Bolivar suddenly chuckled. It was a deep, rumbling sound full of humor. 'I see Lopez doesn't trust you as much as I do. You must be careful of him, Piers. He is a hunter.'

The moment for action was gone. Lopez turned to look at Piers and uncannily seemed to sense what Piers was thinking. He moved his chair so that he faced Piers directly, and he pushed the butt of the automatic farther around, so that it would be difficult to reach.

Piers slumped back in his chair. He touched his temples. They ached. There was nothing he could do except play the detached observer of a tragedy which was about to unfold itself. Yet, he knew, it was too late for that also.

'Now let's see the Aguada tape.' Bolivar returned the video, and Piers fitted in the new tape. It took Bolivar only a few minutes, and then he handed back the video.

Video Report: Tape continued . . .

You ask how long they will stay, Piers? They are here for good. Unless . . . I can return to power. It is going to be harder than I thought. With American and European personnel in key positions, the generals will have a strong hold on the country. I will have to fight a conventional guerrilla war, and that will take years. And so many more people will die.

But why have they been sent in in such large numbers?

What did you see on your way to Cochos?

Nothing.

Not nothing. You saw empty land, thousands of square miles of empty land.

If you're trying to say, Señor Bolivar, that the people we saw are taking over all this newly emptied land, why should they bother to depend on the generals. Given the same situation, they could have come in to aid the country and remained without their help.

The generals are a facade of this nation's liberty. By keeping the generals up front, the West will be able to maintain the impression that they were only trying to aid this country. I know Odu and the other Third Nation leaders believe this is what is happening. I would have believed it as well, if the generals hadn't been so stupid.

Who would you believe is responsible, Señor Bolivar?

I suppose the governments of America, Europe and Russia. Maybe through the Council.

I know that the people in the West will be as repelled as I am when they hear what has been done in their name.

Piers . . . Piers, you are an idealist. Of course your people don't know, maybe they never will. That depends on you and whether you can get these tapes broadcast. I only hope you can, and I also hope, like you do, that they will react. I am cynical of people, Piers, and the Council is too strong. And ruthless.

If it's the last thing I do, I will get these tapes broadcast.

Don't try to predict your own destiny, Piers. I can feel time running out. Lopez, pack all these away and tell Santos.

A last question, Señor Bolivar. Don't you feel any anger?

It's spent and it's too late. I need to remain cold and calm. What happened was inevitable. If there was only half a square mile of barren rock in a dead sea, I would kill you in order to survive just that much longer, Piers. Man has run out of rocks to cling to; someone has to be pushed into the water. But I'm still swimming, and all I ask, Piers, is that you give me one day before you use those tapes. Why do you take so long to answer, Piers? Poor Piers. You are trapped between two landslides, and there is nothing you can do.

All right. I will wait one day, Señor Bolivar.

You may have to wait forever to broadcast those tapes, Piers, but the moment you start trying, the Council will know what I am going to do. Come, let us drink the last of this good Scotch and part.

This is Piers Shatner, Channel 14, New York, with Juan Jesus Bolivar in Sao Amerigo.

Piers took the glass, and Bolivar poured out three fingers of Scotch. He gave himself a bit more. They touched glasses and drank. It burned Piers' throat, but it helped to drive some of the numbness he was feeling away. It seemed to kick his body back into life, and he was grateful to it.

'Remember when you were here last,' Bolivar said, and threw his arm around Piers. 'We drank a lot of bottles, and the women . . . I suppose they're all dead now. Their beauty lost forever. My wife always understood me. I am a primeval man, Piers. I stand with my feet apart on this earth and look up in awe at the sky. The earth feeds my body, and the sky my primitive mind.'

Santos entered with a coat over his arm. Lopez handed Bolivar the briefcase.

'No, my good Lopez,' Bolivar said. 'You will carry out another order. You will kill the generals, you will kill their wives, you will kill their children, you will kill their dogs. You will even kill the rats that run in their homes. I will

135

return soon to take back what is ours, and you must be ready.' He embraced Lopez first and then Piers.

Lopez led Piers out of the room. Before the door closed, he turned. Santos was tenderly helping Bolivar into his coat.

'He's a great man, a great man.' Lopez wept as they found their way out of the tunnel and into the street.

The soldiers were still in their positions. By the time they checked again, Bolivar and Santos would have gone.

Piers and Lopez walked back in silence. Both were deeply absorbed in thought, but not so much that they became careless. The route back seemed much shorter, and Piers guessed it was because his mind was so busy. He was relieved when Lopez stopped and pointed.

'Your hotel is there. Maybe we will meet again, only God can tell. You must keep your word to Bolivar, otherwise I will kill you.'

'You never stopped trying,' Piers joked. Lopez smiled. They wanted to embrace each other, but all they could finally do was shake hands.

'Best of luck,' Piers said, and Lopez waved.

Piers started toward the hotel. He'd moved only a few yards when he heard the echoing crack of a gun. He fell to the ground and peered through the video. The night lens turned the street bright as day.

Video Report: As Colonel Lopez and I parted a few seconds back, a single shot from a gun was fired. It came nowhere near me, and I can see no sign of movement anywhere. There is another shot, and this time the bullet hits the wall three feet to my left. I cannot see Colonel Lopez . . . just yet. There he is. He is on his knees. Maybe he can see who's firing, but without cover he is in a very dangerous position. He starts to turn toward me. He's been hit . . . Another shot is fired, and it slams him back toward me. There's a blur of movement at the far end of the street, but I can't see who it is. It's gone now. In the distance I can hear the roar of a patrol. It should be here within a couple of minutes . . .

Tape pause . . .

Piers ran to Lopez. The patrol was getting nearer. Lopez was still alive, but just. Piers could see life slipping slyly out of the corner of his eyes.

He smiled briefly at Piers. 'I did my job, I served Bolivar,' he whispered. 'It isn't a bad time to die, is it?'

Piers nodded, but Lopez didn't hear him anymore. The patrol was a block away, and there was nothing more he could do. He grabbed the video, and as he sprinted back to the hotel, he wondered who would kill the generals now.

9

The Amerigo Hotel was in darkness. Piers lifted the video and slowly scanned the building and the driveway. Nothing was moving. The video shook, and the scene blurred. He forced himself to steady his hands. He was shaking from head to foot and sweating from the exertion and the punch of fear he'd experienced at Lopez' death.

He would have to risk it. He took a deep breath and sprinted for the rear door. He hit it with his shoulder. It didn't give; it was locked. He tried again; he was positive he'd wedged it open. He looked back and ran along the wall to the front entrance. The large, elegant foyer was only dimly lit and looked deserted. The light didn't even reach the front door. He slipped in and edged along the wall to the stairs. There was a clerk on duty, but he seemed asleep. It was pitch black in the stairwell, and Piers studied every corner through the night lens as he slowly climbed. He had no doubt that whoever had shot Lopez would be gunning for him as well. He'd been missed once. It wasn't the army; he knew that. They would have been open and been waiting for him in the hotel.

There was one light on in the corridor. It was near the stairs. He quickly knocked it out and scanned the corridor through the video. Nothing, except ... He stopped. There was a wafer-thin edge of light showing under a door. Piers moved cautiously to it. He could hear movement and the murmur of voices. He knocked and stepped back.

Harris opened the door. He was dressed the same way he had been a couple of nights back – pajamas and tie. 'What do you want, Shatner?' he asked irritatedly. 'I'm doing a transmit to London.' He studied Piers more carefully. 'You look as if you've been out again and run the mile on top of that. You going to tell me what you're up to? Or else—'

'Have you been out just now?' Piers asked. He had no time for Harris' games. He pushed past him and examined the room.

Harris' video was standing facing the curtained window. A table and a chair had been set up in front of it. He was making a transmit. Piers checked the bathroom to be sure. It was empty.

'You going to tell me?' Harris asked insistently. He suddenly smiled ingratiatingly, and picking up a bottle of cognac, poured Piers a drink. 'You look as though you need one. I always have a couple of shots before taping; steadies the nerves, you know.' He stopped. 'I know you've got a story. Just give me a sniff of it, that's all I'm asking for.'

Piers swallowed the drink. He knew Harris wouldn't tell Geddes anything; all he wanted was something to keep his editors in London happy.

'I've got a story, all right,' Piers said as he went out. 'But it's my exclusive. You will hear about it soon enough.'

As Piers passed Marion's room, he stopped and listened. He could hear the shower, so he waited until it stopped and then knocked.

'Who is it?'

'Piers.'

'Let me dry off,' Marion called. 'I'll come to your room.'

In his room, Piers rewound the tape to start and tiredly lay back on the bed. He wanted to get up and do something, anything, but he knew that all that was left for him was to wait. And wait.

Marion came into the room. She was wearing a dressing gown, and her face was scrubbed shiny and her hair was pulled back into a ponytail and fastened with a rubber band. She looked younger than her age, and like all women, vulnerable in her dressing gown. She was ready for bed, with him or alone.

'You're up late,' he said. She bent, and he kissed her, tasting the sweet smell of soap and perspiration.

'I couldn't sleep.'

'You never will now. Lopez was killed outside the hotel.

139

They took a shot at me, but missed. I have some tape on it, but you can't make anything else out.'

'I'm sorry about Lopez.' Marion took the video camera. 'Next time, the soldiers won't miss, Piers. They'll get you.'

'Wasn't the army.' Piers swung out of bed and began stripping. 'They could have me in the hotel. There's someone else out there, too.'

'Who?'

'CIA, I guess. Or someone of the Council's.'

'How can you say that?' She seemed shocked. Piers gestured to the camera, and left her to look at the tapes while he showered.

He stood under the shower for a long time, wanting the cold needle spray to soothe him and cleanse him of the memory of Lopez and Bolivar and everything else he knew. Lopez, he realized, had been a man very similar to him. In another time, under different circumstances, they would have been friends. They worked the same way, had the same minds, and if they'd had the chance, would have found that they liked the same kind of women. When he stepped out of the shower, he felt neither clean nor relaxed. The knowledge of what had happened in this country would sear him for the rest of his life, however long that was.

When he returned to the bedroom, Marion had gone. The camera lay on the bed, as if it had been dropped suddenly. Piers picked it up and checked the pictures. The shrunken image of Lopez dying slid by his eyes. He carefully placed the camera back in its case, lay down on the bed, and switched off the light. He heard the door open, and saw a bright orange glow float toward him. He moved over, and Marion slid in next to him.

'I went for my cigars,' she whispered. He felt her shivering. 'What are we going to do, Piers? All hell's going to break loose when Bolivar tells what happened here.'

'I don't know, I just don't know. Right now, I want to sleep forever.'

It was as he lay in the darkness that he thought of what he'd said. He looked at his watch. The 'forever' could be for another twenty-one hours. He wondered whether he would ever be able to run his story, and felt an enormous well of futility. It felt as if his mind was locked in a lightless vacuum, and that it was hurtling him toward some unknown. It was the touch of Marion that broke the despair that held him paralyzed. They looked at each other; there was such youth and innocence in her face, and he wanted to love her. Not tenderly and gently or even mechanically as he'd done with women all his life. He thought of Bolivar looking up at the sky with his primeval awe and the gross appetites of the man for things of the earth. In comparison, his own life had been so detached and empty.

They touched, gently at first, kissing, caressing. Marion knew how he felt. There'd been other times when she'd felt herself teetering on the edge of death, and all that she'd wanted had been to greedily satiate all her senses. To have the danger fucked out of reach. They spoke no words, but communicated only by noises, guttural and primitive. They fought each other with a matching ferocity that finally left them both exhausted and bruised and totally drained.

In the last moments of waking, Piers looked at his watch. There were nineteen hours left, and he could feel sleep sliding through his body.

He woke in a blind panic. At first, he couldn't understand why he had such a heavy feeling of foreboding. The light in the room was a mute soothing glow, and he could see Marion sleeping beside him. He sat up and remembered. There were fourteen hours left. He got out of bed and pulled the curtains; the sun was just beginning to glare, and the sky looked a burnished blue. It was a banal sight, yet he stared at it for a long time until he heard Marion wake and sit up. He turned. Her body was blotchy from the bruises of their lovemaking.

'You look pretty good.'

'Macho bastard.' She reached for her dressing gown and put it on; for a minute she just sat on the edge of the bed. Finally she shrugged. 'Well, another day ...' She turned. 'What do we do today, boss?'

'Wait and see what happens.'

'After breakfast I'll do a short tape on O'Brien leaving.'

'He's leaving?'

'So I heard.' She moved to the door and let herself out.

Piers dialled his recorder in New York and transmitted all his tapes. He erased everything once he finished, except the footage on Lopez' death. If he had the equipment, he could have blown up the pictures and maybe recognized the killer. He was just entering the shower when the phone rang. It was a call from New York and Piers knew what it would be about. The blast down the line tingled his good ear.

'Shatner! What the hell are you both doing down there? Having a vacation? I haven't heard from you now for four days. Four days. I've been having to take tape from Chicago. I didn't send you down there to sulk. You there?' Frank Kolok stopped uncertainly. The silence from Piers was very uncharacteristic. They usually screamed at each other.

'I'm here, Frank,' Piers said quietly.

'What's wrong with you and Marion?' Kolok asked worriedly. 'Both ill?'

'Nothing. Whenever we transmit our tapes you don't use them. So I figured I may as well not bother.'

'You let me do the figuring, you bastard,' Kolok shouted. 'I'm spending good money on you two and the big man is already mad at me about your tapes.' He stopped to catch his breath, and then pleaded, 'Haven't you got anything for me?'

'I've got you a story, the biggest.' Piers looked at his watch. Thirteen hours left. 'But you won't use it, Frank, I know that.'

'I'll decide what I use or not. Just send it.'

Piers dropped the phone and went down to breakfast. He wondered whether Frank would use the tapes once he saw them. He needed more than good intentions. He needed a cast-iron guarantee that they would be aired coast-to-coast. At the moment, it looked as if he had a snowball's chance in hell.

He and Marion had just finished breakfast when Geddes came in. The lieutenant looked very cheerful, as if he'd just been given a promotion, as he moved toward Piers. A few feet behind walked two soldiers carrying machine guns. It was as he got nearer that Piers noticed the folded sheet of paper in Geddes' hand. Piers held his hand out, palm up, and Geddes dropped the paper on it.

'You know what it is, then?' he asked.

'Do I have time to pack, or is it a fast ride to the airport?'

'You have time,' Geddes said. 'There's no flight until tomorrow morning. Aren't you interested why we're expelling you?' He seemed disappointed at Piers' lack of curiosity.

'I breathed on the general's sunglasses. Why else?'

'It is not a laughing matter,' Geddes said stiffly. 'We do not like your hostile attitude toward our country and her leaders. That is why you're being expelled. One of these men will be watching you. Or else' – he became hopeful – 'you can stay in the barracks.'

'I'm allergic to uniforms. I'll behave.'

'If you don't . . .' Geddes didn't complete the threat.

'What about me?' Marion asked indignantly.

'We have no objections to your presence in this country, Señora Hyslop,' Geddes said gallantly, and nearly clicked his heels.

'If he goes, I go,' Marion said.

Geddes' shrug was infinitesimal, before he turned to the other journalists. 'General Peres has called a press conference for noon. He is going to make a very important announcement.'

'What about?' Marion asked.

'That is for General Peres to say.'

'Are we allowed to attend?'

Geddes hesitated and then nodded. He gestured to one of the soldiers, and the man sat down abruptly at the next table. He was obviously taking his job very seriously, for he fixed his eyes on Piers and looked as if he was never going to take them off until his job was over.

It was all so pointless that Piers laughed.

'What is the joke?' Geddes asked.

'You wouldn't understand it.'

At 11.30 they left the hotel to walk to the assembly hall.

In his preoccupation, Piers at first didn't notice anything wrong. It was when they were stopped by a small crowd standing in the middle of the pavement that he saw the utter stillness of the people. They were standing on street corners, huddled in doorways, in large groups and in twos and threes. They weren't talking at all. It was as if they were listening to something that Piers couldn't hear. A sound so fine and distant that it could only have been a vibration. It was passing from person to person, and from group to group, and those it touched seemed to be left a breath smaller.

Video Report: Tape continued . . .

It is 11.35 and there is something wrong. I can feel it everywhere as I move to the assembly hall. There is this silence, this hush, this waiting for something that cannot be seen. It is not only the people on the street who aren't moving. It feels as if the wind itself has stopped. The cars have halted, and the buses have parked in the center of the road. It feels as . . . as if . . . the plague has returned. A man sits down on the pavement, his head hanging down; a skinny peasant woman turns her weather-torn face to the wall. I can feel something now. A stirring, a whispering . . . yet there is nothing being spoken. You would have to put your ear to the hearts of the people who stand so silent and still in order to draw out the message.

Lieutenant Geddes, what has happened?

You will find out soon at the press conference.

We enter the Plaza Bolivar – or at least try to. We are blocked by a vast crowd which remains frighteningly silent. They are staring at the assembly hall with such intensity that it seems they can see through the marble and steel and concrete and into the very central chamber itself . . . This is Piers Shatner, Channel 14, New York, in Sao Amerigo.

Soldiers cleared a path through the people for the journalists. It was as easy as pushing aside stunned sheep. Piers suddenly knew what they were looking at. He knew what was inside. He could hear the sound, the vibration was running through him now. It left him out of breath, like a punch to the heart, and filled him with pain. He stumbled and momentarily shut his eyes.

They reached the entrance to the assembly hall and stopped and looked down. The dais, in front of the huge seal, was empty. Below it was a table, and on it a coffin.

Video Report: The coffin is simple. It isn't made of brass or gold or mahogany. Just ordinary planks of wood nailed together. There is a single candle, but no priests intoning prayers. The mourners wait outside in awesome silence. This vast building with its trapping of power, this magnificent city, this huge fertile country which he snatched from the primeval jungle in which he was born and which he fashioned into his dreams, are now his tomb. Juan Jesus Bolivar is dead. Bolivar is dead, and lesser men now file onto the stage to take his place. Their brass medals shine dully in the lights, their gold epaulets look like snakes curled over their shoulders, their uniforms are pretty and neat, their empty faces mere caricatures of warriors. General Peres does not look at the closed coffin. He intends to read a prepared statement.

It is with deep regret that I have to announce the death of ex-chairman of Menaguay, Juan Jesus Bolivar. His remains were found by an early-morning patrol approximately five miles outside the city limits. As far as I can gather, the car he was traveling in was involved in an accident, and in the resulting fire, Señor Bolivar died. There was a companion with him, but we have been unable to locate the man. We hope to find him soon and get the exact details as to what happened. Señor Bolivar, I believe, was on the way to a private airfield, where his personal plane was waiting to take him out of the country. In memory of this great leader of ours, I declare a week's mourning. His remains will lie in state so that his people may pay their last respects. The funeral will take place the day after tomorrow. I wish to assure all those who are assembled here that this government will continue to uphold the tradition and the principles and the ideals of

Señor Bolivar. Menaguay has suffered a double tragedy in the last month. I pray to God that I and my cabinet be guided by the spirit of Señor Bolivar. Thank you.

General Peres now sits down, and there is a long minute of silence in memory of Juan Jesus Bolivar.

Shatner, Channel 14, New York: What time did this . . . accident . . . take place, General Peres?

At approximately two-thirty A.M. *Due to the badly damaged condition of the body, it is impossible to make a more accurate calculation.*

Is it possible to see the remains of Señor Bolivar?

We would rather not allow his remains to be seen. The fire completely destroyed his body. It was with great difficulty that we managed to identify the body. There were certain characteristics and personal possessions that finally made it possible.

You are sure it is him?

Absolutely positive. And I would like to assure you, Mr. Shatner, that it was an accident.

Alexeyev, Tass, Moscow: You are certain he was on his way to his personal plane and that he intended to leave the country, General Peres?

I believe that was his plan. The accident occurred two miles before the airfield.

Schmidt, Radio Hamburg: Why would he want to leave? You were, after all, temporary chairman. You had stated that once the situation was under control, you would vacate the office.

I do not know why he should want to leave. I will also repeat my promise now. I shall, when the emergency is over, leave this office.

Shatner, Channel 14, New York: What personal effects were found in the car?

The usual. Clothes, books, papers . . .

This is Marion Hyslop, Channel 14, New York, in the Grand Assembly Hall, Sao Amerigo.

Piers turned his back before General Peres finished and walked back up the sloping assembly floor. He didn't look at the coffin as he passed. Bolivar was really dead, and he felt numb.

He stopped halfway and sat down. Below him, the charade was still going on. As the numbness wore off, he began to feel an enormous futile rage at the death of the man. It kicked in him like an angry child trapped in a womb, wanting to escape its physical confines violently. The rage passed soon, and he was left sad and spent. He didn't doubt for a moment that the generals now had the flask and that it and the other evidence would be buried with Bolivar in some, cold, grandiose tomb. He looked at his watch. Ten hours. It had ended there for him, but not for the others. For them, time was running out, and there was no Bolivar to warn them.

He looked at the generals and wondered about them. If only men could have shown on their faces the evil and the good they had committed. A symbol, even a letter, would make it so easy. The forehead, the cheeks, the noses would be permanently scarred with the symbols of their evil. But nothing showed. Conscience wasn't the master of all men; especially those who held power. The anger returned; a cold anger. Bolivar had given him a story, and he would force it to be broadcast. The documents and the flasks were no longer available, but he had his tapes, and he was sure he would find other proof. There was Whitlam, a dead man with no past. But Piers was sure that if he looked hard enough he would find a trail that would lead him to the Council. He wondered how much time he had left. Even now, it could be too late . . .

Meunier came and sat next to him. She was a woman in her forties with the brittle surface hardness that all women in his profession had. Piers only nodded an acknowledgment. He was too preoccupied with his thoughts to do more.

'Makes you sick,' he heard her say. 'Stupid generals playing games when their country is suffering so much . . .' She went on, and Piers grunted each time she expected some comment. '. . . and they still haven't found what the virus is. It could break out in some other country tomorrow. No one's safe. I hope O'Brien can crack it by the end of the week.'

'Once he gets back to America, he won't have much chance.'

'Who said he's going back?' Meunier asked.

'That's what I heard,' Piers said, and straightened.

Meunier shook her head. 'I wish they'd tell me these things.'

The generals were filing off the stage, and the press conference was breaking up. Geddes and the others were slowly coming up the aisle. Piers stood up. He frowned. Who'd told him about O'Brien? Marion. He tried to remember exactly what she'd said, and gave up. He trailed the others out and stood on the steps looking down on the plaza. The crowd seemed to have grown, and it remained as silent as before. Soldiers kept them back from the steps, though they were making no effort to push forward.

'Has his death been announced?' Piers asked Geddes.

'No,' he said. 'It doesn't need to be.'

A narrow path was cleared by the side of the building, and they filed singly through it. Piers studied the faces of the people. Because of the common sadness haunting their eyes, they all looked the same. Their individual identities seemed to have dissolved, to create a huge, single being. As he reached the outer edge of the crowd, he felt someone reach for his hand. A piece of paper was thrust at him, and he closed his fist. He tried to see who it was, but all the heads were turned toward the assembly. He couldn't take the risk of looking at the scrap of paper at the moment, and he shoved it into his pocket, where it seemed to burn his thigh like a piece of live coal.

When they reached the hotel, the soldier was waiting for Piers. He followed him up to his room and would have entered if Piers hadn't shaken his head. The soldier hesitated and then pulled a chair out of Piers' room. He set it up opposite the door and sat down heavily. He was going to be there all day.

Piers shut the door and looked at the note: 'The Church of St Teresa, twelve.' The writing was faint and spidery. He wondered who it was from, and what it was about. It was going to be a long day waiting for the answer.

The room seemed to grow smaller with each hour, and Piers tried to keep himself occupied by going over his tapes and mentally editing them for the broadcast. He ran the tape of Lopez' death and froze it the moment he saw the blur in the far background. He couldn't distinguish anything. In between, he would pace the room restlessly. The confinement was driving him mad. He was running out of time, and here he was locked in a room. There was only one other exit – the balcony leading off the room. He was four stories up, but it was just possible to jump to the next balcony and let himself into the next room. He would need someone to distract the guard. He could only think of Marion. Piers checked the address of the church in the phone book and then studied the street map. He had to be absolutely sure, as this time he had no one to guide him around in the night.

Marion and the relief soldier joined him for dinner. It was an awkward meal, as they both felt inhibited by the silent, hungry man who wolfed everything down and constantly refused the wine. Piers had hoped a bottle or two would have made him drowsy enough to fall asleep, but Geddes must have threatened the man with death if he neglected his duty. When Piers took Marion up to his room after the dinner, the soldier grinned enviously and settled himself down in the chair. The machine gun pointed straight at the door.

They didn't make love but lay silently together.

Every now and then they would hear the soldier cough and spit.

'I'm sorry about Bolivar,' Marion whispered. 'You liked him a lot, didn't you?' She felt Piers only nod. 'What do you think happened to the flask?'

'I guess those . . . bloody generals have it.'

He had thought all day about showing Marion the note. If anything happened to him, it was important that she should know. He passed her the scrap of paper.

'Are you going?'

'Yes.'

'You're going to get killed. Don't go, Piers, Please. They're setting you up.' She held his face and turned it toward her. He could see the deep worry wrinkles scarring her forehead and eyes.

'Suppose it isn't a setup? I've got to find out.'

'I'm coming with you, then,' Marion said, and sensed Piers was about to argue. She raised her voice. 'I'm coming, and you know damned well you've never ever been able to stop me before.'

Piers knew how stubborn Marion could be. 'Okay, but you've got to distract the guard some way. I'll go out by the balcony and wait for you by the rear exit.'

'What'll I do?'

'Show him your tits or something.' He kissed her and got up. He checked his camera and moved to the balcony as Marion went out into the corridor.

Piers slung the camera over his back and hauled himself up on the ledge of the balcony. The jump was about ten feet, but the four-story drop made it look twice as wide. He tensed, crouched, and pushed into black space. He hit the opposite ledge chest-high, hooked his arms over the top, and slowly hauled himself up. It had been a bad jump, and he felt winded. There was no time to feel sorry for himself. He let himself into the darkened room, crossed to the door, and peeped out. Marion wasn't showing the guard her tits, but she was showing a lot of leg and blocking the guard's view of the corridor. Piers slid out of the room and ran silently to the stairs, not daring to look back. He rested and massaged his bruised chest while he waited for Marion by the rear exit door. He knew that if he went on alone, she would remember the address and only follow him.

He had to wait ten minutes before she managed to join him. It was 11.30 when they set off with a thin sliver of a moon throwing the faintest of shadows. The curfew was still in force, though Piers had heard that those people standing in the Plaza Bolivar had been allowed to remain, with a cordon of soldiers around them. Piers missed the comforting presence of Lopez. Marion was company, but it was a case

150

of the blind leading the blind. It took them twenty-five minutes to reach the small church, and they stopped across the street in surprise. It looked as if the interior was on fire, and the light pouring out of the windows lit the street and the other buildings. There wasn't a sound to be heard, and it had the eerie feeling of a hastily abandoned palace.

'I think it's a trap,' Marion whispered.

Piers only studied the streets and the shadows carefully. There was only one way to find out.

'Wait a minute and then follow,' he whispered, and suddenly sprinted for the door.

He cringed at every step, waiting for a burst of gunfire, and the few yards he had to cover seemed like miles. He hit the door and fell in and found himself in an empty church. He squinted into the glare of thousands upon thousands of candles, each a prayer burning quietly and steadily. It was hot and stuffy, and Piers felt the sweat pouring off his body. He heard a scuff behind him, and Marion ran in. She looked around in bewilderment and then at Piers. He shrugged. It was five minutes past midnight. They prowled the small church for five minutes; there was no one to be found. Piers had his back to the front door when he caught a glimpse of Marion's face. Her eyes were wide and staring at something behind him.

At first he could see only the barrel of the heavy Magnum pistol. A moment later a fist appeared, and then a face. Piers didn't recognize the youth who cautiously edged into the church. His pistol gestured for them to move closer together; his eyes flicked nervously around the church. Satisfied, he backed and opened the door a bit wider. Santos, Bolivar's bodyguard, stepped into the church and closed the door. He held a Beretta in his fist and looked vastly different from the last time Piers had seen him. His face was smudged and unshaven, the right lens of his glasses were cracked, and the left side of his shirt, from shoulder to waist, was stained and caked with dry blood and dirt. He looked exhausted, but the cruelty in his eyes, still strangely feminine, looked even more menacing.

'Where's Colonel Lopez?'

'Dead.'

The gun in Santos' hand shifted and steadied; it was pointing straight at Piers' belly. Piers could see the knuckles whitening.

'He was shot near our hotel last night,' Marion said quickly.

Santos ignored her. 'First Bolivar, then Lopez. You were the only one who was with both of them.'

'So were you.' Piers knew he was a split-second away from death, and then Santos quite suddenly relaxed.

'I would have given my life for Bolivar,' Santos said softly. 'I've no use for it now without him.' He moved to a pew and sat down. The youth, however, remained by the door and kept them both covered.

'What happened?' Piers asked, and out of the corner of his eye he could see Marion lift her camera to her eye and point at Santos.

'We were on our way to the airfield. We take a corner, and the soldiers are waiting for us. They rocket the car. I am driving, and I swerve. The car hits a tree and bursts into fire. I roll out ... I go back and try to save Chairman Bolivar, but I can't reach him.' Santos gestured hopelessly.

'And the flask?' Piers prayed it had been lost in the fire.

'It is safe.' Santos didn't notice Piers slump. 'What worries me is how the soldiers knew. You could have told them, and killed Lopez as well. I warned Bolivar not to trust you.'

'I can prove I didn't kill him. I have some tape.'

Piers hurriedly fitted the short footage into the video camera and handed it to Santos. Santos in turn handed his gun to the youth. Piers showed him how to work the camera.

Video Replay: As Colonel Lopez and I parted a few seconds back, a single shot from a gun was fired. It came nowhere near me, and I can see no sign of movement anywhere. There is another shot, and this time the bullet hits the wall three feet to my left. I cannot see Colonel Lopez ... just yet. There he is. He is on his knees. Maybe he can see who's firing, but without cover he is in a very dangerous position. He starts to turn toward me. He's been hit . . . Another shot is fired, and it slams him back toward me . . .

Santos let the camera fall on his lap. He seemed unsure what to do next and looked like a man who had just been robbed of all his ambitions. Piers was thankful to see the youth lower the gun, and took the camera from Santos' lifeless hands.

Santos stood up slowly, and the youth hurried forward to help him.

'The flask is in Lopez' apartment,' Santos said. 'I went to wait for him, and when he never came, I left it there. It is in the front room, on a table.' Santos studied Piers for a moment and then smiled. It was an unfriendly smile. 'Bolivar was going to show it to the world as proof of what happened here. He trusted you; so shall I. Now you must do it.'

'I can't,' Piers cried in panic.

'You are afraid.' It was said contemptuously. 'You approve of what has been done here?' He waved to the candles and turned away to the door.

'What can I do?'

Santos only shrugged; he appeared to be tiring fast. 'Bolivar could have told you. I'm only a *paisano*.' He straightened with the help of his companion. 'I have work to do. I must kill the generals, now that Lopez is dead.'

He gave Piers terse directions to Lopez' apartment, and then, with the help of his companion, moved slowly and stiffly out of the church.

The silence that followed the closing of the door was heavy and very still. Piers found it difficult to breathe; it was as if a heavy and immovable weight had been placed inside his chest. It took him some time to sense Marion's hand on his arm.

'Let it be where it is, Piers, please,' Marion begged. She tugged at him, and he took a step to follow her. 'There's nothing you can do.' She pulled him another step, and then he stopped. He heard the panic in her voice. 'Piers, if you

153

touch that flask, they will have to kill you, and there'll be nothing achieved.'

'If I let it be, what happens?' Piers asked dully.

'It will just stay there. Maybe no one will ever find it.' Marion's voice was urgent now.

'Not to it.' Piers shook his head. 'Somewhere else. What happened here was done with the consent of all the Industrial Nations countries. It must have, otherwise Russia would have . . .' He stopped and blinked. 'The Council must have worked this. We take out Menaguay; the Soviets take out China. No questions asked.'

'And what are you going to do, Piers?' She shook him as if he were a silly child. 'Halt nations?'

Piers gently released himself and sat down, facing the large oil painting of Saint Teresa. 'Bolivar told me I was trapped between two landslides moving toward each other.' Marion shook her head; he was talking to himself. 'The Council and him. That's no longer true. I have the flask now, and I am the other landslide, with Bolivar dead. Look at these candles. I wonder how many churches look like this one. All of them, I guess. Oh, God, what do I do? I could leave the flask where it is. I could try to forget Bolivar, the people, everything. I can destroy my tapes. I am not responsible for what happened here; I am only responsible to myself. How do I erase all the knowledge? Press a button? It won't work; the pain will be like a knife, twisting and gouging . . .' Piers bitterly wished he was another man, one who could walk out and never look back.

Piers stood up, and Marion knew what he was going to do. She wanted to scream at him not to, but he wouldn't hear her. 'Suppose,' Marion pleaded for the last time, 'that these people died from a natural plague. There'd be nothing you could do. Think of it like that.'

'I can't.'

They walked out of the church side by side. Marion looked back at the haven; her eyes glistened in the light. She knew there would be no return to this point of their relationship. Three years of friendship, of loving, was coming to an end. They walked in silence, almost not even looking where they were going. From some distant point they would have resembled two machines, moving in two separate worlds.

Piers found Lopez' apartment block, and when he reached the apartment door, he stopped. The door was slightly ajar, as if someone was expecting them. The open door puzzled more than worried Piers, and he couldn't understand why. By the time he did understand, it would be too late.

They cautiously stepped into the long hallway, and Piers walked straight into a table, knocking it over. They waited tensely, trying to listen but hearing only the echo of the fallen table. Piers reached back and took Marion's hand. He was surprised. His palm was sweaty and hot, hers cold and dry. He moved into a room. A table was neatly laid for a meal, and there was fruit decaying in a round, wooden bowl. It looked like an old painting. They tried three other rooms before coming to the front room.

On the table by the chair was the can of deodorant. Piers picked it up, forced off the top, and slid the flask into his hand. It was so smooth and cool that his fingertips couldn't feel the metal at first. His hand shook. Like Bolivar, he had an insatiable urge to open it and peer inside. Marion took the flask from him, and Piers' glance fell on a silver framed photograph on the table. It was of Lopez, an old woman, a young woman with a man, and two children. They were sitting around a table in the garden and smiling at the camera.

'We better go,' Piers said, and turned to take back the flask from Marion. 'What's . . .' She was no longer near him, but standing by the door. The flask was in one hand, and a small automatic was in the other. She was shaking her head and inching back.

'Why don't you ever listen, Piers? Why don't you ever listen?' She was angry and shouting at him, and he couldn't understand.

'I kept telling you and telling you. You're a stubborn bastard.'

Piers couldn't think. His mind was refusing to accept what he was seeing with his eyes. He wanted to talk, to say something, but all he could hear himself articulate was, 'Stop fucking around.'

'I am not fucking around,' Marion shouted. 'You still don't understand. I can't let you walk out of here brandishing this bloody flask to the world, and showing your tapes.'

Piers backed a foot, felt the edge of a chair against his knees, and sat down heavily. The gun in Marion's hand followed him downward. Piers held up a hand.

'What are you telling me?' he asked gently.

'I can't let you take the—'

'No,' Piers said. 'Not that. The gun, and you not being able to let me leave.'

The gun made a gesture of apology. 'I worked for the CIA, and then I was transferred to the Council. I swear, Piers. I've never done anything against you for them before.'

'How long?'

'Five, six years. I promise, Piers. This is the first—'

'Why?' It was a half-articulated scream.

Marion shook her head. It would be impossible to explain, and he would never understand, or forgive. The warp of her life – a happy childhood in Champaign, college at Michigan State, where she'd partly despised her acquaintances involved in the radical movements of the sixties, the need to serve, to heal her country, which, when she first became a journalist, was one of the reasons she'd allowed herself to be recruited by the CIA – was so different from his. She'd never wanted to be sent to Sao Amerigo and had pleaded, but her job was to keep in touch with reporters like Piers. This was the 'first time' only because in their three years he had done nothing important enough to disturb her intelligence chiefs. She couldn't tell him; it would be too cruel. This time it was, and she'd known the moment would come, and prepared herself. The pain would come later, much later, when she allowed herself the luxury to think about it.

'Oh, Christ.' Piers sat back. He had seen it so many times: youths and men and women and children, American, Vietnamese, Arab, Israeli, Indian, Pakistani, countless other races, bewildered, placing open palms against the gaping, shell-torn wounds in their sides and watching their fists sink into their bodies; and never known how it had felt. Like a whole side has been taken out of you, he thought, and you know you're dying but you can't halt it. He tried to think back over their three years together; so many places and so many stories. Which ones had been true; which ones had been set up? He had been controlled, used, channeled; a fucking puppet not knowing it dangled on strings.

'Did you kill Lopez?' He thought of her showering and the familiar odor of soap and sweat.

'Yes, I was trying to warn you.' She was visibly shaking, and Piers felt sorry for her. She was trapped, like him, between two forces. She came nearer to him.

'If you never did it before to me, why this time?'

'Because it's not a game anymore, it's for real. It's not just digging up corruption or bringing down a president. This will bring down the world, destroy everything we have. We will have to go to war with the Third Nations once this is known.' Marion bent slightly toward him. Her voice was patient, like a mother explaining to a child. 'We had to do it, Piers. Bolivar was right, you know, there is no room, no food, no materials for both them and us. One of us has to survive, and today we are still the strong one. We have to preserve our culture, our civilization, our achievements. That's why we did this.'

'Are we really worth saving?'

'I think so,' Marion said. 'That's why I can't let you . . .' She didn't finish.

They looked at each other for a long time. Marion's eyes were sad and searching. Piers was angry. Not at Marion, but at those who had used her, used him, and calculatingly destroyed a country. He moved his foot and he felt something. His hand dangled between his legs, and his fingertips explored the object absent-mindedly. They touched a ball of wool and a heavy, cold needle.

'You told them about Bolivar?'

'Yes. If Santos hadn't escaped with the flask, it wouldn't have come to this. We could have gone home . . .'

He tugged at the needle and felt it come free. 'We can still go home.'

Marion shook her head, and her hair fell over one eye. 'You'll never give up this story, Piers. It would never let you go,' she said gently. 'I'm sorry, I am . . .'

Piers knew he was going to die, and he didn't want to. He had to reach those who had hurt both of them so badly. He brought the needle up quickly, aiming for Marion's gun, but his aim was bad. She screamed as it went through her forearm and struck there like an arrow. The gun and the flask fell on the floor, and he made no move to pick them up, but Marion, suddenly afraid of him, turned and ran out of the room. Piers ran after her. He had to stop her, for he knew she was too committed to preventing him carrying the flask and the tapes out of the country.

'Marion,' he called as she turned down the stairs. He wasn't sure how he was going to stop her talking once he caught her. He knew he couldn't kill her. He took the stairs three at a time, stumbling and tripping. She reached the street door, while he still had a flight left and knew he'd lost her. He ran out onto the pavement; she was moving diagonally across the street and was nearing the opposite side.

In the distance he heard the sudden menacing roar of a jeep and knew he'd lost his chance. Marion was veering toward the sound. The jeep took the corner, and the headlights silhouetted her sharply. She held up her arms, and Piers heard her shout and run toward the soldiers. He backed into the doorway.

A soldier stood up; his machine gun was at hip level and pointing straight at her. Piers suddenly knew what was going to happen and wanted to shout a warning. Marion also understood what was to happen. Piers saw her check, swerve, and turn halfheartedly in his direction, as if she wanted to come and shelter by him. The soldier was only following his orders. The first bullet punched her around toward Piers; the others slammed and bounced her on the street. Piers didn't move. The jeep stopped near her body, and the soldier jumped down, touched her with his foot, and climbed back into the jeep. She would be collected in the morning.

Piers waited until the patrol had gone and then moved slowly to her body. He crouched beside her. He didn't look at her torn body but only at her face. Her eyes were shut, and her face was beautiful in its peace. He didn't know for how long he knelt and stared at her face, but when he straightened, his knees hurt and his back ached. He looked around. A piece of paper scraped by in the gentle breeze, and he felt very alone. He couldn't leave her in the street. He bent, and gently picked her up. Her blood soaked through his shirt and touched his skin, warm and sluggish, as he carried her back to Lopez' apartment. He found a bedroom and put her down and covered her with a sheet. He was about to cover her face, when he stopped suddenly. He was looking down on a total stranger. In three years, he'd only scraped the surface of her life; there were twists and turns and labyrinths to her mind which he'd never have a chance to explore and discover. On death, as the one person falls and recedes further and further away and the other remains steady, the delicate threads connecting them both reveal themselves as they snap. The ones he never knew existed came into view; the ones he thought were there, never really were. He wondered who she was, whether she was Marion Hyslop, as he covered her face.

Piers left the room, shut the door, and locked it. He returned to the front room and found the flask and replaced it in the can. Her video camera was on a chair. He removed the tape and hesitated a moment and then carried the camera to where she lay and placed it gently by her side. There was nothing more he could do for her. He scooped up his own camera and glanced at the photograph on the table. There was no one to look at the happiness in those people, so he turned the photograph down on its face before leaving the apartment.

10

Piers was woken rudely by a loud banging on the door at five o'clock. It sounded as if the soldier was using his gun butt, and Piers winced as he sat up. He ached all over. 'Okay,' he shouted. 'I'll be out.'

The banging stopped, and he slowly got out of bed. He examined himself in the mirror. He was covered with welts. It had taken half an hour of sheer physical pain to get back to his room the night before. The soldier had been wide-awake, and this time there was no one to distract him. Piers had had to climb out of the stairwell window onto a narrow ledge about fifteen feet along and half a foot wide. It led to the balcony of the first room, and the only hold was a drain-pipe. With geometric precision it had been placed exactly between the window and the balcony.

He had slung the video over his back and edged slowly along the ledge until he reached the balcony. Then came the hard part – jumping the six balconies to reach his room. At the first two jumps, he'd only barked his shins and scraped an arm. At the third, he'd misjudged and nearly fallen. His fingers still ached from holding on to the edge and hauling himself up. He had taken his time over the last three jumps and reached his room exhausted. Before collapsing into bed, he'd transmitted the tapes to his studio and erased them.

Piers dressed carefully, wincing each time he touched a bruise, packed his camera, and dropped the deodorant can carelessly at the bottom of his suitcase. There was no use trying to hide it. Piers stopped with his hand on the door-knob. The pain inside him was sharper and deeper than the superficial bruises to his body. He thought of Marion, but the thought itself was quick and over, as if he had willed himself not to remember more. The wound she had inflicted, however, would remain. With her gone, Piers felt alone, but he also knew that now there was no one controlling him, manipulating him like a puppet.

The guard began to hammer, and Piers opened the door. The man grunted surlily and led Piers down to a waiting jeep. There were three other soldiers and Geddes in it.

'Where is Señora Hyslop?' Geddes asked.

'She decided to stay on,' Piers said softly and climbed in.

Geddes tried to hide his pleasure, and signaled the driver.

At the airport, Geddes had Piers and his luggage searched and the tapes checked. He seemed puzzled when he found the tapes blank, but said nothing. 'I will personally escort you to the aircraft,' he said.

'No guard of honor?'

'They double as the firing squad, and they're busy this morning,' Geddes said quietly as they hurried to the waiting 747.

Piers glanced at Geddes' face. It was expressionless, and then he caught his eye. There was a grin in it, and Piers realized in surprise that Geddes had actually cracked a joke. Piers was still shaking his head in wonder when he boarded.

He forgot about Geddes the moment they were airborne. He tried to think what he was going to do with the flask and with the tapes, when he retrieved them from his studio in New York. Show them to Odu and Liu and Sadat and the other Third Nation leaders? They were too far away, and there wasn't much time. 'As wide an area as possible ...' was a chilling expression. Who had told him 'it isn't a game anymore, it's for real'? He tried to remember but couldn't. All he knew was that he had to prevent the Council from killing millions more people. The only way he knew how was to have his story told. But who'd run it? Channel 14? The *New York Times*? And then what would happen?

That was as far as Piers could think. His mind ran around and around in circles, and then finally he gave up brooding. His bruises were beginning to throb in sympathy with his head, and he decided to stretch his legs with a walk down the aisles. At first glance he didn't recognize O'Brien. It looked as if the aging process in the man was accelerating. His fists were clenched tightly, and there were dark, deep circles under his eyes. His hair was uncombed, and he'd dressed without caring. The man, Piers realized, was very near crack-up. He thought of joining him, and then stopped. His companion, a young man of about thirty, wearing glasses and a neat suit, had too watchful eyes. O'Brien was being escorted back to America. Piers hoped he would be able to reach him later on in his office at Rockefeller University.

Mercer narrowed his eyes in surprise as he stared at Solotov. He was seeing Solotov angry for the first time. It wasn't a passionate, verbal anger, the type Darrigan liked to indulge himself in. In fact, to a stranger, Solotov looked as poker-faced as ever. But Mercer could see the rigid ripples on the side of Solotov's face. The man was actually clenching his teeth to keep his self-control.

Darrigan had had his tantrum five minutes back and was now sitting stiffly erect in his chair. Mercer had been briefly angry, but not for exactly the same reasons as the other two.

'Who the hell gave them permission to kill Bolivar?' Darrigan repeated himself for the third time. Each time he said it, a slightly larger note of puzzlement crept into his voice. He was genuinely baffled by someone taking an action without his permission.

'They should have warned us before taking such an extreme measure,' Solotov said. The ripples in his face thickened.

They have grown so accustomed to their power and being obeyed, Mercer realized, that they are now both behaving like children who have suddenly been defied. He had to admit, however, that he himself had been taken aback by Bolivar's death. We are so used to treating humans as units of production who obey our every decree, that we're surprised and shocked when one of them decides to be stupid on his own volition. He regretted Bolivar's death. The run had been short, and it was ironic that this time the Council hadn't been responsible. They had been cheated by a tin soldier.

'They acted like nineteenth-century bandits,' Darrigan said.

'Well, that's what they are,' Mercer said. 'We knew that when we negotiated with them. You surely didn't expect them to change overnight because the Council demanded it.'

'We had no alternative,' Solotov said coldly. 'We needed to make use of them. Someone had to take over from Bolivar. If there hadn't been an alternative, it would have been impossible for us to exploit the country without raising the suspicions of the other Third Nations.'

'All hell's going to break loose now,' Mercer said with some satisfaction. 'We'll be suspected, of course, but General Peres may now lose control of the situation. Bolivar was loved by his people.'

'It was mere emotion,' Darrigan said. 'He gave them a dream and economic independence.' He sneered. 'And then he tries to pull a dumb thing like the embargo on us.' He pushed his button and snapped at the aide on the monitor, 'What's the situation in Menaguay?'

'Still stable, sir,' the aide said. 'The people are still in mourning, according to the last report.'

'If only they'll stay that way.'

'There is a report from General Peres just come in, sir.'

'Run it. I want to see what that son of a bitch has got to say. He's going to bullshit us about Bolivar starting a secret revolution against him. And he'd better have recovered the flask.'

Video Replay: General Alvaro Peres to the Council. Recorded 16/7 at 1145 hours.

As you have no doubt heard, Señor Bolivar is dead. Neither I nor my cabinet was in any way responsible for his death. I repeat, we were not involved in his death. As I stated in the press conference, a patrol found the remains of his car and his burned body. Army doctors have run tests on the body and found it to be Bolivar's. We believe that he was on his way to his private aircraft when the accident occurred. We are not sure where he was going to fly to. My guess is Cape Town. Nor am I sure he had the flask with him. We searched the area and failed to locate it. It is possible his companion, Santos, may now be in

163

possession of the flask. We are of course speculating, as we were at no time sure Bolivar did receive it in the first place. The patrols all over the country have been alerted and are searching for Santos. Once we find him, we shall extract the information we need. The situation here is stable, and I would like to assure the Council that as long as I remain in power, it is the only chance for the situation to remain so. The army is loyal to me. Before I end, I wish to repeat, as I did in reply to the question from your New York reporter: Neither I nor the cabinet were in any way responsible for Bolivar's death. It would in no way have benefited us, just yet, nor would it have benefited the Council.

Darrigan, Solotov, and Mercer stared at the monitor in surprise. They continued to stare for a long time after the screen went blank.

Mercer was the first to speak. 'You think he's lying?'

'He could be,' Darrigan said, 'but I don't think he is.'

'Then how did Bolivar die?' Solotov asked. 'I don't believe the car he was in just had an accident.'

'It could have,' Mercer said dryly. 'We didn't issue any instructions to it.'

They both ignored him. The puzzlement was gradually turning to worry. The Council didn't like things to just 'happen'; there had to be an explanation.

Darrigan punched the button and ordered the aide: 'Have that car Bolivar was traveling in checked. I want to know why it crashed, and I want to know *now*.'

'Yes, sir,' the aide said, and started to fade. Darrigan recalled him.

'The reporter from New York is Shatner, I presume?'

'Yes, sir.'

'I ordered his expulsion days ago.'

The aide looked worried, and Mercer felt sorry for him. He wondered what his name was and what else there was to him, apart from the face on the monitor.

'Sir, we relayed your orders to General Peres. His ADC informed us that General Peres would make his own

164

decisions on the expulsion of people from his country. Shatner has since left Sao Amerigo, sir, and is due in New York within half an hour.'

'Good.'

'Before you go,' Solotov said quickly, 'I want a replay of part of General Peres' tape. I'll tell you what I want.'

'Yes, sir.'

Video Replay: General Alvaro Peres to the Council. Recorded 16/7 at 1145 hours.

As you have no doubt . . .

. . . The situation here is stable, and I would like to assure the Council that as long as I remain in power, it is the only chance for the situation to remain so. The army is loyal to me. Before I . . .

'Thank you,' Solotov said, and the monitor blanked out.

'You see . . . he's threatening us. We cannot permit that. Who would take over if anything should happen to General Peres?' He opened the file in front of him, and Darrigan did the same.

Mercer closed his eyes. Another man was about to be removed. At the beginning, the Council was first created only to negotiate with the Third Nations. Power doesn't corrupt, Mercer thought, it just hardens the arteries. It stiffens the mind and cuts out the tolerance.

'He's only threatening us because he's frightened of us,' Mercer said.

'We have not threatened him in any way,' Solotov said, briefly looking up from the file. 'We have always cooperated.'

It would be impossible to explain anything to the two men, Mercer thought. It's not that, he corrected himself, I don't want to. In another way, I am frightened of them too. They just steamroller along. And although he didn't want to stand in the way, Mercer knew he just couldn't summon enough courage to take the step. And even if he did, they would just veto him and push him back.

'Bardez,' Solotov said, and Darrigan nodded, and they both closed their files.

Before they could give the order, the aide appeared on the screen. 'Sir, we've picked up a broadcast by Odu. Would you like to see it?'

'Yes,' Solotov said.

Video Broadcast: Odu. Recorded 16/7 at 1215 hours.

It is with deep regret and sadness that I have heard of the sudden death of Chairman Juan Jesus Bolivar. I send the condolences of my people to the people of Menaguay, who have suffered so much in the last month. I do believe that there are a number of questions to be answered by the army junta as to how he died. I shall be awaiting the results of their investigation, as will the other Third Nation leaders. We shall be keeping this and other questions in mind when we convene in Cape Town next week.

'He's taking over from Bolivar,' Darrigan said, 'and he's going to form the embargo against us.'

'We've no time. We must expand the area,' Solotov said.

'We have a week,' Mercer said. He had to stall them as long as he could. Give Odu some time. 'He still isn't sure about Bolivar and what happened in Menaguay. If he gets hold of that flask . . . then we better start sweating.'

'We can't afford to give him that chance,' Solotov said.

'I don't know,' Darrigan said thoughtfully. 'They've given us a time – next week, if we time it right.'

Solotov hesitated and finally nodded. 'We must send out the instructions, and I believe we should reply in some way to Odu, and General Peres.'

An aide appeared on the monitor.

Video Record: Solotov on 16/7 at 1300 hours.

It is with regret and sadness that the Council has heard of the death of Señor Juan Jesus Bolivar. We would like to convey our condolences to General Alvaro Peres and his people. The Council is sure that General Peres will continue to bring stability to his country and put to rest the doubts of those who believe that Señor Bolivar's death was other than an accident. The Council is confident that the leaders of the Third Nations will understand the nature of the crisis that has occurred in Menaguay and will react with their customary wisdom.

Solotov looked at Darrigan and Mercer. The nods he received were noncommittal. Darrigan preferred to make the broadcasts, as he believed he had the best image of the three. However, Solotov had increasingly begun to enjoy his appearances, and for the moment Darrigan thought it wisest to indulge him. No doubt the leaders of the Industrial Nations would be taping similar messages right now.

'Sir,' the aide reported, 'Shatner has arrived in New York. He was on the same flight as Dr O'Brien. We have Dr O'Brien under surveillance.' The aide hesitated for a moment. 'Shatner tried to transfer to a flight to Cape Town. As he did not have the necessary visa, his request was refused.'

'Where?' Darrigan demanded.

'Cape Town, via Paris and Rome. sir.'

Solotov leaned forward eagerly. He and Darrigan could at times resemble eager bloodhounds which had suddenly caught a scent.

'First Bolivar tries for Cape Town,' Solotov said quietly.

'Now Shatner . . .'

'The unpatriotic bastard,' Darrigan shouted. 'He's going to contact Odu.' He stopped and looked faintly surprised. 'But he can't do that without any evidence. He's got the goddamned flask or something else that he can show Odu.'

'Wasn't he under surveillance in Sao Amerigo?' Solotov asked the aide.

'Yes, sir. We have not as yet been able to make contact with our agent. She's been missing from the hotel since this morning.'

'Forget about her and forget O'Brien,' Darrigan said. 'Get Shatner immediately.'

'What happens if he resists arrest, sir?'

'I didn't say arrest, did I?' Darrigan said coldly, and pressed the aide off the screen.

Piers closed his eyes. He was exhausted, and his body ached. He had tried to sleep, but his mind had refused to rest. It had chased every problem he had until he felt dizzy with thinking. He winced as the cab hit a bump, and he was thankful that the freeway into New York wasn't jammed. The economic stagnation in the West had at least achieved one good result – cut out traffic jams. This made movement easier but very expensive.

He picked up the video and focused on the car which had been following him since the airport. He cursed himself for having made the request for transfer to Cape Town. If he hadn't been tired, he'd never have made that mistake. He knew it would have been only a matter of time before the Council realized he had the flask. All he'd done was make their job easier.

There were two men in the car. The passenger had an object in his left hand. Piers steadied himself. It was a phone, and the man was obviously receiving orders. He spoke only in monosyllables that looked like yeses. He dropped the phone and spoke to the driver. The car immediately accelerated. Piers turned back quickly to his driver. They were nearing Queens Midtown Tunnel, and New York was sliding down below the horizon.

'Can you step on it?'

'For forty bucks I could squash it,' the driver said. Piers passed over the money, and the cab immediately accelerated.

Piers glanced back. For a moment the car following seemed to slow down, but it speeded up immediately, and the gap began to close. Piers focused the video. The passenger now had a gun in his hand and was leaning out. The cab overtook a car, and for a moment Piers lost sight of the gunman. He caught sight of him again as the car swung out to overtake the car caught between them. Maybe the driver of the third car didn't realize he was being overtaken, but when the gunman's car was halfway past him, the third car suddenly swung into its side. Piers winced. The gunman's car slammed into the glistening white side of the tunnel, cartwheeled, and skidded along its back, scattering sparks. The third car straightened, slowed, and then accelerated.

'We've lost him,' Piers said as he saw the third car swing off the freeway.

'Well, you're not getting your money back,' the driver said, and glared defiantly at him in the mirror.

'Keep it. Drop me off on Park and Forty-fourth.'

Piers didn't wait at the corner. He moved quickly through the revolving doors of the Pan Am Building, crossed the vast, gloomy foyer, and down to the Grand Central level. The station was crowded, and Piers pushed his way to some lockers. He opened his case, took out the can of deodorant, and slid the case into the locker. He had no doubt his apartment on Sixty-second Street was being watched. He needed time to think, and though he had none, he decided to have a coffee. It wouldn't take long for the two men who'd been tailing him from JFK to send out word they'd lost him and have his trail picked up. He felt panicky and claustrophobic. Everywhere he turned there was a flowing barrier of faceless people and he longed for the space of Cochos. There was land and emptiness and a distant horizon. He understood well what Bolivar meant. New York always reminded him of some great, wounded animal, bewildered by its own mortality, dragging its entrails behind it. He could see the decay not only in this city but in all the urban areas in the West. They were overcrowded and broke, and the buildings were neglected and the streets unrepaired. There was a sense of lethargy everywhere.

His hand shook as he tried to drink the black coffee. It was hot and awful, and some reached his mouth. He was tired and afraid. He had to do something with the flask and his tapes, and he bitterly regretted Bolivar's death. He himself was incapable of making a decision. Bolivar would have done everything, and all he, Piers would have had to do was record the events that followed. He was now at the very center and couldn't understand how it had happened.

Piers finished the coffee and found an empty phone booth.

His eyes kept moving, trying not to be seen, yet waiting for someone, anyone, to catch his eye and move purposefully toward him. The operator answered and gave him the number he wanted. There was just sufficient change to make the call, and Piers punched out the number in Washington.

'May I speak to the ambassador?' he asked when he got through. Piers had decided to contact Odu and let him take over the situation. Another voice came on the line, and Piers repeated his question. 'He's away,' the man said. 'Maybe I can help. I'm the first secretary, Charles Ndolo.'

Piers hesitated; he had no alternatives. 'I am a friend of Bolivar's. He gave me something to give to your president. It's very, very urgent.'

There was a long pause, and Piers guessed the man was thinking. It took an age for him to reply: 'Bolivar is dead.'

'I know,' Piers said patiently. 'I've just come from Sao Amerigo, and he gave me something before he died. Odu must see it.'

'What is it?'

'I will tell you when we meet,' Piers said. 'Your president should know what to do with it. I can catch the three-o'clock shuttle and—'

'That would be unwise,' Ndolo said. 'I will come to New York, if my president thinks we should meet.'

'Okay, I'll wait for you at one o'clock. You will be parked on the north side of Grand Army Plaza on Sixtieth, fifty yards west of Fifth. I'll come to you, okay.' Piers rang off as soon as the man confirmed he understood. If anyone was tailing Ndolo, it would be fairly easy to spot him in such an open space.

There were two more calls to make, and though it was dangerous, he would have to reverse the charges. He punched the zero and gave the operator the number, and heard Frank Kolok accept the call. 'What the hell is happening, Piers?' he shouted immediately. 'There are a lot of heavy guys looking for you. You okay? How's Marion? What have you been doing to get this pressure?'

'Marion's . . .' Piers stumbled. 'She's fine; she's still in Sao Amerigo. You wanted a story . . . well, I've got it. That's why those guys are looking for me. You've got to run this story, Frank, if it's the last thing you do.'

There was a long pause. 'It better be good, Piers. We've seen all the pictures on the plague down there, and the public won't want any more South America stories. One a year is enough.'

'This one's got to do with the Council as well.'

'So that's why the heavy guys are out looking for you.' Frank said. 'When can I see the tapes?'

'Give me a day to wrap it up.' Piers rang off and moved quickly away from the phone. Frank would try his best, but he didn't run the station. As Piers came out of the Pan Am exit, he saw the police cars pulling up on Vanderbilt and Forty-second Street. Dozens of men were pouring out of the cars and running into Grand Central. Piers kept moving, trying hard not to run. In the heat – it was ninety-two degrees by Citibank's temperature reading – Piers doubted whether he could have covered a block without collapsing. He stopped at a phone booth when he'd covered five blocks. He figured if they had thrown a cordon around Grand Central he was well clear of it. Piers had the operator connect him to Hal Ginsberg.

Hal was a tubby, bearded man who worked as a financial writer for a small but prestigious firm of investment counselors, Beresford and Seligmann. Hal constantly threatened he was going to quit and join a proper publication, but since he'd married, he was too nervous to make a move.

'First you get thrown out of a goddamned country, then you have me shelling out a quarter for your phone calls,' Hal said the moment he came on the line. Most times, he was rude in a defensive, humorous way.

'Sorry, Hal, I need some information out of the top of your head.'

'In which case it won't be worth much. I only keep sexy pictures in the top of my head. The brains are farther down below.'

'I'll take my chances,' Piers said. 'What would happen if this country had access to unlimited and cheap energy and raw materials?'

'You ever seen a missile take off? ... Well, that's what would happen. From a real growth figure of around 0.5, which is what we have now, we'd shoot up to say 4 to 5 percent real growth.' Hal stopped for a moment and then said quietly, 'Funny you should ask that, Piers. I'm getting vibrations that something like that could happen. Some country is going to denationalize all US property and they are signing an energy deal. What's your source?'

Piers ignored the question. 'What would happen to Europe if the US economy recovered?'

'What the hell do you think would happen? They'd start eating again. You know something, Piers, give.'

'Just one more, Hal. You ever heard of OT?'

'It sounds like a bad drink. No, never heard of it.'

'Thanks.' As Piers replaced the phone, he heard Hal screaming at him. Piers grinned. He liked Hal and didn't want him involved.

Piers teetered on the corner of Forty-seventh and Fifth. He took a deep breath, and felt a momentary release from his panic and exhaustion. He held the breath, tracing the familiar odors of New York trapped in his lungs. The heat of the street, the sweat and perfumes of nearby people, the dust, the smell of bagels from a vendor a few feet from him. The smell of gasoline was faintest. There wasn't enough traffic to sour the air, as with the crisis people were using the subway and the buses and leaving their cars garaged.

A taxi pulled up for the light, and Piers made up his mind. He jumped in and ordered the driver to Rockefeller University. He had to take a chance that O'Brien was back in the lab and, possibly, unwatched. The cab stopped a block from the white three-sided building, and Piers paid the driver off. The grass lawn in front of the university looked a cool, inviting green, and as he crossed it to the entrance, Piers had a boyhood urge to take off his shoes and wriggle his toes through the grass.

O'Brien, according to the information board, was on the third floor. Piers ran up the stairs and met no one. As the university was totally devoted to research, there was a sort of deserted, holy air about it. Piers carefully looked down the corridor. There was no one sitting out. He had to be sure, and moved quickly into the nearest room. It was an office belonging to a Dr Atkinson. By the side of the telephone was a list of extension numbers. He found O'Brien's and tapped it out.

'Are you alone?' he asked as soon as he recognized O'Brien's wavery voice.

'Yes, who's that?'

Piers put down the phone and moved out into the corridor. O'Brien was on the far north side, the last office, and Piers covered the ground quickly. He wasn't sure why they'd left O'Brien by himself. It could be a trap. He hesitated outside the door and then quickly opened it and stepped in.

O'Brien was sitting at his desk and didn't even seem to notice Piers. He was staring straight ahead of him, cracking his knuckles constantly.

Piers took the cylinder out of the can and placed it carefully on the desk in front of O'Brien. O'Brien's eyes gradually returned to focus and hesitantly dropped to the cylinder; they made contact and then flicked away like frightened bees. For a moment he looked as if he were about to cry, as if a childhood fear had been conjured up from his deep subconscious. His hands hovered above the desk and then fell heavily just inches short of the cylinder. 'Oh, my God,' he whispered, for he knew his nightmare had followed him across the world. He hadn't slept for days, weeks, months, years; time was just a heavy numbness that kept him nailed to his fear. He wasn't a brave man, and he'd hoped that by closing his mind, the nightmare of what he'd discovered in Menaguay would eventually fade away.

'You don't have to pray, doc.' Piers was unsympathetic. He knew if he showed O'Brien any compassion, the man would crack; and there was no time for that. 'Just test it and confirm it was the virus released in Menaguay.'

It seemed an eternity before O'Brien picked up the flask; he seemed mechanical and remote as he crossed the hall to his laboratory. Piers guessed the man was in a state of shock and that maybe even an interior death had occurred.

The laboratory was a gleaming sepulcher filled with glass

and electronic equipment. O'Brien placed the cylinder in a container cabinet and sealed the glass cover. Piers noticed that the cabinet had two knuckle-shaped openings just below the line of the cover; inside, a pair of mechanical hands hung stiffly in midair.

O'Brien's whole demeanor changed while he worked. Piers saw him visibly straighten and grow more confident as he efficiently worked his machines. He ignored Piers for the most part and spoke only tersely, in a very academic voice, when he thought it necessary.

'I'm pumping liquid nitrogen around the flask. It will liquefy the gas, and make it easier to handle. . . . Now I'm attaching a vacuum line and an infrared cell which is connected to a spectrometer. No two compounds have the same structure, and the spectrometer gives us what you'd call a fingerprint of what's inside the flask.' O'Brien moved to the spectrometer and peered at the chart, and like a toy doll drained of all its sawdust, sagged. 'I could,' he said tonelessly, 'feed the information through a computer, but . . .'

Video Report: What is in the flask, Dr O'Brien?
 I'll have to run more tests on the sample I've taken.
 You already know, Doctor, so stop hedging. What is it?
 In the fifties, we invented a virus called Sarin. It's code name was GB. It paralyzed and killed anyone who breathed it. It remained in the atmosphere approximately twenty-four hours before becoming ineffective. This, I believe, is a more sophisticated strain of Sarin. It works more quickly and dissipates quicker. I'll have to confirm this opinion, naturally.
 Naturally. Thank you, Dr O'Brien.
 Tape pause . . .

They waited half an hour for the flask to be thoroughly sterilized, and in that time O'Brien never moved. He just stared at the chart. He spoke once, tonelessly. 'I hated Saò Amerigo. I hated the dead, and then I hated myself once I had an idea how they'd died. I've spent all my life here in a laboratory doing my research. Useless. I didn't know this would happen . . . I didn't know.'

When the sterilization time was up, O'Brien reached into the side of the cabinet and took it out. It was damp, and he wiped it on a towel and handed it to Piers.

'What will you do with it?' He sounded uninterested, and Piers didn't reply. O'Brien was no man to confide in.

Piers stood on the steps and looked across the lawn. Shadows had begun to stain the grass black in patches, but there was still an air of cosseted quietness about the university. It was a world he had lived in a long time ago, and it seemed as if he were watching the replay of a dream filled with lazy silences. He longed to remain in it forever. Tiredly, he moved across the lawn to York Avenue. It was only five, and he had a long time to fill before meeting Ndolo. He needed rest desperately; his legs and back ached, and the side of his face was throbbing.

However, beyond these signals of pain, Piers felt and thought nothing. There were odd times, seconds at most, that he tried to wonder what he was doing. He had a flask, tapes, he was carrying it to somebody – Ndolo – and then? He didn't know. It seemed to him that he was interested in something dark and soothing; and this thing was shutting down parts of his mind, like lights being switched off one by one in a skyscraper at night.

On Third Avenue he stopped and stood for a long time outside a movie house. The film, he gradually understood, was a rerun of Pasolini's *Gospel According to Saint Matthew*. He had seen it before, and walked in. It would be good to sit and rest and just stare at a screen.

It was eleven when he awoke with a start. He stared uncomprehendingly at the images tumbling in front of him, panicked for a moment, and then got up. There were two hours to kill, and as he hadn't eaten since leaving – he paused to remember . . . Sao Amerigo – he thought of food. There was a steak house across Third Avenue on the corner of Sixty-seventh, Burke's, and Piers crossed the street, not seeing the traffic, and walked in. It was cool inside, and the sweat on his face dried and hardened. Most of the tables were empty, and half a dozen men sat at the bar nursing beers. At the far end, a large television set shone down on their faces like a Technicolor moon. Piers ordered steak and a beer. The glance the waitress gave him made him aware that he hadn't shaved for a couple of days and that his eyes felt gritty. In the washroom, he studied his face curiously. The eyes were red and the pouches deeper, and lines around his mouth looked like chasms. He washed and returned to the table.

It was a good meal, and when he finished he let the languor of a full belly soak through him. He leaned back and stared at the television. He wanted to sit where he was forever, watching the pointless images sliding in and out in front of his eyes like a mesmeric pendulum. This half-empty little room was a refuge he'd never be able to return to once he left. As it neared midnight, he reluctantly stood up and paid his check. He was near the door when he heard the familiar jingle. It was the late news.

Video Broadcast: *This is Robert Wylie with the twelve-o'clock news. First the headlines. The Dow Jones climbed another fifteen points but just before closing dropped by five. The pulse of the nation quickens as more industries open their doors and recall their work force. The president confidently expects a return to growth and predicts a boom period ahead. In Menaguay the plague continues to be brought under control, and with the help of the Industrial Nations, life returns to normal. However, two generals were assassinated. At home, American national law-enforcement agencies hunt a killer. I will be back in a moment.*

Piers sat down on a stool nearest the door and ordered a rye. The Dow Jones taking a drop, he was sure, wasn't part of the script. Obviously the generals had been important to the Council, and Piers wanted to know who they were. He had no doubt Santos had fulfilled his vows, and Piers wondered whether he'd survived to fulfill the rest of Bolivar's orders.

Robert Wylie returned to the screen. Piers smiled at him. He'd known Bob for over five years and liked him. The screen was filled with graphs and figures, and Piers only half watched. There was another break, and then Ralph Minor of NBC came on screen.

Video Broadcast: *Today at four-thirty, General Alvaro Peres, chairman of the emergency government of Menaguay, and two members of his cabinet, General Bardez and General Villar, were assassinated as they drove from the Grand Assembly Hall to army headquarters. The attack took place on Avenida Peron. The group of commandos responsible for the attack first raked the car in which the generals were traveling with machine-gun fire and then threw grenades. Apart from the generals, a chauffeur and two soldiers were killed. The killers got away. General Viterbo, a junior in General Peres' cabinet, has taken over as temporary chairman. This is Ralph Minor, NBC news, in Sao Amerigo.*

Piers hurriedly finished his drink. He silently toasted Santos; a few more generals would no doubt die soon. As he opened the door, he glanced back. He felt a shock. His face was on the screen, and out of the corner of his eye he could see the barman turning toward him.

Video Broadcast: *Piers Shatner, an ex-Channel 14, New York, television reporter is today being hunted for murder by law-enforcement agencies throughout the country. Shatner earlier today brutally murdered the eminent microbiologist Dr Kevin O'Brien and . . .*

Piers slammed the door and ran up the street. He looked back, but no one came out of the steak house in pursuit, but he could imagine the barman on the phone. He needed time to think before he met Ndolo. O'Brien was dead, but when he'd left him, he'd been alive, just. He'd been taken care of now, and by pinning the killing on Piers the Council had made the hunt for him legitimate. He stopped and felt like giving up. He didn't have a chance of surviving in the streets now, and the odds of him having his tape broadcast were now incalculably against him. The Council had out-maneuvered him. Walking made him feel vulnerable; it seemed that every passerby was staring at his face and re-cognizing him. He had to find himself a car. Though his own, a Mustang, was garaged only a few blocks from where he stood, he sensed it would be dangerous for him to use it. As he walked up Third, and then east on Seventieth, he tested the door handles of the parked cars as surreptitiously as he could. The button of a Ford outside an antique shop below First Avenue gave under the pressure of his thumb, and without looking around he opened the door and slid into the seat. There was no key in the ignition, and he quickly bent below the dashboard and wrenched out the wires. The car started immediately when he made the con-nection. The fuel gauge was a fraction above empty, but it would be enough for his purposes.

He cruised the streets until 12.45 and then turned west up on Sixtieth. He parked east of Fifth Avenue within sight of Grand Army Plaza. There was still a long line of horse-drawn carriages standing by the curb along Central Park, the flags outside the Plaza Hotel fluttered fitfully in the warm breeze, and the lights from the foyer lit up the square in front of the hotel.

There was a car parked across Fifth Avenue, ten yards up Sixtieth Street. There were a couple more cars parked far-ther along past it. The plaza itself was still quite well popu-lated with, what seemed to Piers, tourists making their way back to their hotels. Piers took the camera out of its case and carefully focused on the first car.

Video Report: Tape continued . . .

I am waiting to hand over the flask to First Secretary Ndolo. I want to sprint across the street and like a baton runner hand everything over to the man and let him carry the burden. But I doubt whether this would stop the Council hunting me. The man in the car looks African, and it could be Ndolo. I watch him for a minute. He suddenly turns his head and nods. Either there's someone else in the car or he has a radio link. The crowds I'd first noticed are only a deception. Through the lens I can catch a lot of movement. I can count ten men . . . It feels as if a hole has been punched in my gut and it's filling with hopelessness. I am up against a black, endless wall and I'm too tired to negotiate it . . . Two men step out of the shadows and start toward me. They walk warily, like men expecting the earth to open up . . .

Tape pause . . .

Piers hit the accelerator at the same moment as he heard a shot. He didn't have time to notice, but it came nowhere near him. The men moving toward him turned, startled, and then began running toward him. For a frightening second the car didn't respond to his foot, and then it bucked and shot forward. The lights were against him, but he had to take the chance. He came onto Fifth and heard the cars moving south brake and skid into each other. As he entered the west side of Sixtieth, he heard more shots. This time they were for him, and he cringed. The rear window cracked and blurred opaque. A car suddenly pulled out from the shadows blocking his exit into the park, and he swung left toward the plaza. Another car had begun to move, but there was a gap about eight feet wide. Piers aimed at it, hit the side of the curb, and spun awkwardly onto Central Park South. He glanced into the mirror as he straightened; a car had begun to give chase. He crossed the Avenue of the Americas with the lights; the car behind him was catching up. Suddenly it began to weave, at first slowly and then faster. The driver finally lost control and spun across the road into the eastbound traffic.

Piers swung wildly down Seventh Avenue and saw no more. The car choked, stalled, and Piers grabbed his video camera and slid out of the seat before the car came to a complete stop. As he took the steps down to the Fifty-seventh Street subway, he heard it crashing into a shop, and people scream. There was no time to buy a token, the train was at the platform. He jumped the turnstile and ran down the steps and into the train as the doors closed.

At Times Square he changed trains and came out on Thirty-fourth Street. The sidewalks were crowded with drifters, the pizza parlors and delis were bright with lights and people. Piers hurried to Thirty-first Street and turned west. Halfway down was a cheap apartment hotel, the Amersham Grand. He knew the man at the desk fairly well, and hoped he would be safe until the morning.

It was a small, shabby place. The lobby was furnished with a few battered couches, and there wasn't an unfrayed spot on the threadbare carpet. There was a permanent gray haze in the air, and the stale odor of tobacco. The whole building looked as if it were visibly dying.

The man dozing behind the counter was old and black and fat. His huge hands, resting on the mound of belly, rose and fell rhythmically. Piers rapped on the wood, and the man opened one eye.

'Got a room, Gus?'

Gus reached behind him, unhooked a key, and tossed it to Piers.

'How's business?' He moved to the elevator and punched the half-broken button.

'Sheet, what business? Nobody can afford to stay in a plush joint like this. Even the hookers are broke.' Gus laughed; it was a deep staccato sound. 'God knows what they're doing for money.'

'Working standing up.' The door opened noisily.

'You do that murder they say you did?' Gus opened the other eye and studied Piers.

'No.'

Both Gus' eyes began to close.

'You don't believe me, do you?'

'I'm not saying I don't believe you. And then I'm not saying I do. I'll say this: I ain't seen you at all.' He seemed to fall asleep as the doors closed.

The room was small and with the same still air as the

lobby. It was going to have to be his home for at least a night or two, depending on his luck and what happened next. There was nowhere to run anymore, and he would have to make a stand. Piers didn't think about that. He opened the window – it looked out onto the next building – dropped the camera in the closet, and without bothering to undress, flopped down on the bed.

11

Darrigan looked out of the window. It framed a near-perfect bright-blue sky with little puffs of soft clouds around the edges. It was a kind of day when a man his age should be playing a gentle round of golf instead of sitting around a conference table. He tried to think when he'd last played. Eight months ago, when he'd spent a short vacation in California.

He heard Mercer snort irritatedly and knew it was because he was drumming the table with his fingers. To hell with you, he thought, they're my worry beads, and I've a lot to worry about. Unlike you, who's just a round, soft bag of jelly who's falling apart.

He drummed louder. It was all going wrong. When he'd been told of OT, he knew he and the Council had only one course of action to preserve the Industrial Nations. The price was high, but someone had to pay it, and he was damned if it was going to be them. His job was to preserve and protect it, not destroy it because he was just too weak, like Mercer, to take a strong line of action. They'd worked out all the details, and by now the extension of the area should have taken place. But it hadn't worked quite that way. The Cape Town conference was going to take place, and though he had confidently suggested that it would be the ideal time to extend the area, he wasn't too happy. He hated improvisation. It led to mistakes. He liked planning his movements out in minute detail.

Solotov interrupted his thoughts. The solid, patient Solotov. What is he planning in that buttoned-down mind of his? Darrigan thought, as he came out of the reverie.

'Who is General Viterbo?' he asked quietly, and looked at Darrigan expectantly.

'I've never heard of him,' Darrigan confessed uneasily.

'He's fifty-one and a career officer who worked his way up through the ranks.'

'I know that,' Solotov said, and touched the file in front of him. 'But who is he in relation to us?'

Darrigan drummed harder, and he could feel Mercer studying him. He was sure there'd be a soft smile on his face. The man seemed to enjoy working against the Council. He would definitely suggest that he be replaced. He made a note of it immediately.

'We're trying to find out,' Darrigan said.

'But I gave the order that only General Peres be removed because of his threat.'

'We had nothing to do with it,' Darrigan said unhappily. 'It happened before any of our people could carry out the order. I would think the killers were some of Bolivar's followers.'

'Well, they did do us a favor,' Mercer said.

'But we had a good man in Bardez,' Darrigan snapped. 'And we've no idea in which direction Viterbo is going to move.' He punched the button, and an aide appeared. 'Have you had any more news on Viterbo?'

'No, sir. He has not made any statement as yet. We are standing by to pick up any broadcast.'

'And I presume Shatner has been found, and the flask recovered?' Solotov asked softly.

The aide shifted uneasily. He avoided Solotov's question and passed the buck. 'I have a report from Anderson of National Security in New York, sir.' And before Solotov could repeat himself, the aide switched to the report.

Video Report: Anderson, National Security, to the Council. Recorded 18/7 at 0930 hours.

We are making every effort to intercept Piers Shatner, a journalist, as the Council ordered. The phone of every friend and acquaintance and fellow worker of Shatner's has been tapped. We have broadcast his picture on four newscasts, blaming him for the death of O'Brien, who committed suicide at approximately 2015 hours last night. At 0100 hours last night, Shatner endeavored to pass the

*flask to a man who he thought was First Secretary Ndolo.
We had told Ndolo that Shatner was dangerous, and one
of our agents took his place. Unfortunately, Shatner got
away. This was the second time he'd escaped my men
within a day. As I could not understand how this happened, I ran a complete test on the car that had been in
pursuit of him at 0110 hours down Central Park South.
The two front tires of the car had blown. On closer examination my men discovered that the tires had been shot. I
firmly believe that some persons are running a defense for
Shatner. In the first instance, our pursuit car was side-
swiped in Queens Tunnel. We had no reason to believe
then that this was other than an accident. We have since
traced that vehicle and found it abandoned. As you can
see from these pictures...*

Darrigan hit the switch and began to drum. The sound
was much faster than before. Solotov was blinking at the
monitor, and even Mercer had begun to look interested.

'Get me that man ... Anderson. Now,' he ordered the
aide.

The room was silent as they waited for the connection to
New York to be made. It took two minutes, and then Anderson appeared on the monitor.

'What the hell do you mean, someone is running a defense
for Shatner?' Darrigan asked. 'It's just an excuse for your
incompetence.'

'No, sir,' Anderson said stubbornly. 'You saw the video
tape on the tires and the car. Someone is running a defense.'

'Who?' Solotov demanded.

'We don't know as yet, sir, but my men are investigating.'

'Is Shatner aware of this ... defense?' Mercer asked.

'I'm not sure, sir. I've a feeling he isn't.'

'Where is he now?' Darrigan asked softly.

Anderson looked very unhappy. 'We've lost him, sir.'

'If you have, so have the others,' Darrigan shouted. 'Find
him before they do, and find out who they are.' He hit the
button and broke the nail on his finger.

Darrigan forcibly calmed himself. Think, he ordered his

mind, think coldly and think fast. The other two were doing the same.

'Somebody' – Mercer smiled – 'is taking us for a ride.'

Darrigan nearly ignored the remark and then thought about it. Yes, somebody was taking them for a ride, and he felt a brief burst of anger at the impudence. He stopped it. Okay, he thought, who? Who knew that Shatner had the flask? Odu didn't. He may suspect something, but he still doesn't know for sure. The flask would be the only proof he'd have. He wouldn't run a defense, he'd get it from Shatner. And Shatner would give it. He'd been trying to do that last night. The son of a bitch, doesn't he know what's at stake? He's trying to destroy his own culture and civilization for a bunch of peasants. Darrigan pulled himself up. It wasn't getting him anywhere. Now, who else knew Shatner had the flask? The Council, of course, and security agents. Darrigan shook his head. He doubted they were being double-crossed from the inside. Who else? Who else? He tried not to think about it, but he kept returning to the same answer. The person who'd given Shatner the flask in the first place: Bolivar. But Bolivar was dead.

Darrigan glanced at Solotov. The Russian seemed to have reached the same conclusion. He hit his button. 'Has the report on Bolivar's car come in as yet?'

'Yes, sir. We're just setting it up.'

Video Report: Bozeman, Central Intelligence Agency, to the Council. Recorded 18/7 at 0810 hours.

On orders from Mr Darrigan we have run a thorough check on the vehicle in which Señor Bolivar was travelling at the time of his death. The car was hit by several rounds fired from a machine-gun at relatively close quarters. We calculate, and as you can see, approximately thirty rounds were fired in all. They damaged the steering mechanism of the vehicle, destroyed the tires, and hit the gas tank. Eight rounds were found lodged in the passenger and driving seats of the vehicle. The bullets which hit the steering mechanism no doubt sent the car out of control, and those that hit the tank would have caused it to catch fire. But the fire was more extensive than it normally should have been. Investigation has revealed that further gasoline was added to the fire in order to totally destroy the vehicle and the passenger.

Darrigan reached his button before Solotov could touch his. 'I want a medical team flown out to Sao Amerigo immediately,' he ordered the aide. 'They will exhume Bolivar's body and report to the Council immediately whether it is him.'

When Piers woke, it was ten o'clock in the morning. It looked bright outside, but from where he lay he couldn't see the sun, and he doubted whether the grim little room had ever been touched by sunlight. He still ached, but the pain was less. He ran the water in the basin in the hope it would become hot. It didn't, and he washed his face and parts of his body in freezing-cold water. He wished he could change his clothes, but he knew it was impossible. His apartment would be watched, and no doubt, Grand Central as well. He dried himself with the coarse top sheet and stood at the window. By peering straight up, he could just catch a glimpse of blue sky.

He took out the video camera and placed it next to the flask in front of him. His actions were mechanical, like a man thinking of something else while he worked.

And yet he wasn't thinking at all. His mind, to all intents and purposes, had ceased functioning beyond the narrow limits of the immediate objective: to complete the story and broadcast the tapes. Somewhere, O'Brien's confirmation of the virus, his own exhausted, lonely running, Marion's death ... His mind had tipped. The long accumulation of anger and sadness, threads of steel and silk, had knotted hard in his belly. The broadcast would be his personal delivery of justice. He no longer had need for sleep or hunger or love or people. He had all that he needed on the bed. His smile was soft and very distant as he caressed the flask. He touched it longingly, as if he wanted to become a part of it.

He picked up his camera, pocketed the flask and left the

room. Gus slept in a bed at the end of the corridor, and Piers knocked. A sleepy grunt answered, and Piers went in. The room was cluttered with clothes, beer cans, and ashtrays.

'I want to keep my room, Gus.'

'You'll have to pay, then,' Gus said, and took the money Piers gave him.

'You see the morning news?' Piers asked. 'Anything about another plague breaking out?'

'Jesus, I hope I never see that one again.' He shook his head. 'They're still looking for you.'

There was a pair of sunglasses lying on the table, and Piers put them on. He looked into the mirror. With three days' beard and the glasses he didn't look too much like the clean-shaven Shatner on the news.

'You okay?' Gus asked worriedly as Piers went out.

'Sure. Why?'

'You look as if you're in some kind of a dream.'

'I'm okay,' Piers said.

He had a coffee in the deli a block from the hotel. No one gave him a second glance, and he felt somewhat safer. He finished his coffee and walked a block to a corner telephone. He had made up his mind sometime during the night while he'd slept what he was going to do, but first there were a couple of things to tie up. He rang Frank Kolok at the office. He muffled the mouthpiece to stall identification until Frank came on.

'He's not in,' the secretary said.

'When are you expecting him?'

'He's on vacation. Who's calling, please?'

Piers dropped the phone. Frank had taken a vacation a week before the Sao Amerigo trip. He was too worried a man to take a second one so soon. Piers moved a farther two blocks from the hotel and then tried Frank's home number.

'Frank,' he said when he recognized the voice. 'I've nearly got the whole story tied up. There's just one more lead . . .'

'That's great,' Frank said. His voice was enthusiastic and hearty. 'I can't wait for it. By the way, I won't be able to make that party you'd planned at Pearls.'

Piers didn't hang up this time. He let Frank talk to an

empty booth and hurried to a doorway half a block north. He looked at his watch and waited. It took three and a half minutes for half a dozen cruisers to scream up to the phone. Piers turned and started walking. He had a long way to go.

He was sweating by the time he reached Thirty-fifth Street. He looked for the number that had been given as Whitlam's address on the carbon. He found it, but there was nothing there. It was an empty lot growing weeds and garbage. The buildings on either side were apartment blocks. Across the street was a solitary delicatessen. It was spotlessly clean and empty and smelled of good, wholesome food. There was an old man cutting sausages behind the counter, and Piers waited until he'd finished.

'What happened there?' He pointed across the street.

The man leaned on the counter and studied the vacant lot. 'I was standing here one day, and this guy wearing baby-blue leotards and a big S on his chest comes down, picks up the building, and flies away with it.'

'He should have dropped it on this place.'

'I should be that lucky. I could have claimed insurance and moved to Miami.'

'When did it happen?'

'One year ago.' He picked up a slab of Polish sausage. 'All my life I've been seeing them knock things down and put them up. I knew one day they'd knock it all down and just walk away. They started across the street from me.' He squinted at Piers thoughtfully. 'I've seen you somewhere, haven't I?'

'The Johnny Carson show last night,' Piers said, and went out.

The address was a fake and Whitlam seemed to recede even further into a state of nonexistence, and Piers wondered whether, in fact, he really did see him in that car outside Cochos. It could have been an illusion. He shook his head. It was on tape. Whitlam was a real man, and he had to find out who he'd been. It was the only loose end in the story.

Piers walked along Forty-third Street and half a block west of Broadway turned into a narrow doorway sandwiched between a camera store and a steak house. He moved cautiously up the flight of carpeted stairs, hesitated at the door at the top, and opened it. The briefly clad Chinese girl behind the desk smiled automatically at him, took his money, and pointed him to the rear door. The Paradise massage parlor claimed that it was the very height of luxurious decadence. It all looked a bit worn and shabby. Piers undressed quickly, refused the services of the girl, and plunged into the sauna room.

Half an hour later, Frank Kolok, thin and pale, with a neat beard and fogged glasses, groped his way into the room. He sat gingerly down on the hot wood about one foot from Piers, and like Piers, ignored the girls. They'd spent quite a few evenings together in the parlor, sometimes with the women, often just to relax. Johnny Pearls was the owner of a chain of parlors, all with exotic names, and as both knew him, they preferred to use his name rather than name the parlor.

'The phone was tapped,' Piers said.

'I guessed it.' Kolok blinked owlishly at Piers. 'You kill that O'Brien guy?'

'Come on, I don't go around killing. I need your help, Frank.'

'With the heavies looking for you, I'd try God. He's the miracle worker around this part of the world. But you better tell me what the story is.'

'I will, as soon as I can tie up the loose ends.'

Frank studied Piers. Even with fogged lenses, he could sense a disturbance in the man near him. Piers seemed remote, and his eyes flicked, not restlessly, but stared steadily and unblinkingly straight ahead. Like a child mesmerized by some distant, glittering spirit, which only it could see.

'I haven't heard from Marion, nor can I get her in the hotel.'

Piers only shrugged; it seemed as if Frank was talking about a total stranger.

'Okay, what do you want?'

'I need to find out two things. They should be in the studio library.'

'Shit,' was all that Frank said.

'You can get me in by the alley on Fortieth.'

'Tell me what it is, I'll find it for you.'

Piers shook his head. 'It's hard to explain what I'm looking for, but I'll recognize it when I see it.'

Frank didn't like the idea at all as they moved up Broadway to the studio. Piers wasn't saying much, just moving silently beside him. Any attempt at conversation or to probe what the story was, was met only by monosyllabic answers. They parted at the corner, and Piers went down Fortieth, cut down the alley, and waited for Frank to open the rear door. It was the lunch hour, and Piers guessed most of the studio staff would be out. It took Frank nearly ten minutes, and when he did finally open the door, Piers pushed impatiently past him. Frank nearly told him to get the hell out, but he knew what Piers was like with a story. He was the best reporter he had, and if Piers said the story was big, and with the Council involved, important, he'd play ball for a while.

They moved quickly down the thickly carpeted corridor to Frank's office. It was a small, sparsely furnished room, lined with books and three television monitors.

'I've got three abbreviations; they're lines on a graph I found in a hotel room. The first is OT, the second IRS systems, and the third is CPG.'

Frank sat at his desk and tapped the monitor buttons. The library computer would find the information faster than any human. It took about five seconds before the monitor lit up and began to print out the information it had.

Video Printout: OT requested Frank Kolok.

OAS

OCED

OPEC

ORA

OTM

OVA

The list was fairly long, but Optimums Terminated wasn't

in the computer's memory bank. Piers shook his head.

Frank wiped the screen and punched out the next initials.

Video Printout: IRS systems requested Frank Kolok.

IAC
IBM
IRS

'Check that,' Piers said.

It came up: 'Internal Revenue Service.'

They worked through the list, and again there was nothing.

Video Printout: CPG requested by Frank Kolok.

CAA
CAB
CPG

'Check that one.' Piers waited patiently.

CPG: Curtailization of Population Growth: See Pickard Report.

'Frank, can I see that last one?'

Video Printout: CPG requested Frank Kolok. Curtailization Population Growth, Pickard Report.

A Study on the Necessity for the Curtailization of Population Growth by Dr Hedley Keylor [Stanford], Dr Peter Ways (Harvard), Professor I. Korda (Moscow), P. Zokor (Moscow), Dr Andre Bruyere (Paris), Dr Jack Stephenson (London).

Piers knew it was what he was looking for. The report ran to four hundred pages and was filled with statistics, tables and graphs. On the back cover of the report was a small photograph of each author and under that a brief bio-data.

Video Report: Tape continued . . .

I have finally discovered what CPG means. The Curtailization of Population Growth. It is an urgent report put out by the prestigious Pickard Institute on the historical necessity to drastically curb the population growth in specific key Third Nations. In brief, the report analyzes the population and political situations in these key countries and projects the possible future Territorial Expansionist policy these countries will follow. TE is, according to the report, a psychological point in a country's growth when the necessity for extra territory becomes of prime importance. In order to deactivate TE, drastic measures have to be taken in order to relieve the pressures within the country.

But far more important than this dry study on the historical factors dictating the territorial ambitions of nations are the photographs at the back of the report. As you can see, there is a very, very close resemblance between Dr Peter Ways of Harvard and the dead man found outside Cochos, Charles Whitlam. I find it puzzling that a man like Ways should be involved in the destruction of a large population, for at no time in the report does he recommend death as the final solution to the problem. He suggests compulsory birth control and variations on that theme, but not destruction.

Tape pause . . .

So why did he journey all the way out to Cochos with two lethal flasks if at no time did he believe in killing people? Piers brooded. Ways must have believed he had something else in those flasks which would have solved the problem easily and harmlessly. The flasks must have been switched without his knowledge. He would have to go to the Pickard Institute and interview the other authors. They would be able to help him.

Frank shook Piers roughly to snap him out of his brooding. 'What the hell are you talking about?' He was worried now for Piers; the man looked as if he was about to crack. 'Destruction of a large population . . . Charles Whitlam . . . Ways . . . Piers, what in hell is it?'

'That's the story.'

'What story?'

'The plague in Menaguay wasn't caused by nature – it was man made for economic reasons.' Piers patiently explained everything he'd found out.

When Piers finished, Frank sat slowly back in his chair. He stalled for time to think. It was frightening, but . . . He studied Piers. How long had they known each other – fifteen years? They'd worked together on the *Times*, and then both had made the transition to television. In that time, Piers had become famous, while he'd kept to the background. In those years, Piers had often been troublesome, a pain in the ass both to him and the studio, but he'd never given them a fake story. There was always a first time: it could be an ego trip, or he may have – and this seemed possible – cracked at seeing so many people dead.

'You can prove all this?'

'I've got it all on tape.' Piers lovingly patted the video camera.

In which case it wasn't an ego trip. Frank tried to marshal his thoughts. It was some story, Christ, but how the hell did one handle it? Delicately, very delicately. He'd had to make countless decisions in his career – city corruption, Watergate, CIA assassinations – and he knew none of those were as tough as this one. The others had had internal repercussions for the most part, and a lot of thought and soul-searching, days, weeks, before they were run. This one . . . Frank didn't want to think what would happen if this one became known. Who'd be affected? America, Europe, Russia, South America, China, Africa, Asia – the whole bloody world. Frank knew that sometimes – and he stirred uneasily, because there had been quite a few of those times – the truth was best not revealed until one was sure no one would be affected. He'd have to talk this one over with the studio chiefs, the president (does he know? Frank wondered) and then, of course, Darrigan and the Council. Frank wished to God he'd never heard the story. No wonder everyone was out hunting Piers.

'Where's the flask and the tapes?'

'Hidden.'

Piers' glance suddenly was sly.

'Look,' Frank said, 'maybe it isn't going to happen anywhere else. You're just guessing.'

'We can go to the Pickard Institute and ask the others.' Piers stood. 'And I have to find out what Whitlam – Ways – thought was in the flask.'

Frank kept his eyes on Piers' face. 'And what happened to Marion?'

Piers ducked his head as if avoiding a blow. He was struggling to remember, and then he said it suddenly and garbled: 'Machine-gunned on street . . . ran from me . . . working for CIA and Council. I didn't know.'

'Oh, Christ.' Frank hadn't either, but he was more affected by her death than her connections. She had been shaping up as a good reporter, and he had gotten on well with her. He'd get the news team to put out an item on her. 'How are you going to get to this institute?'

'Drive.'

'They've got roadblocks on the tunnels and bridges. Eleven-o'clock news.'

'The ferry?'

'We can try.' Frank stood up and moved to the door. He shouldn't even be seen with Piers, but he had to find out whether the plague was going to break out in another country, and when. Maybe some strong pressure in the right place could control the situation. He also wanted to stick close to Piers; there was no telling what he would do.

He stuck his head out into the corridor, nodded to a technician, and waited until there was no one in sight and signaled Piers. They moved quickly out into the alley, and Frank made Piers wait until he fetched his car from the garage across the street.

Piers was about to slide into the passenger seat as Frank backed into the alley.

'You better get in the trunk.'

It was hot and stifling, and Piers lay curled, like a child in a womb, in the trunk. He held the trunk open an inch or two to let in air and some light, but not enough to see where they were going. At times Frank seemed to be driving over the biggest potholes in the city, and Piers tried his best to cushion himself against the cruel bumps. He peered at his watch as the car slowed and dipped downward. It had taken half an hour. He could faintly hear the water lapping against the piers, and then the car hit a bump and stopped. It rolled gently and soothingly. Cautiously he began to raise the lid, when he felt it pressed down again, hard.

'There are cops up on deck,' he heard Frank whisper fiercely. 'I'm going to sit in the car in case...'

Piers closed his eyes and tried to make himself comfortable. He could feel the beginning of a cramp in his right leg, and the sweat was pouring off him in rivulets. The heat made him drowsy in a restless way, and in between fitful snatches of sleep he wondered what he would find at the institute. Maybe the answer as to what was in the flasks; that depended on whether Keylor, Korda, and the others were there to give him the answer.

He felt the ferry wallow to a stop, and then the cars start up. It took Frank about ten minutes to hit the ramp and climb up the incline onto the road. He drove for about five minutes and then stopped. Piers blinked at the evening sunlight when Frank suddenly opened the trunk.

'It should be okay on this side of the river,' he said. 'You must've lost a few pounds in that hot box.'

He helped Piers climb awkwardly out of the trunk and watched him massage and stretch his legs. His clothes stuck to his chest and back, and his face glistened with sweat. He also smelled, and Frank guessed he hadn't bathed for a couple of days.

They drove in silence, each wrapped in his thoughts, along the freeway through the unending suburban sprawl of New Jersey. Each town flowed into another, and they all looked so much alike that it was impossible to distinguish where one ended and the other began, or even remember the names of them. Frank swung off onto Passaic Avenue and passed a green sign: West Caldwell. It took them ten minutes of driving around in circles before they found the Picard Institute. It was opposite a large, new industrial estate that covered over twenty acres, and the reason they'd missed it was because it looked so much like one of the factories. It was only when Frank swung into the driveway that they saw it stretched at least half a mile back off the road.

The institute was the foremost 'think-tank' complex in the West, and was totally subsidized by funds from the Industrial Nations. There were scientists from all over the Industrial world working on every problem ranging from pollution to how man would civilize the moon in the year 2001. It was a cold, antiseptic-looking place, fringed on all sides by strips of green lawn and neatly spaced trees.

'You want to wait?'

'I'll come with you,' Frank said, and followed Piers to the entrance. 'I'll do the talking, okay.'

The security guard was doubtful whether they could enter, but Frank's press card got him an invitation from Keylor's secretary.

'That was a crazy thing to do,' Piers said as they followed the guard's directions down the long, carpeted corridor. 'They'll both remember you.'

'How could we have gotten in otherwise?'

Piers shrugged, and when they reached Dr Keylor's office, he stepped aside to let Frank enter first. The secretary was waiting for them, poised and inquisitive. She was a woman in her early thirties, pretty and plump, with dark hair.

'Can I help you Mr . . .' She looked from one to the other and stopped when Frank nodded. '. . . Kolok.'

'I was wanting to see Dr Keylor.'

'He's away on a field trip. Maybe I can help?'

'Dr Korda?' Piers asked sharply.

'He's away as well. If you tell me . . .'

'And Ways and Zokor and Bruyere and Stephenson, I suppose.'

The woman studied him carefully. She tried not to show her exasperation at Piers' impatience. 'Yes. I can put you in touch with the institute's director.'

'Where is Dr Ways?'

'I believe in Alberta.'

'For the institute?'

'No.' She spoke slowly and began to frown as if trying to place Piers' face. 'The institute is always commissioned either by industry or a government organization. This was by the Council of Ind ...' She stopped. 'You're the one—'

Piers hit her. She went back, hit the edge of the desk, and slid to the floor, crumpled like a toy hurled petulantly to the ground. Piers gestured. It was an apology which never reached his lips.

'Oh, shit, did you have to do that?' Frank asked.

Piers didn't reply. He moved into Keylor's book-lined office. There was a monitor on the table. Alberta was a long way from Cochos, and he was sure that all the others would also have false destinations for 'field trips'. It was a slim chance. Slowly, he tapped IRS out on the keyboard. The small screen lit up.

Printout. IRS systems. Involuntary Respiratory Sterilization. Formula, tests, results, analysis, summation, use of.

Piers and Frank sat down and watched the information printout on the screen. It was nearly all in jargon and statistics, and at first Piers couldn't make head or tail of them. He calmed himself and patiently began to read through the information for a second time, and gradually began to make sense. He knew now what Ways had thought he had in the flask and why he'd opened it so confidently. It had been used already in the Industrial Nations.

Video Report: Tape continued ...

IRS. *Involuntary Respiratory Sterilization is the ultimate birth control. As long as seven years ago, medical scientists had perfected an odorless gas which would have the same effect as the pill and the injection on the human being's ability to reproduce. While the other two have to be administered either orally or by injection, both of*

197

which have to have the human's consent, this method of respiratory sterilization needs no such permission. If released over a specified area, it is possible to sterilize for a period of two and a half years 78 percent of the women who breathe the gas. This is according to the tests that have already been carried out over a wide and varied area of the Industrial Nations. Parts of New York, Chicago, Los Angeles, and other cities in America, as well as London, Paris, Milan, Lisbon. The tests have been carried out mainly in urban areas which have a high density of low-income population groups. The birth rates in those areas, which were running at thirty per thousand, dropped over a year of testing to five per thousand. The gas will be released every two and a half years in order to control the growth of undesirable elements within society. It is this IRS that Dr Peter Ways, using the name of Whitlam, went to release near a village called Cochos. But instead of it, a sophisticated form of Sarin was used. All Optimums had been terminated, and there was no time, in the view of the Council, for a gradual decrease in the number of people in the world.

This is Piers Shatner, Channel 14, New York, at the Pickard Institute.

When he finished the report, he felt completely emptied. He sat there for a minute not thinking or doing anything. The story was over. He heard a moan from the next room. The girl was trying to sit up. He picked up the tape dispenser on the desk and gently bound her arms and legs and carried her into the office. He laid her down on the couch and touched her face in apology but wouldn't meet her eyes. Frank, helpless in the face of what Piers had done, futilely straightened her skirt. By the time he turned, Piers had left the office and was well down the corridor on his way back to the car. Frank found him sitting in the passenger seat, staring straight ahead of him, his fingers rhythmically tapping his camera case.

'You saw what they've been doing?' It was a rhetorical

question, and Frank sensed the repressed rage under the words as he slid into the driving seat. 'For three years they've been secretly sterilizing the poor, weeding them down until one day they will no longer trouble us.'

'Sterilizing. That's a strong word,' Frank protested. 'The effect lasts only two and a half years.'

'For Christ's sake, two and a half or two thousand, people should be told what's happening to them. You just don't use women, humans, as guinea pigs for the greater good of' – he spat – 'society.'

'Stop being so goddamned naive. For a thousand years, governments, societies, whatever have been eroding individual liberties for the sake of society. It's got to be done so that the whole body survives, rather than just one part. I agree with you that those sections of society which are being used as guinea pigs should be told that they're being sterilized, very gradually, in order that they have a better chance of survival. But if you do tell them and ask permission, they're going to refuse.'

'They have to the right to, for God's sake. We're interfering with the very way they breathe and function.'

'The gas – IRS – doesn't destroy them; it controls their reproduction.' Frank started the car and moved onto the street. 'Instead of six, eight kids, they have one, two, whom they can care for better. And it can be here or in London, Rome, or India.' They came off Passaic Avenue and headed toward New York.

'But they're being manipulated and controlled, like sheep.'

'We all are,' Frank said angrily. 'Whether it's by God or our own greed or by an authority.'

'I'm ...' Piers thought of Marion, and felt alone and strangely free. He could see, but not be seen anymore. 'I'm not.' The freedom was, though he was unaware of it, really a sense of power. He had knowledge that no one else possessed, and he had a weapon to force this knowledge onto those who were ignorant.

For the first time, he saw which way they were heading.

199

Frank sensed the sudden tension, and smiled quickly to calm him.

'They're only blocking the route out of New York, not in. You can get into the trunk when we're a mile or so from the tunnel.'

'You going to run the story now?' Piers said. 'It's urgent, we've got to stop Keylor and the others from releasing the virus.'

Frank had been expecting the question for hours and still wasn't sure how to answer. He had hoped that Keylor and Korda and the others would have been in the institute and this would have postponed the decision for a few days. They'd both reached the end of a road. Piers had his story complete, and Frank had to say yes or no.

'It's not that easy.' Frank stalled. 'You know damn well that we make joint decisions on something like this. It's not a news item that I can judge; it's a fucking bomb.'

'Frank, either you're going to push it out or I will.'

'How?'

Piers only smiled and waited. Momentarily, Frank was puzzled. How would he push it out himself? Show it to CBS, NBC, or the *Times* or *Post*? He'd get the same reception there. No one took a running jump into a story like this. Frank guessed Piers was bluffing.

'I've got the truth,' Piers said patiently. 'So?'

'Well, you either use it like a scalpel or a bludgeon. And you're doing the bludgeon act. You don't understand the implications of your story, Piers. The moment it comes out—'

'Bullshit. You're just feeding me words.'

'I'll discuss the story when I get back, with you along.'

'No chance. You do it by yourself,' Piers said.

'Maybe,' Frank said carefully. 'We could take the angle that Whitlam acted alone. You know, a nut. The world would understand that better. The moment you pull in Darrigan, a secretary of state, Mercer, the European foreign minister, Solotov, a representative of the Kremlin, you're pulling the roof down on the world. I'll play it that way, okay?'

'And what about Keylor and the others. More nuts?'

'Once I start getting word up the ladder that we've got this story, they'll be pulled back.'

'And in a hundred years, when everyone's forgotten – that's if they're still around – we can tell the truth.'

'I guess so.'

Piers thought: It could work; it could force the Council to recall the others from wherever they were. It wouldn't resurrect all those who'd died from the virus, nor Bolivar and Marion, but it was a start. After that, the box would be opened wide.

'Okay, but I've got to know by tonight.'

'I'll ring you.'

Piers shook his head.

'You ring me.'

Again the head shook.

'How?'

'All the phones will be tapped. When you announce ... Marion's death, which I guess you will, just say ...' He paused in thought. '. . . she didn't die for nothing.'

Frank nodded and glanced at his watch. He had four hours to go for the ten-o'clock news show. There just wasn't enough time, but if he could even get something started, it would stall Piers; and more important, stall the Council. He slowed the car and ppulled over. They waited until there was a lull in traffic, and then Piers climbed into the trunk.

As he neared the Holland Tunnel and stopped momentarily to pay the toll, Frank thought of racing through the city and delivering Piers to the police. He passed a lone cop, watching the traffic entering, and then he was inside the white insides of the tunnel. When he came out the other side, he saw the traffic jammed for blocks as the police searched the cars leaving Manhattan. Once he gave Piers in, he wondered what would happen to the story. Vanish?

Frank worked his way up the Avenue of the Americas, and wondered where he should let Piers off. It was going to be awkward with all the traffic. He stopped for a light at Christopher and felt the car suddenly spring up fractionally.

He didn't turn around to watch where Piers would run.

Piers moved hurriedly down Christopher and then cut into Bleecker. He stopped to stare into a discount bookshop on the corner, studied the faint reflections he could see in the window, and then hurriedly let himself through a door jammed between the bookshop and a leather store. He ran up the four flights of steps and unlocked a door at the end of the short corridor. It was a small studio apartment with iron bars on the window and a steel-reinforced door. There was a studio couch, a desk, and a chair squeezed into one portion of the room. The rest of the room was filled with his video equipment. There was an Ampex videotape editing machine which took up most of the space. It was fairly old, the gray paint was scratched, and stood about five feet high and five across. The left-hand side of the panel was dominated by a television screen, the right by two empty videotape spools. Below was the control board. The Ampex was one of the best machines on the market for editing, as it could also improve on the quality of the videotapes. On a table, connected to the telephone, was a Sony video recorder, almost out of tape. There was also an RCA color television set, and two video cameras.

Piers wound back a part of the tape on the recorder and connected it to the television set. The quality of his pictures sent in from Sao Amerigo wasn't perfect, the colors were too bright, but the Ampex could rectify that on the final master. He drew the blinds and switched on the light. As far as he knew, no one was aware he had this room and equipment. This was his escape, this was where he played with his tapes and juggled images. He set the alarm for ten o'clock and settled down to editing the tapes.

At ten, when the alarm startled him out of his concentration, he switched to Channel 14, and sat back. Bob Wylie and Sally Fabic came on the air. He kept working, no longer interested in the economic-recovery story or the fact he was still hunted by the law-enforcement agencies. He stopped only when Bob, a moment before the commercials, announced that Channel 14 would be paying tribute to two members of its staff. Piers stared blankly. Two?

The moment the two photographs came on the screen, one of Marion, on the left, and the other of Frank, on the right, and Wylie's deep voice began the voice-over announcing that Frank Kolok had been killed by a hit-and-run driver, Piers switched off. Somehow, he didn't feel any surprise, only deep sadness. Fifteen years ended so suddenly, and he was once more responsible.

He bent his head for a moment. It may have been tribute or just tiredness, but the moment was soon over, and he returned to his work. He was trapped in his role of a landslide, and by tomorrow night he would find out who would win.

By morning he'd finished. His body ached with exhaustion, but he refused to allow it any rest. His eyes looked feverish and almost bulged out of his head. If he lay down, he'd never wake. The tapes and the equipment were given a final test; not perfect, but adequate. He fitted tapes into the three cameras, checked them, and left the room with two of them. The streets were filled with people, basking in the sun, strolling, talking. Piers passed them silently, quickly. He caught the subway to Thirty-fourth Street and made his way to the Amersham Grand. The receptionist, a young fat man, didn't look up as he took the elevator up to his room. He spent half an hour in it, testing and checking; then, locking the door carefully, he left with the remaining camera.

He hesitated outside the hotel, and then made up his mind. The cabdriver who drove him to Union Square never had a chance to see his face. Piers paid him off quickly and then was lost in the crowd. He wandered around until he found what he wanted. A small, clean apartment hotel, the Greenwich Palace. He paid for the room in advance and spent half an hour in it. When he finished, he hung a 'Do Not Disturb' sign on the knob and left the hotel by the fire escape, empty handed.

By the time he reached his apartment on Bleecker, he was humming to himself. It was a wild, tuneless sound over which he appeared to have no control; it just rose out of him, a crescendo of notes that clashed and collided with each other. The narrow studio couch looking inviting, but he didn't have time. He returned to his work, and when he finally finished, he clapped gleefully to himself. He stopped suddenly and frowned. If only Marion and Frank could see what he'd done. He smiled. They would tonight. He was ready for the Council.

12

Mercer was whistling softly to himself when he entered the Council room. He stopped on the threshold. Darrigan and Solotov were in their seats and turned irritatedly toward him. Normally he would have stopped and quietly taken his chair. This morning, however, he continued his whistling as he took his place. He was happy because he was about to leave the Council. He had seen Darrigan's recommendation of the day before. It had also been signed by Solotov. The days he had on the Council were numbered, and he didn't care a damn anymore. He'd be able to retire to his villa in Cap Ferat and write the memoirs of a man who had held one-third power over the lives of the people in the Industrial Nations countries. It was, he knew, going to have an interesting ending.

He opened the file in front of him. Statistics, reports, production figures. He glanced at them quickly and pushed them aside. He didn't feel like the dreary routine of the day-to-day negotiations with the Third Nations. He glanced around. Neither were the other two. All three were waiting, and they weren't sure for what. Mercer smiled suddenly. He had a feeling that it wasn't only his days that were numbered. The other two looked as if they were counting as well.

'We've received a videotape from Shatner, sir,' an aide announced on the monitor.

'Run it. Did Anderson trace it?'

'There wasn't enough time. It lasts only 20·6 seconds.'

Video Report: Piers Shatner to the Council. Recorded 19/7 at 0700 hours.

This is Piers Shatner. You know who I am, so I will not waste time. I have the flask, and I have the tapes of what really happened in Menaguay. It is not, repeat not, going to happen anywhere else in the world. On the nine-o'clock news tonight, Keylor, Korda, Zokor, Bruyere, and Stephenson will be seen arriving in New York from wherever they've been sent. At ten o'cock, you will give me one hour's air time on Channel 14 for my story. If these conditions are not met in full, I will open the flask. These terms are not negotiable. Repeat, not negotiable.

'He's mad,' Darrigan said softly. 'Did you see him? He's mad.'

Solotov nodded, and Mercer gave a slight shiver. In the light the video had been made, Shatner's skin had looked chalk gray, his eyes had seemed to be gouged out of his head, and his voice had been shaky. The five-day beard growth made him look menacing.

'He means it,' Mercer said, and pressed the button. The aide came on and looked at Mercer in slight surprise. 'Get me whoever is the expert on that ... goddamned virus immediately. He will tell me what effect the release of one flask will have on New York and its environs. Immediately.' He raised his voice when the aide started to glance toward Darrigan. He punched the button before the eyes could shift a fraction of an inch. He remembered and recalled the aide before he'd quite faded.

'Contact Keylor and the others and have them return immediately. They must reach New York by the latest at eight o'clock. Lay on special transportation where necessary. Move.'

The other two hadn't moved. They were watching him curiously.

'Now, what are you going to do about the broadcast?' Darrigan asked sarcastically. 'Let him do it, I presume.'

'Of course,' Mercer said calmly. 'We have no alternative.'

'Like hell we haven't,' Darrigan said. He punched the button and told the aide, 'Get Anderson to put every available man he has on looking for Shatner. He has permission to search every building in the city. Send him the authorization.' Darrigan sat back satisfied. 'They'll have him in half an hour.'

'And what happens if they don't have him by ten to-night?'

'We are in trouble,' Solotov said quietly. 'If the national leaders and the people see the broadcast, we will be ... destroyed. We moved without authorization from the national leaders. And when Odu, Mrs Gandhi, Liu, Sadat and Sheik Zaheer see the broadcast ...' He didn't finish, but closed his eyes for a second.

Darrigan hit his button. 'Inform Channel 14 of the possibility that they may have to broadcast Shatner's tape. They will wait for permission from me before they do. The broadcast, if it is made, will be limited to New York area only. Outside, the programs will be normal.'

'Why don't you order every New Yorker to shut his eyes between ten and eleven?' Mercer suggested. 'It would be easier.'

'I don't like your jokes, either,' Darrigan snapped.

'It wasn't a joke,' Mercer snapped back. He sat up in his chair and glared at Darrigan and Solotov. His face was turning red. 'We've been ordering the people to do just about every other goddamned thing. We try to tell them when to work, where to work, what to work at, how to work. We manipulate them as to what to think, when to think, and how. Soon we'll tell them what books they should read and what programs to watch. We've deprived one-third of the people the right to have children, without their consent. All in the name of political and economic unity and strength. Telling them when to open and shut their eyes is only the next logical step. And we've already done that permanently to the people of Menaguay, and we're planning to do it to other people, all because we want to preserve this fucking "civilization" we've created.' He fell back exhausted.

'A grand speech, Mercer,' Darrigan said with contempt. 'But don't waste our time. Save it for your memoirs.'

'And I'll get a permission denied.'

An aide appeared on the monitor and looked at Mercer. 'I have Dr Vernon Mitchell of Fort Omaha, sir.'

Video Report: Dr Vernon Mitchell to the Council. Recorded 19/7 at 1100 hours.

As requested by the Council, I have computed the possible effects of the BZ virus if released in New York. The city itself will suffer fifty-five percent fatal casualties, as it is the target area. The effect of the virus outside a twelve-mile radius depends entirely on the direction and strength of the wind. At 1045 hours, for instance, the wind was N.NW at five m.p.h. We could draw a curve starting at Ottawa going through Toronto and Chicago and to St Louis. Within that area the fatality rate will equal New York's. That is, between fifty and sixty percent. As the virus remains active for a period of twenty-four hours, it could affect other parts of the country if the wind should change direction. This in turn . . .

Mercer pressed his button, and Vernon Mitchell faded. 'Stop all air and surface traffic entering the area suggested by Mitchell from 1800 hours. Extend that line down to Jacksonville. North of New York, draw the line from Quebec to Halifax. And from 1800 hours report on the weather conditions in the New York area every half-hour. And from 2100 hours, every fifteen minutes.'

The aide nodded and faded off the screen. His young face was beginning to crease with worry.

'Why don't you evacuate New York?' Solotov suggested quietly. He glanced at the clock. It was 1130 hours.

'We can't move twelve million people out in twelve hours,' Darrigan said. 'It's impossible.' He pressed the button. 'Any word from Anderson?'

'He has been in contact, sir,' the aide said. 'But the results are negative. I have a preliminary report from Dr Fulton, sir.' Darrigan looked blank, and the aide added, 'you sent him and a team to Sao Amerigo to perform an autopsy on the remains of Señor Bolivar.'

Video Report: Dr Henry Fulton to the Council. Recorded 19/7 at 1050 hours, Sao Amerigo.

As requested by the Council, I have carried out an

autopsy on the remains of Señor Juan Jesus Bolivar. I
will not go into details here. A separate written report on
the autopsy has been sent by a courier. The body which I
examined bears a very close physical resemblance to that
of Señor Bolivar. The dental work, for instance, exactly
matches the records we have of the dental work done on
Señor Bolivar. It took us some time to locate the dissimi-
larity. Señor Bolivar had a three-eighths-inch gap on the
bridge of his nose. The cartilage had been badly broken
and never set properly. The body we examined does not
have this gap in the cartilage. The skin grafts we took . . .

Darrigan was the first to speak in the silence that followed. 'He's alive,' he said simply and quietly.

'I thought so,' Solotov said, and nodded to himself. He
seemed pleased that he'd guessed right. Then he shook it.

'But why did he allow everyone – his people, the generals,
us – to believe he was dead?'

'Alive, he was much more of a threat,' Mercer said with
the same puzzlement in his voice.

The three men fell silent, and Darrigan began to drum his
fingers. He hated being puzzled.

'Okay,' Darrigan thought aloud. 'Let's figure out what
would have happened if Bolivar hadn't "died". If he remained alive and in Sao Amerigo, his movements were
totally restricted. If he'd escaped and remained alive, the
army would have hunted him down. By "dying", he had
the army forget him, and he can move freely around the
country. Even we forgot about him.'

'But he may not have remained in the country,' Mercer
said.

'With the flask, he would have gone to Odu . . .'

'And what would Odu have done?' Darrigan said triumphantly. 'I'll tell you – nothing. And the other Third
Nation leaders the same – nothing.'

'I don't agree,' Mercer said. 'They would react very
strongly once they found that we had been responsible for
what happened in Sao Amerigo.'

'Of course they'd react strongly,' Darrigan said. 'They'd

be scared they'd be next on the list, but what exactly would they do? First tighten their border security to ensure no virus is let off in their country. And it wouldn't have, either. We would have not extended the area once we knew positively that Bolivar had reached Odu with proof. Let's take the next step. Attack the Industrial Nations. Negative. They know they don't stand a chance – as yet. And if they did decide to attack, we could have retaliated. The western governments will only declare war if we can prove that we're under attack. One missile in this direction is sufficient proof for us to retaliate. And that's the last thing the Third Nations want. The only move Odu and the others would have made would be to sit tight and wait for OT.'

'Or an attack from us,' Mercer said.

Darrigan shook his head. 'We've studied that one before. By the time the radiation dispersed, it would be five years, and all that we'd find would be contaminated earth and water.' A note of awe reluctantly crept into Darrigan's voice. 'Bolivar had figured this out. He knew it would be a wasted journey to Cape Town.'

'And he'd also figured out,' Solotov said softly, 'how we'd react if we were made to think he was trying to get that flask to Odu. Because of what we'd done, we'd do everything to prevent it, and concentrate our efforts on this.'

'So he decides not to go to Odu for help,' Mercer said, 'and he's got the flask. He can have it released in New York or London or Rome – anywhere he wants – in retaliation.'

Darrigan shrugged dismissively. 'That's not Bolivar's style. A few million dead in the West would have achieved nothing . . . for him. In fact, a plague breaking out in the Industrial Nations would have erased all doubt that Odu and the others would have had about it in Menaguay. And they would have lowered their guard. The bastard's a lot cleverer than that.'

'Shatner,' Mercer said in the silence.

'Shatner,' Darrigan spat. 'What's he got that is more powerful than the flask? The tapes. He's got all that information on tape, and he's going to broadcast it at ten tonight.

The virus, IRS, Ways and the others. Bolivar knew what kind of man Shatner was. They'd met before. So what does he do? He gives him the story and knows that he'll run until he drops dead. But in order to broadcast that story, he needs a lever to get permission. Bolivar hands him the flask and says whatever. Deliver it to Odu or something. But he makes goddamned sure that Shatner will never be able to, and he runs a defense on him. It would have worked both ways. Protect him against us; and prevent him from handing over the flask to someone else. Shatner's a peculiar man. He's a loner, and he's got a half-cocked idea of justice and truth. He's going to broadcast those tapes, come hell or high water; and he'll use that flask if we don't give permission.'

Absorbed in their thoughts, Darrigan, Solotov, and Mercer looked like dummies set up around a table. They didn't move or even blink. They seemed to have stopped breathing.

'We've not only been taken for a ride,' Mercer said. 'But to use a colloquial term, we've just been set up for a hit.'

Darrigan pulled himself together. He wasn't going to be beaten by a South American peasant who'd never even completed his schooling.

'Any word from Anderson?' he shouted at the aide who came on. 'It's twelve o'clock.'

'No, sir.'

'If he needs more men, he can have them. He must find Shatner.'

'Yes, sir,' the aide said. 'We have made contact with Keylor, Zokor, Bruyere, and Stephenson, sir. They are now on their way to New York.'

'There's one missing,' Mercer said.

'Korda, sir,' the aide said. 'We are still trying to reach him.'

'Where is he?'

'In Shenyang, sir.'

Darrigan looked at Solotov. The face as usual was a mask. The shoulders gently shrugged, and his eyes glanced away. Darrigan felt a frightening stillness in him. He sensed that Solotov knew something that he didn't know.

'Can you reach Korda? He's one of your people.'

'He's an Institute man, like the others,' Solotov said blandly. 'The Council sent him there, and I'm sure the Council will be able to bring him back.' He turned to the aide. 'Keep trying to reach him.'

Darrigan sat back and stared at Solotov, and then looked out of the window when the other man ignored him. The sky was cloudy. Rain, most probably, Darrigan thought. It wouldn't necessarily spoil a game of golf, and he wished he was out on the course. Suddenly he felt very old and trapped. First he'd been outthought by Bolivar, and now his instincts told him that Solotov was working on something. If only he could reach Shatner, he was sure he could reason with him and dissuade the man from committing such a stupid action. No one knew where Shatner was. Anderson was one of the best men he had. He sat up. Maybe he could broadcast to Shatner. Tell him Bolivar was alive and that he'd been ruthlessly used. No, he'd have to prove Bolivar was really alive, and there was no time for that. Time, time, time. There was no time for anything.

'A report from General Viterbo, sir,' an aide said.

Video Report: General Viterbo to the Council. Recorded 19/7 at 1430 hours.

I have just heard of the report made by Dr Henry Fulton. I and my cabinet should have been informed of your suspicions earlier. Bolivar being alive changes the situation temporarily. My cabinet and I have decided to halt further flights of aircraft carrying personnel from the Industrial Nations into my country until the situation has cleared. Those who are already here will come to no harm and will work with us for the good of Menaguay and the world. At a later date they may be evacuated.

A collective sigh arose from the three men. The economic lifeline they'd thrown out looked as if it were about to break. If they sat still enough, maybe General Viterbo wouldn't insist on an 'evacuation'. He was reacting out of pique. Generals liked to be consulted and made to feel important, and in their worry over Bolivar they'd forgotten to inform him.

Video Report: The Council to General Viterbo. Recorded 19/7 at 1600 hours.

We deeply regret having not informed the general about our suspicions about Bolivar's death. At that time they were only suspicions, and we thought that we should not disturb you with them. We were aware that with the death of General Peres you would be very occupied with forming your cabinet and taking control of the reins of government. We quite appreciate your decision to temporarily halt the flights. Once the emergency that has now arisen is over, we are sure that you and your cabinet and the Council will be able to negotiate an agreement that will be beneficial to both our countries.

'I hope that will hold him,' Darrigan said, and fell silent. There was still no word from Anderson, in spite of almost countless men searching for Shatner. He had gone aground in some hole that no one knew of; and there wasn't time to search the whole of New York for the particular hole. It must, Darrigan thought, be a warren of rooms and basements and holes.

At 1700 hours the aide came on. 'The figher jets that have picked up Keylor, Zokor, Bruyere, and Stephenson should be arriving within the next hour, sir.'

'And Korda?' Mercer asked, and waited without breathing.

'He has left Shenyang, sir,' the aide said, and Mercer took a breath. 'And our agents inform us that he is on his way to the drop zone. There is no way of reaching him.'

'But didn't he also receive our orders to hold, which we sent two days ago? The others must have, since they were located so easily.'

'We did send your instructions to all of them, sir,' the aide said. 'I don't understand why he didn't receive them.'

'Never mind,' Darrigan said. He was watching Solotov. The man looked too bland. 'I think I may have some idea.

You have to recall Korda,' he said to Solotov. 'If he isn't on that nine-o'clock newscast, Shatner will open the flask.'

'I'd do everything possible to prevent Shatner from opening the flask.' Solotov sounded as sincere as he could. 'But how can I reach that man when our aides can't? It is too late to fly there, and I have no idea why he didn't receive our earlier instructions. Communications most probably broke down. Shenyang is like that.'

Darrigan knew he could accuse Solotov of interfering with Korda's instructions until he was blue in the face, and Solotov would keep up his denials. There was no way to prove anything until something happened in Manchuria. Darrigan hoped to God that nothing would. Mountains were crashing all around him, and he was beginning to feel dazed. Like a fighter trapped in a corner, he wanted to swing out in all directions. Except, the enemy was proving to be too elusive.

'What the hell has happened to Anderson?' Darrigan shouted at the aide. 'Order him to have the Channel 14 building in New York under tight security. Shatner still has to deliver his tape, and we'll get him there.'

Mercer felt strangely sorry for Darrigan. The man was battling against insurmountable odds. And yet, he deserved the defeat. For three years he had held enormous power and bullied and cajoled everyone. He was learning humility the hardest possible way. And in order to be taught that, a lot of people were going to die, and there was little they could do. Unless they located Shatner.

At 1830 hours the aide came on. 'The wind is NNW at 3·5 m.p.h. I have a report from Anderson, sir.'

'Put it on immediately.'

Video Report: Anderson, National Security, to the Council. Recorded 19/7 at 1825 hours.

I have not as yet been able to locate Shatner. We have broadcast his picture continuously, as he has changed his appearance. There have been countless sightings reported by people, but none of them have been correct. Somebody is obviously hiding him, and my men are checking out every possible contact of his. With regard to your request to tighten security around Channel 14, New York, I have consulted Carl Mott. He is here with me.'

Mott, the president of HBO, was a big man with a red angry face.

Carl Mott to Mr Darrigan:
What the hell's happening? I've been ordered by this Anderson guy to preempt my ten-o'clock schedule. You know what we're sending out – Muyer's De Sade, first coast-to-coast hard-porn movie. We've got 110 million viewers out there, they're gonna go mad. I checked with my chief engineer. We can confine this, whatever it is, only to the New York area. Shit, they're gonna go berserk. Bob Bush, the engineer, says we'll have to use the earth station on the roof of our Twenty-third Street building. The movie will go out to the RCA microwave link, and then through Valley Forge for the rest of America. I don't know what will happen if this . . . nut . . . has someone monitoring in LA or wherever. He's already contacted Bush, and he's not delivering this film of his. Bush has been given the wavelength on which Shatner is going to transmit, direct from his video camera. It has a range of five to ten miles, and we can pick it up and boost it. If he was using a line, then he could be anywhere, but then you'd be able to trace him, I guess. I'll cooperate, but I should have you here to listen to my switchboard.

Darrigan punched out Mott angrily. 'Get me Anderson immediately.' He drummed while he waited. 'Anderson, how long will it take to locate Shatner's video once he starts his transmits?'

Anderson turned away from the screen to consult someone and returned. 'Approximately ten minutes to get a fix on the signal, sir. It should take another five to get to him.'

'Saturate the five-mile area with your men and make that one minute, if you can.' Anderson looked harried and doubtful. 'As soon as you can, then, and knock him out before he uses the flask.'

Darrigan turned triumphantly to the other two. 'We've got him. Shatner's not going to have more than ten minutes with his broadcast.' He sat back and relaxed for the first time that day.

At 2100 hours the aide reported the wind speed and direction. It had veered west and had the same speed.

Video Broadcast: *This is Robert Wylie with the nine-o'clock news. First, headlines. The economic situation in the West continues to improve. The Dow Jones holds steady. The president announces that we are over the last hurdle at a speech to students of the University of California. Law-enforcement agencies in the country continue the hunt for Piers Shatner. In Menaguay, General Viterbo takes over from the assassinated General Peres. Doug Hayward wins the Masters by one stroke. Four scientists from the Pickard Institute return to New York from a worldwide expedition. One moment ... we are receiving reports of a plague outbreak in the Manchuria province of China. I'll be back in a moment ...*

'Get them to kill that last item,' Darrigan shouted at the aide. He glared at Solotov. 'I wasn't wrong. You and your government planned this.'

'And the Council gave its permission,' Solotov said quietly. 'As it did for the operation in Menaguay.'

'We withdrew permission,' Mercer said angrily. 'You've defied the Council. There was no vote on it either by me or Darrigan. You've now jeopardized the lives of millions of people in the New York area and God knows what else.'

'I suppose you wanted me to sit on my hands and nod my head like a doll,' Solotov snapped. 'While North America and Europe gained an enormous economic and political advantage.'

'But you would have gained the same advantages as us in the supply of raw materials and other resources,' Mercer said patiently. 'You knew that. It is part of the under-standing.'

'And we'd have been dependent on your goodwill for the continued supply of these resources while you stalled on our expansion plans.' He shook his head. 'We had to do it. We face a bigger threat from that border than you did econ-omically from the Third Nations. I am sorry for those people in New York. But it cannot be helped.'

They argued, even though they knew it was futile. Once Shatner knew what had happened in Manchuria, he would open the flask. The item had been killed, as Darrigan ordered, but had Shatner seen it?

At ten o'clock the screen went blank for a moment and then came on again. Darrigan looked at the clock.

Video Broadcast: The plague of Cochos. Reporter Piers Shatner.

On the sixteenth day of June this year, a man calling himself Charles Whitlam arrived in Sao Amerigo, the capital of Menaguay. He looked a totally harmless man. He was in his mid-fifties and had a scholarly face and thinning hair. When he passed through customs that day in Sao Amerigo, the inspector must have seen the two large cans of deodorant packed in his suitcase. Most prob-ably he even handled them, unaware that the cans were dummies. Inside each one was a flask of virus. Strangely enough, Whitlam himself, though aware of the flasks, did not know their contents. He believed that the flasks con-tained a gas known as IRS. This gas . . .

The three men stopped watching the program. They sat mesmerized by the numerals flicking by on the electronic clock. Ten minutes was up. Then eleven. Twelve and a half. Thirteen minutes forty-five seconds. At fourteen the screen went dead.

'He's got him,' Darrigan shouted. 'He's got him . . .'

At fourteen minutes and thirty seconds, the screen came alive again.

A frightening discovery has been made by Colonel Lopez, chief of SOMIS, the internal-security organization of the country. On orders from Señor Bolivar, the ex-chairman of Menaguay, who had private information that the present junta may have possibly had some involvement in the plague that has devastated this nation. Colonel Lopez started his investigations. Colonel Lopez . . .

'Get me Anderson fast,' Darrigan shouted. Anderson came on the monitor looking even more worried. 'He's back on.'

'We located the video he was transmitting the tape from, sir,' Anderson said. 'It was in a small hotel called the Greenwich Palace. He'd rented it early this morning. When we raided the room, he wasn't there. The video was transmitting on remote. I now believe that there may be two or three more set up around New York. As one is deactivated, the other starts transmission. My men are locating the one that is transmitting at the moment, sir.'

'The clever son of a bitch.' Mercer shook his head. 'We've just been hit. What he's transmitted so far is more than enough.'

'Before you start a Shatner fan club,' Darrigan said tiredly, 'just remember he's still got the flask.' He didn't turn to look at Solotov. 'And we've given him every excuse to open it, and he's mad enough to carry out his threat.'

An aide appeared on the monitor. He was looking as worried as Darrigan and Solotov and Mercer.

'The wind is now SW. Same speed. The meteorological office says there's a possibility it could shift farther south.'

'Out to sea.' Darrigan smiled. 'We'll beat him yet. Yes.'

The aide was waiting. 'We're receiving reports that the broadcast has been picked up in Baltimore. It's not from HBO, sir. And independent is picking up Shatner's video signal and boosting it to Washington and Chicago. We can't block the signal, either.'

Darrigan nodded and looked defeatedly up at the television screen. Anyone could make a copy of that tape now, and it could pass from hand to hand right around the world.

There was nothing more he could do. The Council's gamble had failed, but he had to save those people in New York. As if on cue, the screen he'd been blindly staring at went blank.

He didn't whoop this time. Instead, he found himself tensely counting seconds. Ten. Twenty. Thirty. It remained blank, and he began to hope. Forty. There were only two videos, and he felt himself smile.

... and so someone pulled a double-cross on this man who was calling himself Charles Whitlam. The flask which he thought contained the sterilization gas contained something far more lethal. Look at it. It doesn't look particularly dangerous, for its size. And yet this killed between ten and fifteen million people. Why did they die? They died because the Council believed that the only way to permanently postpone OT was to destroy large portions of mankind in the Third Nations. This action has most probably bought, and that's the only word for it, the Industrial Nations some time. But OT cannot be postponed until eternity. It will return to haunt us again and again and again. Who's going to pay the price the next time? It could be ...

Mercer reached for the button.

Darrigan looked as if he were hypnotized by the image of Shatner. 'Get me Anderson,' he ordered the aide. Anderson took a few minutes to come on. 'I think he's on live now, Anderson. It's the last video. You've got to find him before he opens that flask.'

'We're trying to get a fix on the signal now, sir.'

'Best of luck,' Mercer said softly. He didn't doubt that Anderson was well aware that if Shatner opened the flask, he was also a dead man. He'd given no hint of his fear.

'Mr Darrigan, sir,' the aide spoke softly to the dazed man. 'The president wishes to speak to you, sir.'

The tape was being seen on a golf course in California. Mercer knew he was going to be next. In one way he was pleased and relieved that it had all gone wrong. As Shatner had said, the price was too high. But they'd had no alternative. There wasn't going to be any retirement for him. He had been one-third responsible for what had happened and for all the consequences that were to come. Both for the Council as well as for the Industrial Nations.

'Mr Mercer, sir,' the aide said, 'the chief minister wishes—'

Mercer waved the aide away. 'Tell them both to hold for a minute.'

Solotov smiled coldly at both men. For the first time in years, he actually looked pleased with life. He was, Mercer realized, enjoying what was happening. No doubt he'd return and receive the Order of Lenin for his day's work.

Solotov pressed his button and ordered the aide 'Get me Moscow.' He waited, disinterestedly watching Shatner moralize on the screen. It was taking a long time. 'I said I wish to speak to Moscow,' he repeated angrily.

The aide looked flustered. 'I'm sorry. None of the lines are functioning, sir. We are also receiving reports of a device having been detonated in that area, sir. The report cannot be confirmed as yet, but I believe that . . .'

Solotov wasn't listening anymore. He looked white as a sheet, and as he took his finger off the button, his hand shook.

Darrigan turned to him. It seemed as if he was wanting to say a lot to the Russian, but only a single word was spoken: 'Tough.'

. . . When I made my demands for this broadcast time, one of the non-negotiable conditions I had stipulated was that all five men who'd been sent to extend the area of the plague be immediately recalled. Otherwise, I promised, I would open this flask on the completion of my program. I am truly sorry that the Council ignored my condition. I had hoped that by doing this broadcast alone I would prevent further suffering. But on the nine-o'clock newscast I saw that one of the men, Korda, had not returned with the others. No doubt, like Charles Whitlam, he lies dead in some remote corner of Mongolia. And with him have also died millions more people. I will say sorry to all those within range of this virus, but it is necessary that I do open it. The Third Nations must understand that the people of the West feel deeply repugnant over the actions of the Council. The future, I hope and pray, will provide a more humane answer to our problems. This is Piers Shatner . . .

The screen went blank, and no one spoke for a minute.

'Do you think Anderson got him in time?' Darrigan asked softly.

Solotov didn't reply, and Mercer only shrugged his shoulders.

PETER DICKINSON

King and Joker

If Prince Eddy hadn't died in 1892 a quite different
Royal Family would now occupy Buckingham Palace:
King Victor II, a qualified doctor prevented from prac-
tising by the TGWU; a lefty Prince of Wales who is also
an amateur zoo-keeper; and Princess Louise who
attends Holland Park Comprehensive. There is also a
practical joker at the Palace, who seems harmless
enough . . . until the discovery of a most bizarre and
unpleasant murder there.

Walking Dead

'A highly intelligent, witty and elegant book'
The Times Literary Supplement

Sent to a remote Caribbean island to experiment on
rats, research scientist Dr David Foxe becomes
enmeshed, rat-like, in a maze of politics, corruption
and voodoo.
In one of his most entertaining novels yet, Peter
Dickinson weaves his usual brilliant web with skill,
originality and cool intelligence.

'His most delightful imaginative exercise yet'
The Observer

'The Tolkien of the crime novel'
H. R. F. Keating in *The Times*

Other Top thrillers available in Magnum

These and other Magnum Books are available at your bookshop or newsagent. In case of difficulties orders may be sent to:

> Magnum Books
> Cash Sales Department
> P.O. Box 11
> Falmouth
> Cornwall TR10 109EN

Please send cheque or postal order, no currency, for purchase price quoted and allow the following for postage and packing:

U.K.   19p for the first book plus 9p per copy for each additional book ordered, to a maximum of 73p

B.F.P.O.   19p for the first book plus 9p per copy for the next 6 books, thereafter 3p
& Eire   per book.

Overseas   20p for the first book and 10p per copy for each additional book.
customers

While every effort is made to keep prices low, it is sometimes necessary to increase prices at short notice. Magnum Books reserve the right to show new retail prices on covers which may differ from those previously advertised in the text or elsewhere.